THE CHRISTMAS NOVELS OF ANNE PERRY

ANNE PERRY'S
Merry Mysteries

ANNE PERRY'S
Merry Mysteries

TWO VICTORIAN HOLIDAY NOVELS

A Christmas Hope

A New York Christmas

Anne Perry

BALLANTINE BOOKS

NEW YORK

2015 Ballantine Books Trade Paperback Edition

Published in the United States by Ballantine Books, an imprint of Random House, a division of Penguin Random House LLC, New York.

BALLANTINE and the HOUSE colophon are registered trademarks of Penguin Random House LLC.

Originally published in hardcover as two separate works entitled *A Christmas Hope* and *A New York Christmas* in the United States by Ballantine Books, an imprint of Random House, a division of Penguin Random House LLC, in 2013 and 2014.

ISBN 978-1-101-88482-9
eBook ISBN 978-1-101-88515-4

Printed in the United States of America on acid-free paper

randomhousebooks.com

246897531

Book design by Karin Batten

A Christmas Hope

To all those who would
carry the light

CLAUDINE BURROUGHS DID NOT LOOK FORWARD TO the party. This November of 1868 it had been bitterly cold, the kind of chill that creeps into one's bones and makes them ache. Now it was early December and warm again. People were predicting the mild spell would last. Here in London there might not even be any snow! Most unseasonal.

Claudine regarded her face in the glass, not because she admired it, but because she must do the best with it that she could. She had never been pretty, and now in middle age she had not even the bloom of earlier years. She had strength, something not always admired in a woman; and character, also not necessarily cared for; but excellent hair, thick, shining, and with a natural wave. When her maid dressed it in a glamorous style, as she had this evening, it always stayed exactly where she wished. It was the one aspect of her appearance in which her husband, Wallace, had ever expressed his pleasure.

Not that that mattered to her anymore. He disapproved of too much that was at the core of her, like answering honestly when she was asked her political opinions—which were definitely more radical than most people's. She laughed at the jokes it would have been more ladylike to pretend not to understand. And, despite Wallace's disapproval, she worked at Hester Monk's clinic for sick or injured prostitutes—voluntarily, of course; she had no need of money, and the clinic had none to offer. She had begun there looking for something better to fill her time with than endless committees. Now she loved it for the fellowship, the variety, and above all, the sense that she was doing something of genuine worth.

She looked away from the glass. There was nothing more to accomplish here. She stood up and, thanking her maid, went out onto the landing and down the stairs, walking carefully so as not to trip over the hem of her rich teal-green gown.

Wallace was standing in the hall with his coat on. He was a big man, more overweight than his expensive and skillfully cut suits allowed to show. The flicker of impatience on his heavy features told her that she had kept him waiting.

He made no remark, no compliment on her appearance, simply held her cape for her and then nodded to the footman as he followed her out of the front door. Their carriage had drawn up to the curb ready for them. The coachman must have known the address to which they were going because Wallace did not offer him any directions.

They did not speak on the journey. They had long ago run out of things to say to each other about life or feelings, and Claudine imagined he did not want to pretend any more than she did. There would be enough of that when they arrived. The other guests were all socially important, which was the reason for their going. Wallace was a successful investment adviser to several people of considerable importance, and she admitted that he deserved his success. Apart from being gifted, he worked very hard at cultivating all the right connections. He never failed in anything he regarded as his duty. It was the laughter, the gentleness, and the imagination he could not manage. Perhaps it was beyond his ability, as well as his nature. During rare moments, she hoped he was happier in their life than he had ever made her.

And yet, it would be graceless not to acknowledge

that she had never gone without any of the physical comforts of life. She had never dreaded that a letter or a knock on the door would be a request to pay a debt she could not meet. He had never lied to her, so far as she was aware, never drank too much, never embarrassed her in public, and certainly had never been unfaithful. She sometimes thought she might have understood if he had been, possibly even forgiven him for it. It would have shown a quality of passion she had never felt him to possess. Instead of admiring his rigid tidiness, it infuriated her. He folded everything, even the discarded newspaper, matching the corners exactly. He put everything away where it belonged as soon as he finished using it.

But that was a self-defeating argument. If he had understood passion and loneliness, the same desperate hunger for warmth, then she might have loved him, despite everything else. She had tried to love him. But here they were.

At least she could behave with gratitude. She would do her part this evening: She would be gracious to the Foxleys and the Crostwicks, the Halversgates and the Giffords, and everyone else it was necessary to please.

They alighted at the entrance to the Giffords' magnificent house. Forbes and Oona Gifford were wealthy enough to entertain in the most lavish style, and seating thirty to dinner was no effort to their staff. Claudine and Wallace were welcomed into the hall, relieved of their outer clothing, and shown into the first of the large reception rooms. They had timed it perfectly: not the last to arrive, which would be slightly ill-mannered or self-important, but very far from first, which made one appear overeager.

Oona was Forbes's second wife, his first having died some ten years earlier. No one knew where Oona had lived before their marriage, and she never mentioned it, which was an interesting omission. She was very striking to look at, some might say truly beautiful. She came toward Wallace and Claudine now, her dark hair swept up luxuriantly and her slender gown the height of fashion. Wide crinolines were suddenly out. No one with the slightest pretensions to style would be seen in one.

"Delightful of you to come," Oona said with a smile. "Thank you, so much. In spite of the clemency of the weather, Christmas will be upon us before we know it. Let us begin to celebrate as soon as we can, I say."

"Indeed," Wallace agreed, forcing a warmth Claudine knew he did not mean. "What better way to begin the season?" He spotted Nigel Halversgate and moved toward him, realizing Nigel was standing with his wife, Charlotte—known as Tolly—only when it was too late to change course.

Oona saw what had happened and shot a surprisingly candid look of amusement at Claudine.

"Beginning to gain the Christmas spirit, I see," Oona said ambiguously.

"Such a party is definitely the best place to do so," Claudine replied, equally ambiguously. She was thinking of the discipline it took to be agreeable to a number of people she did not know very well or especially care for, but she certainly would not say so aloud.

"Goodwill to all men," Oona murmured under her breath. She sighed. "And women." Lifting her chin a little, she turned as Euphemia Crostwick approached, a delicately blond woman whose pretty face was always at attention, looking this way and that to be sure she missed nothing.

"I'm sure you know Mrs. Burroughs," Oona said, motioning toward Claudine.

"Of course." Eppy Crostwick smiled brightly. She looked up and down at Claudine's dress; it was a very handsome one, but it certainly would have overwhelmed her own diminutive figure, and its dramatic coloring would have bleached her skin. "It seems like ages since we last met," she added, letting the underlying meaning hang in the air.

"Indeed." Claudine inclined her head, her good intentions already vanished. "So much has happened. But surely it is one of the pleasures of life to be busy, don't you think?"

Eppy's eyes widened. "I had no idea you were . . . busy. Your charities, no doubt . . . You must tell me all about it"—she waved her hand delicately—"sometime."

"Of course," Claudine agreed. "I should be happy to. However, this is an evening to celebrate our own good fortune, rather than commiserate about the tragedies of others."

Eppy gave a sigh of relief, which was only a trifle forced. "I'm sure you'd love to meet some of the other people here. You know Verena Foxley, of course. Such a good-looking boy, Creighton, don't you think?"

They all looked over at the Foxleys. Claudine did agree that Creighton Foxley was handsome enough, if not quite as superb as he himself imagined—but then, Eppy had not really meant it to be a question. It was an opening for Claudine, who had no children herself—

another way in which she had disappointed Wallace—to argue that Eppy's son, Cecil, was just as distinguished, in his own way. Actually, Cecil was very ordinary looking, but one did not say such things, for Cecil and Creighton were good friends. Occasionally Ernest Halversgate tagged along with them, half disapproving most of the time but reluctant to say so in case he found himself excluded.

Claudine took a deep breath. "Very handsome, in a certain way," she agreed. "But there are others perhaps a little more . . . interesting to look at, don't you think?" She smiled as she said it, allowing her implication to be understood.

Eppy was satisfied. "I do so agree. Have you heard that Lady Lyall is to be married . . . again? The woman is quite . . ." She searched for a word.

"Extraordinary," Claudine supplied. It was the perfect cover-all word for disapproval that could never be quoted against you. Its entire meaning depended upon the expression with which you said it, the degree of uplift in the voice.

And so the early part of the evening progressed: a series of encounters with people Claudine had met on scores of other such occasions, from a world she used to be part of. But since her work in the clinic and her introduction to a different reality, it felt more alien than ever. Did she look as strange and lost as she felt? The thought occurred to her that perhaps everyone felt the same, in their own way; as if each of them were trapped in his or her own little bubble, jostling and bumping with others but never breaking through.

No, that was complete nonsense. There was Tolly Halversgate, elegant in the extreme of fashion, wearing a shade of purple-pink no one else would get away with. She was imparting some confidence to an elderly woman Claudine knew had a title of some sort, but she could not remember what. Countess or marchioness of somewhere. Tolly was a great royalist, always looking upward.

Lambert Foxley was talking business with a couple of hearty men at least ten years older than he. Both of them nodded to emphasize a point.

A couple of girls laughed just a shade too loudly, attracting the disapproval of their mothers, and the interest of several young men.

It was all colored silk, chatter, the glitter of lights from chandeliers, and lots of laughter.

Instead of mingling her way through the crowd

again, as Wallace would have expected of her, Claudine turned away and walked through a garden room. At the far side she opened the French doors onto the terrace and stepped out. It was extraordinarily pleasant: a wide paved area extending all the way to the wall bordering the street. There were flower beds—bare now, of course, but no doubt full of daffodils or hyacinths come spring. There were also ornamental stone tubs at different heights, giving a most agreeable variety, and several attractive holly bushes. The terrace was overlooked by the windows of at least two of the neighboring houses, but they were all dark, leaving Claudine with an agreeable sense of solitude.

It was at that exact moment she realized with a jolt that she was not actually alone. Half in the shadows between the soft glow from the Giffords' lighted windows, there was a man standing watching her. For an instant she was frightened. Then, when she realized he could only have come from the party, since there was no other way to reach the terrace, she was merely annoyed.

"Good evening, sir," she said coldly. "I apologize if I am interrupting you. I did not see you in the shadows."

"I didn't greatly wish to be seen," he replied. His voice was very deep and a little slurred, and yet there was a music in it, a lilt even in those few words. "Then I should have to make polite, inane conversation," he added.

She herself was not in the mood to be polite, or inane. Her eyes were becoming accustomed to the half-light now, and she could see him more clearly. He was of average height, which meant only an inch or two taller than she. It was hard to tell his age. His heavy hair was dense black, with not a touch of gray, even at the temples, but his face was ravaged by some inner wasting. His dark eyes were ringed with what looked like bruises, and his cheeks were blotched and sunken. His features were strong, his mouth generous, but already either disease or drink had marred him.

"That is what parties are for," she said, still coolly. "Polite conversation. What were you expecting?"

"Just one person who can see the stars," he replied, apparently not stung by her tone. "And you never know where you'll find them."

She recognized the music in his voice now. He was a Welshman, probably long left the valleys but never quite forgotten them. Surprising herself, she answered him honestly.

"No, you don't, but they are more likely to be found

among those who are searching than those who would get a crick in their necks if they looked upward." She wished at once she had not said it. It sounded more judgmental than she had intended.

He laughed. It was a sound of pure pleasure.

"Well spoken, Mrs. . . . never mind, it doesn't matter. You will tell me your name and I'll think it doesn't suit. I shall call you Olwen . . ."

She was about to object, then she realized that she liked the name better than her own. She wanted to ask him why he had chosen it, and perhaps what it meant, but that would have betrayed far too much interest.

"Indeed," she said quietly. "And what shall I call you?"

"Dai Tregarron," he replied. "I would say 'at your service,' but I do little of use. Poet, philosopher, and deep drinker of life . . . and of a good deal of fine whiskey, when I can find it. And I should add, a lover of beauty, whether it be in a note of music, a sunset spilling its blood across the sky, or a beautiful woman. I am regarded as something of a blasphemer by society, and they enjoy the *frisson* of horror they indulge in when mentioning my name. Of course, I disagree, violently.

To me, the one true blasphemy is ingratitude, calling God's great, rich world a thing of no value. It is of infinite value, so precious it breaks your heart, so fleeting that eternity is merely a beginning." His bold stare demanded she answer.

"Wild words, Mr. Tregarron," she said, but there was no disapproval in her voice. She recognized his name. He was a poet of some acclaim; she was familiar with several of his works. They all had the same lovely, untamed feeling as the words he had just spoken.

"I'm a wild man," he said with a grin, and she found herself wanting to smile back. "Did you let them tame you, Olwen, put the fires out so you are never burned by them? Do you sit in the dark and the cold and wonder why you were born?"

"You're drunk," she said, trying to ignore the truth in his observation.

"Surely, I am," he replied. "Most of the time. Sober, I'm terrified. The world is too big, and I'm too small and too alone. Drunk, I can see only what I choose to. Can't walk a straight line—but what's so good about straight lines? Nature abhors a straight line. Haven't you noticed that?"

"The horizon is a straight line, at sea," she answered, wondering why she was even bothering with this ridiculous conversation.

"Ah!" He held up his hand to stop her. "Olwen— Olwen—the world is round. Did they not tell you that? And there are flowers in the grass where you have passed; you're just so busy looking ahead at your straight horizon that you didn't see them."

Suddenly she felt she must escape. She wanted to think of some appropriate riposte, but nothing came to her mind. She mumbled something about needing to find someone and turned away.

Inside, it was all exactly as she had left it: the laughter, the half-heard music, the glittering lights and the swirls of colors, all the faces she knew, and the others that were so alike she might as well have known them.

Almost at once Wallace found her. His expression was sharp with irritation.

"Where have you been?" he demanded. "I have some most important people for you to meet. I wish you would pay attention. We are not here simply for fun, Claudine."

"Just as well," she said quietly.

"I beg your pardon?" It was a demand that she repeat herself, if she dared.

"I said, that is just as well," she answered defiantly. "One should not go to a party simply for fun, especially at Christmas."

"Sarcasm is very unbecoming to a woman," he told her, taking her arm with an unnecessarily firm grip and leading her forward to meet the people he considered so important.

A long and joyless hour later, Claudine glanced toward the door to the terrace just in time to see Creighton Foxley stagger in. His handsome face was white and his clothes were torn, dusty, and stained with blood.

Claudine froze, wondering for an instant if she had taken more wine than she thought and that, combined with the tedium, it had affected her wits. Then she realized the buzz of talk was fading in the room. One by one, everybody was turning to stare at Creighton.

One of the young women screamed.

Lambert Foxley made his way through the crowd toward his son. He was a lean and elegant man, a trifle austere looking with his perfect silver-winged hair.

"Good God, Creighton, what the devil's the matter with you?" he said angrily. "You look as if you've been brawling. Are you drunk, sir?" Then, before Creighton answered, Lambert took in the shock on the young

17

man's face, and the fact that he was gasping for breath, keeping control of himself only with difficulty.

"What's happened?" he said more gently. "Are you hurt?"

"No!" Creighton shook his head violently. "No . . . not . . . not much. But I think she's dead . . ."

Lambert Foxley looked as if he had been struck. "What? What are you talking about? You *are* drunk!" But it was a faint protest, made without conviction. He was beginning to understand that something terrible must have happened.

Now Verena Foxley was fighting her way through the bystanders, her head high, her elegant face twisted with fear. She looked first at her son then her husband.

"Creighton! Oh, my heaven! Are you injured? Lambert, call a doctor!" She turned angrily toward Foxley.

"He's all right," he said sharply. "Someone else is hurt . . . a woman . . ."

Martin Crostwick emerged from the crowd. He was small, neat, and seemingly in control of things.

"Come now, Creighton, tell us who is hurt and where. Take a deep breath and tell us what happened."

The words were given in a tone of command, and in

spite of his father's clear resentment, Creighton turned to Crostwick.

"This woman . . . ," he began, his voice harsh with emotion. "I don't know who she is or how she got in here, but she and that . . . oaf Tregarron were quarreling over something. He struck her, and she fell back then came forward at him, fists flying. He struck her again. We . . . we tried to stop him, but he was drunk out of his wits, and very strong. He was . . . completely beyond control. We tried to pull him off her, but I think . . . I think she's dead."

There was a moment of horrified silence.

Several of the women cried out with gasps or sobs.

Verena Foxley stood white and motionless as if she were turned to marble.

"Someone should call a doctor." Claudine broke the silence, moving forward to stand in front of Creighton, demanding his attention. "In the meantime, take me to this young woman. I have some experience dealing with injuries. I may be able to help."

Creighton stared at her.

While she waited for him to collect his wits, she thought rapidly about what might be of use. She grasped some clean linen napkins off the nearest table then a bucket of half-melted ice and a bottle of whiskey. If there were wounds to be cleaned, surgical spirit would be better, but whiskey would have to do.

"What are you . . . ?" Verena stammered.

Claudine ignored her. "Show me!" she said loudly and curtly to Creighton. "Now!"

Lambert Foxley called out something after her, his voice raised and angry, but she took no notice. If a woman was badly hurt, the sooner she was given whatever help was possible, the better.

Creighton led the way toward the terrace where Claudine had been an endless hour ago. He stumbled at the steps and put out his hand to steady himself against the doorjamb. He came face-to-face with Cecil Crostwick, who was pale and whose light brown hair was tousled. His shirt cuffs were also stained with bright scarlet blood.

Claudine was accustomed to both injury and disease at the clinic. Even so, she felt a stab of alarm. She pushed Creighton out of the way and brushed past Cecil and then Ernest Halversgate, who was standing almost in his shadow.

A young woman lay on her back on the terrace paving. Her fair hair was coming out of its pins; her dress was torn and the skirts all over the place. Worse than that, the bodice was crooked, half off one shoulder, and ruined by deep scarlet splashes of blood. Her face, bruised and swollen, under the caked blood, was ashen.

Dai Tregarron was kneeling beside her, a ripped-off length of her petticoat in his hands as he tied it around her arm tightly to stop the bleeding. Relief flushed his face as he saw Claudine. He straightened up and stepped back.

Ignoring him, she kneeled beside the girl and reached for her neck with the back of her hand to find a pulse. After a second or two she found it, but it was erratic, and she knew it could stop at any moment.

She took a cloth and dipped it in the ice bucket then began gently to wipe away some of the worst of the blood and dirt, looking for the other source of the bleeding apart from the wound already bound.

There were several cuts but none of them deep. Very gently, afraid of what she would find, she put her fingers to the back of the girl's head, searching for the wetness of blood, the sponginess of shattered bone.

The main wounds seemed to be the gash in her upper arm and another just below the elbow, as if she had tried to fend off a blow from something sharp enough to tear her flesh.

Claudine used the whiskey liberally and did the best she could with the napkins to make bandages at least adequate to stop the bleeding until the girl could be treated professionally.

She turned to see Lambert and Verena Foxley hovering nearby.

"Has anyone sent for a doctor?" she said somewhat peremptorily.

"Yes, of course," Lambert replied with something of his usual self-control. "And the police."

She had not thought of the police, but of course he was right. They must be notified. She looked around, and it was then that she realized Dai Tregarron had gone.

Cecil Crostwick and Ernest Halversgate shot quick glances at each other. Creighton Foxley was standing close to his father.

"Who is she?" Claudine asked, still on her knees beside the girl.

Cecil gave a helpless shrug. "Tregarron called her Winnie." He looked at Ernest again. "We don't really know her."

"I thought he said Winnie Briggs, but I'm not certain," Creighton added.

Lambert Foxley swore under his breath. "What on earth is a woman like this doing here, Creighton?"

"I don't know," Creighton said defensively. "Tregarron brought her. You'd better ask whoever invited him. It all . . ." He gulped. "It all erupted out of nothing. One moment everything was good-natured, the next she and Tregarron were screaming at each other. We tried to stop it. He was really vicious, and we were afraid it was going to get ugly, but it was all so quick." He looked at the other two young men for support.

"He was totally drunk," Cecil said bitterly. "The man's a lunatic."

Claudine was overwhelmed with a wave of disappointment. Perhaps Wallace was right and she was a naïve fool.

She could do nothing more for the girl, at least for the moment. She climbed to her feet feeling heavy and awkward. No one moved to assist her.

"We should take her inside," she said to Foxley. "She'll freeze out here."

"Where on earth should we put her?" Verena asked, her eyes wide, as if the idea were made in bad taste.

"Somewhere warm," Claudine replied. "What about the housekeeper's sitting room? There'll be a fire there."

"I can't ask the Giffords' housekeeper to give up her sitting room to a . . . a woman off the street!" Verena exclaimed.

Claudine raised her eyebrows very high. "I was assuming that they would tell her, not ask her," she said very coolly. She expected a blistering reply but was angry enough not to care.

Verena's face flamed, but she turned in her tracks and stalked back into the great room. A few moments later, the butler came out with two footmen to carry the still-unconscious young woman.

Fortunately the doctor came within the next ten minutes, but it was a full half hour after that before the police arrived. They were led by a Sergeant Green, a soft-spoken man in his early forties who looked as if he had been on arduous duty all day and had expected to be home at his own hearth by this hour. Nevertheless, he was even tempered and conducted the questioning of the guests with courtesy.

The conclusion he came to was exactly what Claudine had feared it would be, but she could say nothing that would make it any different. Winnie Briggs had joined the party, either from a nearby establishment or off of the street, at the invitation of Dai Tregarron. Nobody else knew her, and unfortunately—but perhaps very wisely for his own survival—Tregarron had fled the scene. No one knew where he had gone.

Creighton Foxley, Cecil Crostwick, and Ernest Halversgate were all agreed that Winnie and Dai had quarreled violently. He had attacked her, and—in spite of the efforts of all three of the other young men to prevent him—he had seriously injured her.

She was removed to a hospital for the poor. Sergeant Green, having noted the Welshman's description, ordered that Tregarron be searched for throughout the neighborhood and arrested on sight.

In the dark, and in some distress and confusion, the party broke up and the guests departed.

"*H*e should never have been invited," Wallace said angrily as their carriage jolted over the cobbles on the way home. "I can't imagine what Gifford was thinking of. The very best he could have got away with was a most unpleasant and unnecessary degree of vulgarity. Tregarron is a boor, and everyone knows it."

Claudine said nothing. She felt wretched about the whole affair. After her concern for the poor girl, the deepest hurt was her disillusionment in Dai Tregarron. Of course, he drank too much; he had not denied it himself, when they had spoken. But violence toward someone totally unable to defend herself was a completely different matter. Of what value was any poetic talent, no matter how beautiful, if you were capable of inflicting such pain on another human?

Perhaps she should have defended Forbes Gifford—or Oona, if it really was she who had invited Tregarron—but she knew it was pointless. In the early days of their marriage she had argued with Wallace, attempting to show him a kinder or more reasonable side to the things that angered him. Looking back, it was surprising how long it had taken her to realize such arguing was futile, at least with him.

"I expect it was Oona," Wallace went on. "Nobody really knows where she came from before marrying Forbes."

His condescension stung Claudine. She liked Oona Gifford, as much as she could like someone she hardly knew. In a sense, she was also an outsider. Without thinking, Claudine sprang to her defense.

"That is an unfair assumption," she said quickly. "She would hardly invite an unmarried man to an important Christmas party without consulting her husband, especially a man who was known to drink."

Wallace was startled. A magnificent carriage passed them, and in the sudden brilliance of its lamps she saw the surprise in his face. Then the darkness closed in on them again.

"Then you clearly know her better than I do," he said tartly.

"I know any woman better than you do," she retorted before thinking. She knew that it would have been far wiser to have given a softer, possibly also less accurate, answer. But it was too late to withdraw it.

"Well, even if Gifford allowed it, you still seem to be saying that where judgment of men is concerned, Oona Gifford is a fool," he said coldly. "Hardly a necessary comment, Claudine. I had noticed. I think, if you recall, that was my original observation."

She was too hurt to retreat. "You remarked that Oona must've invited Tregarron, because we don't know anything about her past," she pointed out. "But you can't know that any more than I do. Therefore your conclusion that she is a poor judge of character is flawed."

"Rubbish! I thought Gifford had more sense, anyway." He dismissed the matter as finished.

"Or possibly Forbes has sufficient charity to extend his hospitality a little more widely at Christmas." She would not let it go so easily.

"Then he should have extended it to us." He glared at her. "And not ruined a perfectly good party by embarrassing his guests with the presence of a man like Tregarron, not to mention one of Tregarron's . . . street women. I don't know what morality is coming to these days."

She thought to herself that there was an enormous amount about morality and human nature that he did not know—an infinity of it—but this time she did not say so.

They reached home in grim silence, dismissed the coachman and footman, and went into the house. After the cool night air, the warmth of the house was physically pleasing, but she felt no sense of comfort at all.

Wallace picked up the subject again as they crossed the hall to go upstairs.

"Even at Christmas it seems we can no longer expect

to see the values of a Christian society," he remarked, a step behind her.

She stopped abruptly, and he trod on the train of her gown. "I suppose you have been too busy with your wretched clinic even to have noticed," he added.

"You are standing on my skirt," she told him.

He stepped back, his face flushed with annoyance. It was clear in his eyes that he had no intention of apologizing. "I didn't expect you to stop at the bottom of the stairs. Am I to be obliged to walk around you if I wish to go to bed?"

"I thought you were about to explain Christian standards of hospitality to me, and I wished to pay it the attention it is due, rather than stand with my back to you," she answered, meeting his gaze.

"At this time of night?" he said incredulously. "Sometimes, Claudine, I wonder if you are quite sane. I don't know why the subject needs explaining at all."

"Because I was under the impression that Christian hospitality was meant to include all kinds of people, not just those we find most comfortable. I remember a number of occasions in the Bible where the Pharisees criticized Christ for dining with sinners."

His face flushed a dull red. "You are not Christ, Claudine, in spite of your charitable work for Mrs. Monk's regrettable clinic for . . . sinners, if you choose to use the word. You already spend more than enough of your time dealing with them. It is damaging your sense of values. At least other women might learn from such an experience, and place even more price on their own blessings. It does not seem to have had that fortunate effect on you. Perhaps you should direct your spare time toward other pursuits, for the foreseeable future."

That blow was deadly. It crushed her completely into silence. She turned, and picking up the front of her skirts so she did not trip, she walked up the stairs, her heart pounding, each step feeling like a small mountain. She loved her work at the clinic. It had saved her from despair. She had begun it at a time in her life when the future spread before her like a long, gray plain stretching forever into the coming night.

She had offered her help, expecting to be given the genteel tasks of mending linen or making lists, and finding no reward in it but that of variety from her usual, desperately repetitive social routines. Instead she had found herself cooking in giant saucepans for dozens of hungry and sick women off the streets, even cleaning floors and heaving laundry around. She had used physical strength she was not aware she possessed, working past the point of what she had thought was exhaustion. She was caring for people in all circumstances, giving practical and emotional comfort without thought of herself—as she would have done for the children she had never had. Her mother had always called her selfish and incomplete. At last that was untrue, and the clinic had made it so. If Wallace took that from her, he would be robbing her of the most valuable part of her life. She should have kept her opinions of Christianity, and the Giffords, to herself.

Even now it would not be too late to apologize. Wallace was always pleased when she did that. But the words stuck in her throat, and she went up to bed in silence.

She did not sleep well, and when she woke in the morning she realized it was rather later than she had intended. She drank the morning tea her maid brought her, and dressed in a plain dark skirt and jacket. It looked a little drab, especially on a gray day, but it suited her mood. She thought about her few minutes on the terrace with Tregarron, the passion in his words, the blanket of stars above them, and the music of the party softened beyond the doors. It had been no more than a colored veil drawn deceptively over the hard outlines of reality. If such a man could beat a young woman to death, what were his wild words worth? No more than any other pretty lie. In fact, less, because they had passed so close to being a greater truth.

Perhaps it was a good thing she had overslept. At least Wallace was gone and she ran no risk of plunging again into last night's unpleasantness.

She ate breakfast, though she wasn't hungry; it was simply a wise thing to begin the day with a decent meal. She had just finished when the kitchen maid, Ada, came into the room. She was a pretty girl, in a dark, unusual kind of way, and Claudine rather liked her.

"Good morning, Ada," she said pleasantly. "You look worried. Is something wrong?"

Ada lifted her chin a little, as if preparing to face a danger. "Ma'am, there was a man come late last night, cold an' 'ungry. I gave 'im some bread an' a cup o' tea an' let 'im sleep in the stable, up in the 'ayloft where 'e wouldn't be seen. I give 'im bread an' tea this morning, but 'e looks that wretched, can I give 'im an egg or two before 'e moves on?"

Claudine felt a sudden warmth spring up inside her. Wallace would be furious if he knew, but this girl had exercised compassion anyway, trusting that Claudine would back her.

"Yes, of course you can," she said quickly. "And perhaps a little bacon as well. As long as he doesn't disturb the horses, he's no trouble to us."

"'E in't no trouble to the 'orses, ma'am," Ada assured her gratefully. "In fact, 'e were good with 'em. Maybe 'e's a tinker, or such. 'E's real dark, like 'e could be one ov 'em, a foreigner, you know?"

"I'm glad you took care of him, Ada. Thank you," Claudine said sincerely. "It's a wretched time of year to be homeless."

"Yes, ma'am. Thank you. 'E looked scared, like somebody were after 'im." She turned to go.

"Ada!" Claudine said suddenly. "Is he hurt?"

"I dunno, ma'am. You think I should ask 'im?"

"No, thank you, I think I'll do that myself." She rose from the table and followed Ada into the kitchen. When the hard-boiled eggs and the bacon between two slices of toast were ready, Claudine took them out to the stable herself. If the man was hurt, or sick, it was very likely she had the ability to help. Since she had worked at the clinic she had learned a lot about people who were destitute, ate too little, and lived on the street.

ANNE PERRY

She walked across the yard to the mews and then into the stable. She looked around for the groom or the coachman and did not see them. Thankful not to have to explain herself, in case either man should feel obliged to tell Wallace about the stranger, out of a sense of duty, she went into the hayloft.

"I have your breakfast," she said quietly. "If you would like it, please come and take it."

There was a moment's silence, then a man appeared and climbed slowly down the ladder. Claudine's eyes widened in shock. It was Dai Tregarron. He was still in his dark suit from the previous evening but now had dust and pieces of hay sticking to him and poking out of his wild, dark hair. He was conspicuously unshaven.

"Thank you," he said gravely, taking the sandwich and the eggs from her. He bit into them hungrily, perhaps for fear she would remove them again now that she knew her fugitive was he.

"How did you get away from the party?" she asked after a beat. She ought to have fled back to the house, she supposed, but she was rather curious. "The police were looking for you. That girl was very badly hurt, you know."

A moment's grief touched his face; he looked tired,

34

and older than she had previously judged him to be. There was an air of desperation about him, and for an instant she felt a brush of physical fear for her safety. What was she doing standing here alone in the stable with a man who had beaten a street woman half to death, simply because he had lost his temper? Claudine was a tall woman, and fairly strong. But if three hardy young men hadn't been able to stop Tregarron, she doubted she would be able to defend herself against him. If he attacked her, he would be long gone before anyone came to help her. Ada wouldn't think to interrupt right away, and the groom did not know either of them were here.

"What are you doing here, and how did you get here?" she repeated more sharply, taking a step backward, away from him.

"In the dark I looked enough like a footman to ride as such on the back of your coach," he replied with his mouth full. "Don't blame your coachman. He's a gentle soul who didn't know the police were looking for me. Thought he was just giving some poor devil a lift."

She was confused. He had beaten Winnie and fled from the scene without even waiting to see if she was still alive, and yet he was asking her not to be harsh on

ANNE PERRY

the coachman. Her confusion made her angry, though. She resented the emotions he aroused in her.

"The girl is in hospital," she retorted. "She was still unconscious when we left."

His eyes widened: great dark pools of misery, depths beneath depths.

"I didn't do that to her, Olwen! Are you too innocent to see the darkness in three elegant young men with their scrubbed-clean privilege and their drunkenness of the soul?" He touched the darkening bruise on his face, which was half hidden by his black hair. For the first time she noticed the blood on him. "That's their work," he went on. "The blood is from trying to defend her from them, not hers to defend herself from me."

She wanted to believe him, but it seemed such an obvious thing to say. Why should he admit to beating her, even if it were true? And why would rich, comfortable, and responsible young men at a Christmas party with their parents have anything to do with a street woman?

Yet she wanted to believe Tregarron. It was perverse of her. Did she like him simply because he had flattered her, and because he, too, was an outsider, excluded in a way that matched her own sense of isolation?

"You'd better leave," she said, as if it were a decision she had suddenly reached. "I'll send the groom on an errand, so you can be sure he doesn't know you were here, or which way you went. The police will still be looking for you."

"What about your maid?" he asked. "Don't get the girl into trouble by lying for me."

"Do you think I'm going to tell her who you are?" she demanded. "To her, you're just a tramp, someone she was sorry for, because she's a kindhearted girl. Give me five minutes, then go."

"And yourself?" he asked, still without moving. "Or are you above the law, Olwen?"

She felt the warm color wash up her cheeks. "Are you going to stand there arguing and asking stupid questions or get whatever coat you have and get away while you can?" she snapped.

"I'll go . . . thank you." He said it with a bow so slight she was not sure whether she had seen it or imagined it.

Without speaking again she turned on her heel and went to look for the groom. She would find some errand that would keep him away from the mews for at least a quarter of an hour.

It was close to mid-morning when the police arrived.

It was Sergeant Green again. Claudine recognized him from the previous evening, although he somehow looked different in the hard winter sunlight. He had with him a constable.

"Good morning, Sergeant," she said politely when the maid showed him into the sitting room. "Have you any news of the poor girl who was injured last night?"

"Not yet, ma'am," he replied. "She was in a bad way. I'm here because we're still looking for Mr. Tregarron. I don't suppose you would know where he might be?"

She did not have to feign surprise at being asked so directly.

"No. I've no idea."

"You see, one of the other guests said you appeared to know him," he explained. "A Mrs. Crostwick. Said you were in quite close conversation with him."

Eppy Crostwick! Her jealous and troublemaking tongue.

"It was a party," Claudine explained. "As far as I knew, he was another guest. It is part of the function of such gatherings that one should make pleasant conversation with people, whoever they are. It is good manners and a courtesy toward one's host to assure that whoever

38

else they invite should be made welcome. Certainly I had never met Mr. Tregarron before."

Sergeant Green regarded her a little skeptically. "Mrs. Crostwick said you seemed to know him quite well," he insisted.

Claudine kept her irritation in control. She was lying to the police about a man suspected of a very ugly crime. She could not afford to let emotion overtake her judgment. She forced herself to smile at the policeman in front of her.

"It was an agreeable conversation," she explained. "About beautiful and inspiring things. Such discussions cause me to smile. Perhaps she mistook that for a greater acquaintance than was the case."

"You met him on the terrace," he pointed out. "Alone."

"Good heavens! I know Eppy Crostwick is an inveterate gossip, but that implication is ridiculous. I went outside into the air for a few moments because the music and the crowded atmosphere were making my head ache. I have no idea why Mr. Tregarron was there, and I didn't ask him. We spoke for a few minutes, and then I came inside again." Deliberately she turned the barb against herself. "Look at me, Sergeant. Do I look like the kind of woman Dai Tregarron seeks out for an assignation on the terrace?"

Sergeant Green was clearly caught on the wrong foot. That was not the sort of response he had foreseen. He decided to retreat with what grace he could.

"I'm sorry, ma'am. Mrs. Crostwick is a bit unfortunate in her suggestions. I should have known better. I didn't mean to offend."

"On the contrary, you flatter me," she said with a faint smile. "I'm afraid I have no idea where Mr. Tregarron is. But please feel free to look anywhere you wish, to be certain. Just don't alarm my staff and make them imagine they are in any danger."

"No . . . of course not. Thank you, ma'am."

She went with both of them, showing them the entire house, from the servants' quarters in the attic to the wine and the coal cellars beneath ground level. She caught Ada's eye once, smiled at her, and moved on.

When he was satisfied, Claudine thanked Sergeant Green and his constable for their courtesy and for assuring that the household was indeed quite clear of intruders of any sort, either a fugitive from justice or a casual burglar. She bade them good-bye and watched them leave with a sigh of relief.

She sat down to a light luncheon with a feeling of peculiar exhaustion, as if she had spent the morning in some dangerous and highly energetic work. Dai Tregarron must have made good his escape, but she knew he was still in very considerable danger. Apart from Wallace—who she hoped would never know about the day's adventure—Tregarron also had against him the Foxleys, the Halversgates, the Crostwicks, and the Giffords. All of them would feel equally aggrieved by his intrusion into their world, even though someone had presumably invited him to the party in the first place. Whatever it was that had actually happened to Winnie Briggs, none of them would wish to be tarred by it, and they had the collective power to make sure that they were not.

What could Claudine do? Tregarron was free for the moment, but the police would catch him eventually. Maybe one of the young men from the party would tell the truth—or even poor Winnie, were she to regain consciousness and have any memory of the night! Of course Claudine assumed that the police would visit Winnie and ask her all the appropriate questions. However, if Winnie was the kind of woman everyone was assuming her to be, then the police were, on many levels, her natural enemy. Claudine, with her work in the clinic, would be a friend. If she wanted to know the truth, then the obvious thing was for her to speak with Winnie herself. Quite apart from that, ordinary humanity dictated that she go and see the girl, who, if conscious, was probably alone and feeling both frightened and in considerable pain. If she had friends they might well not know where she was. Or if they did, but were of her same circumstances, they might fear any kind of authority, enough to keep them from visiting her.

She put money in her purse, in case any purchases were needed—food or clothes, perhaps some small luxury that would ease her distress—then set out for the hospital.

$\mathcal{A}$s she arrived at the large gray building with its long corridors and its permanent smell of carbolic and sounds of echoing footsteps, she wondered who might have been here before her to question Winnie. Would Winnie even remember what had happened? Sometimes a hard blow to the head and a spell of unconsciousness destroyed the memory. Or, if Tregarron was telling the truth, what if Creighton Foxley or one of the other young men had already been here? Would they have persuaded her that it was not any of them who had hurt her? Might they have helped jog her memory with their own accounts and perhaps words of warning as to how difficult life could be for her if she chose to make an unwise testimony to the police?

Or, of course, there was the more humane but equally effective path of a monetary inducement to recall a few events just a trifle differently. Even something like ten guineas would be a windfall to a girl on the street fighting for every penny. Why would she forfeit such a chance?

And then there was the other possibility, the coldest and most realistic of all: that it really had been Dai Tregarron, blind drunk and fragile tempered, who had struck her, possibly not even knowing what he was doing at the time. To say that might not be a lie, just an accurate description of his drunken state, hovering between physical reality and the intoxicated worlds of the imagination, or the darkness where nightmares and vision collide.

Claudine reported to the nurse in charge, who viewed her coldly until she mentioned the clinic and Hester Monk's name. Then the response was quite different: a sudden flash of warmth. She was taken by a more junior nurse, who was hurried and overbusy, to where Winnie Briggs lay motionless on a narrow cot, one in a row of many others just like it. The ward was horribly impersonal, but it was both clean and reasonably airy, a legacy of Florence Nightingale's unceasing battle for improved hospital conditions.

Even so, Claudine was horrified when she saw the young woman lying under the stiff sheets. She was still unconscious, breathing shallowly. Her face was even more swollen now, and the bruises were black-and-blue. The blood had been washed away, but that made the extent of her injuries more obvious. One eye was closed, and—until the flesh resumed its normal proportions—it would be impossible to see out of it. There were also bruises on her slender neck and across her shoulders. One could not judge her age, except that it must be between fifteen and thirty.

Claudine had seen many beaten women before. In

the clinic it was a common occurrence: prostitutes punished by their pimps for laziness, theft, or simply lack of earnings; or beaten by dissatisfied customers who hated them, hated the world, or despised themselves for what they had become.

"Has she stirred at all?" she asked the nurse.

The nurse shook her head fractionally. "Not so far as I know, ma'am."

"Has anyone been to see her?" she pressed.

"Doctor's been to see her, but there in't nothing much he can do."

"I meant visitors. Police, friends, anyone at all?"

"I don't know. People come and go. I don't know as she's done anything wrong. Why would the police want to see her?"

Claudine knew the woman was tired, overworked, and probably underappreciated, but the question seemed stupid. She controlled her anger with an effort.

"Because someone beat her senseless," she replied. "That's a crime, no matter who she is."

The nurse shook her head. "That happens all the time," she said quietly, as if it were Claudine, not she, who was the ignorant one.

"I'm sorry," Claudine responded. "I know that. I

work in a clinic myself. This was different. It happened at a party given by wealthy people, and a man is being hunted by the police for having done this. It's important that they get the right man."

The nurse looked surprised then sad. "Poor thing. Well, she hasn't said a word. Never opened her eyes, so far. I'm . . . not sure as she's going to."

Claudine looked back at the figure on the bed, and a coldness grew inside her.

"I brought a few things for her: soap and a small bottle of lavender water and a clean comb for her hair. If there is anything else she needs, or that would ease her pain, perhaps you would purchase it for her if I give you the money?" She pulled out the bag she had brought and passed it over.

"'Course I will," the nurse said with surprise. "Who shall I say left it for her?"

"She doesn't know me. I was there last night and tried to help her a bit, that's all. I'll wait a little while, just in case she stirs. Can you bring me a chair to sit on?"

"Yeah . . . if you want." The nurse still seemed somewhat doubtful of her.

"I do. Thank you," Claudine said firmly.

46

Less than an hour later, while Claudine was still there sitting, half in a dream, Winnie suddenly began to breathe in a more labored way. She was almost gasping, as if she struggled to fill her lungs.

Claudine sat forward and touched the girl's white hand on the sheets. It was listless.

Within seconds the struggle became more desperate. Claudine got to her feet and ran to the main door of the ward, calling for a doctor, even though she already feared there was little he could do.

As soon as someone took notice of her and ran for help, Claudine returned to the bedside. Winnie was worse, her face as white as the sheets, her eyes still closed. Her breathing was shallower. Every now and then she gasped, stopped, then gasped again, as if the pain were overwhelming.

Claudine held her hand more tightly and touched her face as much as she dared, in between the dark, terrible bruises. She spoke to her, just saying her name over and over. She had no idea whether the girl could hear anything at all, or was even aware that anyone was with her, but she had to try to comfort her.

The doctor came, a thin man with gray hair and a weary face. There was nothing he could do, and within

47

seconds they both knew it. He looked at Claudine, looked at the quality of her clothes and the pain in her face. He did not ask her who she was. At this point it hardly mattered.

In less than ten minutes it was over, and Winnie Briggs slipped into the endless future of eternity.

"I'm sorry," the doctor said quietly as they stepped into the corridor. "I'm afraid there was never anything we could have done. She was too advanced in tuberculosis, and the beating on top of that was more than she could survive. But if it's any comfort, she would not have lasted a great deal longer anyway. A month or two, at best three."

"It wasn't the beating that killed her?" Claudine asked. She was surprised to find her throat tight and aching. She was on the edge of weeping.

"Yes, it was," the doctor sighed. "But it only hastened the inevitable. Did you know her well?"

"No, actually. I suppose I didn't know her at all. I only ever saw her last night, after she was . . . beaten. I tried to help, for whatever that was worth."

"I'm sorry," he said again quietly. "You don't know if she has any family?"

"I've no idea. Probably not, or she wouldn't have been on the street. But the police will find out, I expect. If . . . if there's no one to claim her, I'd like to see that she's buried properly." She said it rashly, without stopping to think of how she would find the money, or what difference it would make to anyone. After all, the God she believed in cared for every soul, and what happened to the body left behind mattered not at all. But she said it as a gesture to the world that Winnie Briggs had mattered, just like anyone else, just like the people at the party so much more concerned about their own welfare than anyone else's.

The doctor nodded. "I believe you left a few things for her. I'll see they are returned to you, Mrs. . . . ?"

"Burroughs. But, please, give them to anyone else who might find them useful. Heaven knows, they're small enough."

"Mrs. Burroughs. Thank you. If you leave your full name and address, I'll see that you are informed . . . if no one else claims . . . Winnie Briggs." He sighed. "Now, I suppose I have to inform the police that she cannot testify as to who did this to her. What a mess. I'm so sorry."

*I*t was a mild and very pleasant evening, but Claudine was unaware of it. Even had it been snowing and carolers had been at the door, she would have been unable to think of Christmas or any other kind of rejoicing. She decided to occupy her mind with writing letters but found her attention wandering, and what she was saying was far from the kind of happy message people wanted to hear at this time of the year.

At seven o'clock Wallace returned home. Over dinner he looked down the length of the carved oak table and regarded her with heavy satisfaction.

"The unfortunate woman died," he told her. "The beating he gave her must have been more violent than we assumed at the time. I imagine now you will not be so eager to defend him." He gave no preamble of explanation, as if she would understand exactly what he meant.

Indeed she did, but his words still seemed to her unnecessarily cold.

"I know she is dead," Claudine replied without looking up at him. "I was there when she went."

"There? What do you mean?" he said abruptly. "Where?"

"At the hospital, of course." She was in no mood to cushion her reply. The situation still felt very raw: the pain, the sheer aloneness of the young woman, as if neither her life nor her leaving of it mattered to anyone.

"What on earth were you doing at the hospital?" he demanded.

Her anger was gone, washed away as quickly as it had come. "Visiting her, to see if there was anything I could do for her. I thought it very possible no one else would," she replied.

He opened his mouth to say something then changed his mind. He ate several more mouthfuls of roast beef before he spoke again.

"It changes the matter, of course," he said, staring down the length of the table at Claudine. "It's not just assault now, it's murder." He waited for her response.

"She was dying anyway," she said without looking up at him. "The doctor said she wouldn't have lived more than another month or two, regardless."

"You amaze me sometimes, Claudine," Wallace said with a wince of pain.

"Do I? Life on the street is hard. Many such women die young. So what is it exactly that amazes you?"

"It angers me"—he pronounced the words carefully—"that you, of all people, should say that since the poor woman was ill anyway, it doesn't matter so much that she was beaten to death a little sooner. I thought you to have some compassion, at least for the fallen ones of your own gender. I'm disappointed that you should be so . . . so filled with uncharitable judgment."

She put down her knife and fork. They rattled on the china from the shaking of her hands. "It matters that we use her," she said between her teeth. "It matters that we leave her on the streets cold and hungry. It matters that we abuse her, shut her out, that we mock her and strike her and then leave her to die alone in hospital. But it also matters if we charge someone with murdering her when they may well not have been solely responsible for her death. And it matters if we are sufficiently hypocritical to say it is murder if Dai Tregarron struck her, but if it had been Cecil Crostwick or Creighton Foxley who did, we would call it an unfortunate accident."

"You omitted mentioning Ernest Halversgate," he said with an edge of sarcasm. "Had you forgotten his name?"

"Ernest Halversgate hasn't the gumption to hit a rice pudding, let alone a living person," she snapped back at him.

"A rice pudding?" He looked at her as if she had taken leave of her senses. "What on earth are you talking about?"

"Hypocrisy. Did I not say so?"

"I think you had better go and lie down. The strain has been too much for you. You should attempt to do less. You are overtired."

She crossed her knife and fork on her plate to signify that she had finished. "I have done nothing at all, except sit with an unconscious woman while she died," she told him. "Perhaps if I had done a little more I would feel better."

Wallace smiled. "You are quite right. I'm glad you perceive that at last. You should busy yourself with the pleasantness of Christmas, keep up with the social acquaintances who matter to us. There will be more parties, the theater, and possibly the opera. It is a season of rejoicing. Perhaps you should see your dressmaker and get one or two more gowns. Something of a warm color would be appropriate. Not vulgar, of course, but perhaps less . . . less plain than you usually get.

"This whole matter is best forgotten as soon as possible. I'm sure the police will catch Tregarron sooner or later. The man's a drunkard. He won't be hard to find. You won't be called upon to say anything. The evidence speaks for itself. But if there's a trial, then no doubt Foxley, and perhaps Gifford, will say all that's necessary."

Claudine could think of nothing to say. He was talking about murder and retribution in the same breath as a new gown for the opera. It stung her like vinegar in an open wound, and yet she sat silent. She despised her own cowardice, but she also realized she had no words to rebut anything he said.

And who was to say Dai Tregarron was innocent, anyway? She wanted him to be, but she had no evidence of it. She was merely a naïve dreamer, without the courage of a visionary.

In the morning the newspapers reported that Dai Tregarron was still on the run, hiding from the police and now wanted for murder. They made much of it because his writing was admired by the literary establishment, even if his life was not. His best work, lyrical with his love of the hills and the skies of Wales, was quoted by way of illustrating how a brilliant mind had been destroyed by immorality and the abuse of drink.

They also pointed out that his flight had not in any way at all helped his case, and pleaded for him to come forward and surrender himself to justice rather than risk being injured—or worse—if captured by force.

Claudine never read the newspapers in front of Wallace. He had long ago given up attempting to make sure she chose only those parts that were suitable for women. Still, she preferred to read in private rather than under his disapproving eye. Today she was glad he had already departed for the work he did so well and so did not see how deeply the comments distressed her. He would have lectured her on the foolishness of concerning herself with people who were both socially and morally beneath her. He might have added, yet again, that she should occupy herself with suitable preparations for Christmas.

Even more dangerous was the risk that he would use the intensity of her reactions to this tragedy to end her work at the clinic. She could imagine the satisfaction in his face as he told her it was entirely for her own good.

She had tried before to tell him how important it was to her, and his incomprehension had wounded her far more than he had realized. It had left her with an awareness that underneath the outward trappings of marriage, the obligations of law and society, they shared almost nothing.

She despised herself for retreating from him, but it was a matter of preserving herself, keeping the small flame of hope alight inside her.

And she was afraid for Dai Tregarron. Public opinion had already judged him and found him guilty. If there was any doubt left, then the Foxleys and the Crostwicks would soon put an end to it. With poor Winnie Briggs dead, Tregarron faced the rope.

For more than two hours Claudine worked on household accounts and petty domestic problems, but her attention was so divided as to make it necessary to do half the jobs again. When she had added a column of figures three times, and obtained three different answers, she finally gave up and admitted to herself that she could not disregard the fact that she did not believe Dai Tregarron was guilty. She must at least attempt to help him. In a sense the die was already cast; she had lied to the police on the morning after the attack, when the case was not murder, although it was certainly assault. She could say she had not believed Tregarron guilty, but that was not an excuse for giving him food and then denying to the police that she had seen him. She could

56

not even claim that she had been afraid for herself. He had been gone by that time, and they would know that as well as she did. Heaven only knew what motive they might attribute to her! Considering his reputation with women, she preferred not to entertain that train of thought.

But what could she do for him—and, for that matter, herself? Where could she find active or useful help?

There were only three people she knew of who could provide any sort of assistance. Ideally, she would've liked to go to Hester and her husband, William Monk. However, Monk was head of the Thames River Police at Wapping. He would therefore be obliged to arrest Tregarron if he could find him, and possibly even to charge Claudine with aiding his escape! All of which would also place Hester in an impossible situation.

Claudine could not do that.

The only solution was the one she had considered first and decided she could not bring herself to adopt. She must ask Squeaky Robinson for his help. Squeaky was the highly disreputable bookkeeper at the clinic. His past was unspeakable, filled with details even he would no longer discuss. At the time of Monk's first encounter with him, he had been keeping a large and thriving brothel in the buildings that were now the Portpool Lane Clinic. How he had been duped out of their ownership was a long and complicated story.

Afterward he had become the bookkeeper to the new enterprise as a means of survival. Monk had given him no alternative, other than losing everything and finding himself on the street, without a roof over his head or a livelihood, painfully vulnerable to his many enemies.

Squeaky had had responsibility forced upon him, but in spite of his many complaints about it, he had over time become rather fond of it.

He had originally regarded Claudine as an ugly and useless woman, only accepted as a volunteer in the clinic because Hester hadn't the steel in her backbone to say no to anyone. Squeaky had learned his mistake in that regard fairly quickly. Hester had nursed soldiers on the battlefields of the Crimea, and he soon found that she had enough steel in her soul to equip an army.

Claudine he had learned to respect rather more slowly, and with considerable reluctance.

In turn, she had accepted him as almost human only when a sudden burst of compassion had driven him to rescue her from a rather spectacular piece of foolishness, which he had never given away to the others at the clinic. She had no choice but to be grateful to him for that.

So it was early in the afternoon of the second day after the unfortunate party, Claudine went to the clinic. This was more or less in keeping with her schedule, and at half past three she found the opportunity to speak to Squeaky Robinson in his office.

He was older than she, though not by much, but life had used him hard. His long gray hair was a trifle stringy and sat on his collar. His face was cadaverous, snaggletoothed. His clothes were those of a dandy with dubious taste: a very well-worn frock coat, a white shirt cleaner than it used to be before the advent of his new respectability, and a cravat that was definitely more expensive and more elegantly tied than those of many gentlemen of means.

She closed the door behind her. "I'd like to speak to you, Mr. Robinson," she said formally. She was feeling awkward already, and she had not even begun.

"If you're wanting to ask about the money, it's all right," he said defensively. "We aren't overspent."

"Good. But I'm not here about the money," she answered. How like Squeaky to be off on the wrong foot from the beginning. "I need advice . . . perhaps help."

He looked at her suspiciously. "There's no money to spare. I can tell you that before you even ask," he warned.

Since he was apparently not going to invite her to sit down, she did so anyway, in the chair on the opposite side of the desk from his rather large high-backed seat.

"I don't want money," she replied. "I told you, I need advice."

He was still cautious, and rather unhappy. "What've you done?"

She would like to have snapped back at him that she had not done anything, but if she did that, she would only have to retract the words later. As it was, this gave her the opportunity to tell him the truth.

"I have accidentally become involved in a murder," she replied, ignoring his horrified expression. His quill pen slid out of his hand and spurted ink over his papers.

"It appeared to be merely misfortune at the time," she continued. Now that she had begun, she was determined not to be interrupted. "A fight that became more unpleasant than was intended. However, the poor young woman died, so now the police believe it was murder. Although I think that that is overstating it a bit."

Squeaky stared at her as if she had suddenly turned into a monster in front of him. "God help us, woman! What have you done?" he squawked.

She gulped. "I have helped someone . . . I helped Dai Tregarron escape from the police, although I didn't know he would be accused of murder at the time," she explained.

"What did you think it was, for God's sake, if the police were after him?" he accused her.

She took a deep breath. "I told you, I thought it was just a fight that got rather . . . out of hand. The girl— Winnie Briggs—she wasn't dead then," she added.

"If she wasn't dead, why were the police after you . . . or . . . whoever?"

"Because it was a nasty fight, and . . . and the wrong person was blamed. I think—"

"You think?" His voice rose higher. "You think! If you had anything in your head to think with you'd have left the whole thing alone and got the hell out of . . . whatever it was! You didn't think!"

She felt angry and vulnerable. She was already perfectly aware that she had not exercised the best judgment. It only made it worse that Squeaky, the one person who might have helped her, had nothing to offer but blame. She responded with the greatest insult she could think of.

"You sound just like my husband."

Squeaky paled. "That's a terrible thing to say, Mrs. B. I'm cut to the heart!"

She consolidated her advantage immediately. "Wallace will not even consider that the wrong man is being accused, because the other three who might have done it are all rich, respectable young men. The man accused, Tregarron, he drinks too much, is older, and has a somewhat dubious reputation," she added for good measure.

His eyes narrowed. "And why is it you think this drunkard is not guilty?" He knew her opinion of strong drink and those who overindulged in it.

She was trapped and recognized his awareness of it immediately. She raised her chin in defiance, but finding the words was less easy. "Because he's a womanizer," she replied. "He has charm—in fact, he's notorious for it. Why would he resort to violence? It's stupid, and it's unnecessary."

"Oh, well," Squeaky said sarcastically, "nobody ever does anything stupid or unnecessary under the influence of drink. Everybody knows that!"

"He's a drinker, so he must be guilty," she retorted. "I forgot."

"There's no need to be snippy," he replied. "What did you do, exactly?"

His tone brought sharp and very unpleasant childhood memories to Claudine's mind, of standing in her father's study while he required her to explain her misbehavior and then be appropriately penitent.

"He escaped from the immediate scene," she replied stiffly.

"How?" he asked at once. "I suppose you helped with that, too, did you?"

"No, I did not! He came as a footman on my carriage, and I had no idea until the following morning . . ."

Squeaky's eyebrows shot up.

"Do you think I look at footmen's faces?" she snapped. "It was dark. The coachman didn't notice, and I certainly didn't. I ride inside my carriage, not on the footboard!"

"Then how did you learn of it the following morning? He wasn't still on the footboard, I presume?"

Having to be this civil to Squeaky Robinson was a high price to pay for anything. She would rather have told him to mind his manners and be about the job he was paid for. But she simply could not afford to. "One of the maids found him in the stable and gave him something to eat," Claudine explained. "She told me. I went out to see what she was talking about, and I found him. I gave him breakfast and sent him on his way." She took a deep breath. "When the police came looking for him, sometime after that, I did not tell them I had seen him."

"Ah. Who looks after your horses?"

"I sent the groom off on an errand. If he knew anything about it, either he has already told the police, or he's not going to."

Squeaky pursed his lips. "And where is this drunkard now?"

"I have no idea—"

"Good," he cut across her. "Leave it that way. If you should be asked by the police and they know he was there, say you didn't recognize him. You can't be expected to know every tramp by sight. Who the devil do they think you are? You found him sleeping in your stable. You fed him out of charity. You have nothing else to add. That's my advice." He smiled with satisfaction and reached for his pen, looking with disgust at its rather bent nib and then at the ink marks on the page he would now have to write again.

"Thank you," she said stiffly. "Now I need your advice to know what I can do to help him, to make sure that the police don't arrest him and convict him, if he is innocent."

He raised his eyes slowly. "You have just crawled out of the fire, and now you want to jump back into it?"

"I don't want them to hang the wrong man!"

"They aren't going to hang anybody until they catch him, and they may not do that if he has any sense."

"He can't live in hiding forever! And he shouldn't have to, if he's innocent," she protested.

"It shouldn't rain on my birthday either, but it usually does. There's nothing you can do about it." He screwed up one of the ink-stained sheets of paper and threw it into the wastebasket.

"When's your birthday?" she asked.

"February," he replied. "What are you going to do about it? It always rains in February."

"Are you going to help me prove his innocence?"

"No. I'm going to do something useful, like pay the bills. Leave me alone to get on with it."

She was disappointed, unreasonably so, and she was also humiliated. She had come in here and interrupted the scruffiest and most disreputable man she knew, a man who had not long ago run a brothel for a living. She had asked for his help, and he had refused her. Worse than that, she could see that his refusal was perfectly reasonable.

She turned and walked away before he could look up again and make some further remark or—worse—see that she was hurt.

*C*hristmas was approaching rapidly. There were now parties, theater performances, opera, and ballet for those who either had such tastes or found these events were appropriate places at which to be seen. Claudine was of the former opinion, Wallace the latter, although he did like certain orchestral concerts, particularly oratorio—the only one she did not care for.

A couple of days after Claudine's conversation with Squeaky, she and Wallace dressed to join some friends at the theater for a gala occasion. Claudine did not have a new gown yet, so she chose an older one. It had been considerably adapted, almost recut, and she felt it was particularly flattering. She had always been tall, and since working at the clinic she had had less time to eat. Actually, if she were honest with herself, she had less time in which to be bored, and consequently eat cake and pastries. As a result, she was considerably slimmer than she had been a short while ago, and it became her.

Wallace looked at her without interest as she came down the stairs to where he was waiting. Then he noticed the peacock-shaded silk over the darker blue underskirt, and his eyes widened. He drew in breath to say something then changed his mind.

"We'd better hurry," he told her instead. "We don't want to be late."

The theater was already crowded when they arrived, with people greeting friends. The sound of laughter, the swirl of bright gowns, and the glittering of lights gave a sense of festivity, as much so as wreaths of holly, the sound of church bells, and the songs of carolers. It still looked like there would be no snow. How perverse of her to be sorry for that! Claudine did not like the cold and was always afraid of slipping on the ice, but the snow was like a soft mantle, hiding the ugliness of so much, allowing one to be willfully blind to it for a season. For a little while the world could be as one wished it to be, reality painted over.

They were inside the crowded foyer, trying not to be jostled. She stayed close to Wallace. She would be most embarrassed to lose him, since he had the tickets. After a moment or two, in desperation, she took his arm.

She passed people she knew, at least by sight. She smiled at them and inclined her head. They smiled back. Wallace bowed. Once or twice they made polite conversation regarding the weather or some uncontroversial subject everyone could express opinions about without fear of contradiction. It seemed unwittingly meaningless, and yet it had some social value.

They took their seats, which were in one of the better boxes, and Claudine thanked Wallace for his generosity.

The lights dimmed, and the buzz of conversation ceased. The curtains were drawn open to gasps of pleasure as the scenery was revealed, and the drama began immediately.

Claudine found her interest in the romance fading after only a few minutes. It seemed clear from the casting exactly who was going to fall in love with whom.

And since the Christmas season was traditionally one of happy endings, the result also was predictable.

Instead she looked across at the people in the boxes opposite and, as discreetly as possible, began to watch them. She held her enameled opera glasses to her eyes, as if studying the stage, but actually looked to the side.

The first people she recognized were Martin and Eppy Crostwick. At this distance, Eppy looked as delicate as a bone-china figurine, with her flawless complexion and dainty features. Her pale yellow hair was piled up precariously. Claudine noticed a few other opera glasses trained in her direction, which would no doubt please her. Eppy loved to cut a dash, and her ambition knew no bounds.

Martin was sitting next to her proprietorially, looking self-satisfied and nodding his head now and then.

A little farther along, at the same level, were Lambert and Verena Foxley. They were speaking to each other and not even affecting to look at the stage.

Claudine was irritated with them for their ill manners. Then, aware of her own hypocrisy, she turned to watch the performance.

Half an hour later, when the plot was proceeding exactly as she had foreseen, she looked along the boxes again. This time she saw something she had not expected: Alphonsine Gifford was staring at the stage as if captivated by the actors. Her face was less beautiful than that of her stepmother, but there was a warmth and a charm in it that was easily as attractive. Her hair had a touch of auburn, which some people might not have cared for but which Claudine thought was particularly pleasing. Alphonsine had dressed in soft colors, which made her vitality even more apparent.

Next to her was Ernest Halversgate. He was a total contrast to her. There was nothing unpredictable in him. Some might have considered him good-looking, but Claudine found him insipid. Watching him now as he stared not at the stage but at Alphonsine, it was difficult to re-create in her mind the horrified expression that had been on his face as he stood on the terrace near Winnie's unconscious body. There seemed to be a faint smugness in him now. Could he possibly have dismissed it from his mind so soon?

Or was Claudine being totally unfair, judging him for what was nothing more than a masterful effort to behave with consideration toward the young woman he was accompanying now? From everything Claudine knew, it would be an eminently suitable match. Both sets of parents would approve it. For the Halversgates, it would be something of a catch. Alphonsine was an heiress of substance. For the Giffords, well, Ernest had a reputation for diligence and sobriety. He might bore Alphonsine to death, but he would never break the rules, either morally or socially, and he would invest her money profitably. He neither gambled nor drank.

Claudine pulled herself up sharply. She was being horribly unfair, and unkind. She did not know Ernest Halversgate. Plenty of people who were interesting and witty were also cruel, and what good was all the entertainment in the world without kindness? She should stop making assumptions about his personality. Dutifully she looked back at the stage until the intermission.

She had not wished to meet the Foxleys and the Crostwicks, but Wallace did, so it was unavoidable. She should have expected it. It was very possibly why they were here in the first place. The romantic comedy was hardly to Wallace's taste, and she knew of no reason why he would imagine it was hers.

Close up, Eppy looked even more striking. Claudine was pleased she had worn something so unusual herself. Her height made her additionally noticeable, and in a manner quite uncharacteristic for her, she enjoyed being noticed.

"How extremely well you look." Eppy said it in a tone of voice that was hardly complimentary, as if Claudine had been fading away the last time they had met.

"How generous of you," Claudine murmured, meaning anything one cared to attribute to it.

Verena Foxley smiled as if nothing ever troubled her. She was rather like a swan gliding above the water, Claudine thought. Such elegant and regal birds, but heaven only knew what their feet were doing beneath the surface.

"What a delightful occasion," Claudine went on. It was only fair to Wallace that at least she try. "It quite puts me in the mood for Christmas."

"I was already in the mood for Christmas," Eppy said, with her eyebrows arched in surprise.

"So I observe," Verena murmured, glancing at Eppy's hair.

Claudine had a ridiculous image of the whole coiffure decked with tinsel and candles, and the desire to laugh was so overwhelming she snatched a handkerchief from her reticule and buried her face in it as if she had a fit of uncontrollable sneezing. She dared not look at Verena.

"I've heard no news of that wretched man Tregarron, have you, Burroughs?" Martin Crostwick said with a gesture of distaste. "I don't know why the devil the police can't catch him. It would seem simple enough. Dammit, even if he wasn't dangerous, the man's a bad influence on others. I can't understand it, but young men are apparently fools enough to admire his ... I don't know what! Disregard for anything to do with decency."

"Don't worry," Eppy comforted him. "Their attention has been well and truly curtailed, and it was slight enough anyway. Tregarron's a fugitive now, and no one will give him food or shelter, let alone friendship. I think the whole miserable disaster happened at a very fortunate time. Decent young men will have had a sharp lesson against keeping bad company." She looked pointedly at Claudine.

Claudine wanted to come up with some scathing reply about fair trial and assumption of innocence, but no coherent words came to her quickly enough.

"I daresay, he'll leave the country," Wallace put in, perhaps afraid that Claudine was going to speak. He avoided looking at her. "After this, there's really nothing left for him in England. All he has is his reputation, and that's gone, as it deserves to be. A lot of it was built on hot air anyway."

This time Claudine did not stop to think.

"It's built on a large body of poetry," she said fiercely, "that is all rooted in the valleys of Wales, the hills and the coastline, the history. Even those with no Welsh ancestry at all find a familiarity in it. He'd die away from his own places. Where on earth could he go? He'd be a stranger always."

"Then he should have lived a decent life, instead of drinking himself half senseless and going from woman to woman," Wallace said extremely sharply. It was intended to silence her, and she knew it.

"Going from woman to woman may be immoral, but as long as the women concerned are willing, it's not a crime," she retorted. "And drinking too much is a vice practiced by half the men in London, at one time or another in their lives. I daresay, it is the same in Paris or Rome or anywhere else."

"Why on earth are you defending him?" Verena said in surprise. "You saw what he did to that poor young woman. She might be of . . . no virtue . . . but she didn't deserve that. I thought your charity work was precisely concerned with protecting women of her sort, at least from disease and attack."

"It is." Claudine felt the heat burn in her face. "And I'm not defending him. If he did that to her, intentionally, then he deserves to be put in prison. But we—"

Wallace lost his temper. He turned toward her with his eyes blazing. "There are no 'buts,' Claudine," he said between clenched jaws. "These highly respectable young men, known to all of us here for years, saw him do it and tried their best to prevent him. What happened is not open to question."

"Three of them?" she responded recklessly, knowing she would pay for it later. "All younger than Mr. Tregarron, and sober, and they couldn't stop him? He must have superhuman strength. I hope if they find him they get at least six policemen to capture him. Otherwise one of them may end up dead, too, like poor Winnie Briggs."

"Who is Winnie Briggs?" Martin Crostwick asked with a blank look on his face.

"The girl Tregarron murdered!" Eppy snapped at him.

"The girl Tregarron attacked in a drunken rage," Lambert Foxley corrected her. He shot an irritated glance at Claudine. "Perhaps we should not preempt a

75

jury by leaping to conclusions. Although I don't see an alternative one, myself," he added. "The sooner the issue is decided, the better it will be for all of us. If I have a word with the appropriate authorities, perhaps we can avoid the necessity of having to appear in court ourselves. A sworn testimony should be sufficient, if it is clear enough that we all agree as to the facts."

"An excellent solution," Martin Crostwick agreed. "Get the matter over with."

The bell rang to warn that the intermission was nearly over, and without further comment—apart from general observations as to how pleasant it was to have met—they returned to their boxes.

The rest of the evening passed by Claudine. Her mind raced, searching desperately for a way to stop Lambert Foxley from essentially ending the pursuit of truth before it even began, which is what would happen if he "had a word" with the authorities. Squeaky Robinson had refused to help. What could she do alone? She certainly could not find Dai Tregarron and warn him. She could not even look in the places Squeaky could have, or ask the people he knew. But she could ask the women who came and went at the clinic if they knew anything of Cecil Crostwick or Creighton Foxley. And

Ernest Halversgate, she supposed, though he seemed more a spectator than a participant in the seamier sides of life. She would hate doing it. It was an unfair pressure to question the injured who came for help, but it was the last option she had left.

And she might learn something of Winnie Briggs that could prove useful, even if it were no more than the name of a prior acquaintance. Anything that kept open the questions surrounding her death would be worth it.

Blast Squeaky Robinson for his stubbornness!

Maybe she could give it one more try? If she went to see him with specific ideas, that might persuade him!

"No," Squeaky said even before she had finished speaking. He looked down at his ledgers, which were spread out on the desk in front of him. "We could use more money for supplies—medical supplies," he emphasized.

"We have plenty," she replied. "At least until mid-January."

"Not if we get a lot of patients in, and people have

overspent themselves for Christmas," he said doggedly. "Then what'll you do, eh?"

"Go out and find some money, of course," she told him tartly. "As I always do."

"Very right an' proper," he nodded. "So go do it."

"By then Dai Tregarron could be in jail waiting to be hanged!"

Always literal when he wanted to be, Squeaky gave her a long, cold stare, and spoke very clearly. "It is December; Christmas is in less than a fortnight. They haven't even caught him yet. They've got to try him and give him three weeks' grace before they hang him. You're good at sums—that's more than a month, at the very least. He has time. We don't. We need more money."

"No we don't!"

"Everybody needs more money," he said reasonably.

"You really won't help me?" She felt despair well up like a dark cloud filling the sky. She had tried to do something like this once before, and Squeaky had had to rescue her. The memory was so humiliating she refused to let it enter her mind.

"No, I won't," he said flatly.

She felt ridiculously as if she were going to weep. She

swallowed hard, a loneliness crowding in on her from every side: in society, at home, now even here. It had been absurd, even pathetic, that a woman of her age and station should find her only real friendship in a clinic for women off the street! And now even at the clinic she was alone.

"Then I shall have to do it by myself," she said with as much dignity as she could manage. She turned and walked out of the office, leaving him sitting at the desk, a pen in his hand and a look of baffled frustration on his face.

Claudine walked the length of Portpool Lane and turned onto Leather Lane, moving south briskly but without purpose. She was angry. She was afraid of doing this alone. Mostly she was afraid of failing.

She realized how perverse she was being. She knew almost nothing about Dai Tregarron, except that he had a poet's vision and the music of words in his brain. He might very well be guilty of having beaten Winnie Briggs and given her the blow that had been the immediate cause of her death, at least in law. He might not have meant to kill her, but it was a foreseeable result— and a wrong and brutal thing to do. Yet he hadn't seemed like a man who would do such a thing. How could one person hold such violent and terrible contradictions within their nature?

Why was she wasting her time at all? And it was a waste. Squeaky was only speaking the truth when he told her she would be far better employed raising money for the clinic. He had not observed that she was on this mission largely to defy Wallace and all the people she knew who were like him. Did she even know why? Yes, she did. Dai Tregarron had called her Olwen, had spoken to her as if she were a creature capable of escape from the commonplace, not the pedestrian, middle-aged woman everyone else saw, incapable of imagination, even less of passion. He had seen who she wanted to be and given the dream a moment's life.

Someone dug hard fingers into her arm. She gave a cry of fear because the grip was strong enough to pull her to a halt. She struggled, looking around the gray street for anyone who would help her, but she saw only vehicles passing by, people hurrying, collars turned up. She swiveled around to lash out with her free hand as hard as she could.

"What's the matter with you?" Squeaky demanded shrilly. He had to let go of her and step back smartly as she swung her arm, stumbling forward with the impetus when there was nothing close enough to strike. "Who the hell did you think I was?"

She was furious, and horribly embarrassed. A man in a morning coat and top hat was staring at them as he approached. He moved aside quickly, as if she might attack him, too.

"Why didn't you say something?" she shouted at Squeaky.

"I did!" he shouted back. "I called your name. You're so busy in your daydreams you didn't hear me. And you're walking like you're going to break into a run any minute. I ain't chasing you all the way along the street!"

"Keep your voice down!" she growled at him. "You're making a spectacle of us."

"*I* am?" he said incredulously. "I just touched you! You're the one galloping down the pavement like the devil's after you, then attacking me and screaming like a—"

"You were after me," she pointed out. "Well, what do you want? I presume you have something better to do than just scaring me half to death?"

"If me speaking to you in the street, in broad daylight, scares you half to death, how on earth are you

81

going to detect where to find Tregarron and why he wasn't to blame for that poor girl dying?" he demanded. "You'll meet a lot worse than me in the first public house you go into."

She looked him up and down, from his cadaverous face and crooked top hat to his skinny legs in striped trousers and resoled boots.

"What do you want, Mr. Robinson?" she said coldly.

"To help you find Tregarron an' find out who killed that poor girl, you daft piece," he replied with total disrespect. "You don't have the first idea as to what you're doing."

She stood motionless, staring at him. She wanted to say something to freeze his impertinence, but she was also astounded with gratitude.

"Thank you," she accepted after a moment. She thought of adding something about his manners but decided against it.

"You're welcome," he said. "Not that it'll make any difference, of course. There ain't a damn thing we can do."

"Then why are you here?" she said tartly.

"'Cos I remember the last time you set out detecting, an' how you near got yourself killed that time."

She did not say anything. There was no reply to make. Instead she asked him what he thought they should do.

"Look for that damn fool Tregarron," he replied, falling in step beside her. "Find out what he says happened, and then tell him to get out of London. Go hide in Glasgow, or somewhere else they'll never look for him. See what else I can find out about the girl, what's 'er name—Winnie Briggs. You should look into the doings of those three young men. And don't get caught at it, like last time!"

She did not reply to that, either, but kept walking, her mind already busy with plans.

❋

Claudine began her own inquiries immediately, but it was much more difficult than she had imagined. She had to find a way to ask people about each of the three young men without appearing to be intrusive, or obviously implying that they were dissolute. That could not be done directly.

She wrote Christmas cards, a new custom but a

charming one. She shopped for small gifts to send to friends and the few relations she had. She bought a leather-bound copy of the history of the Napoleonic Wars for Wallace. All the time she was thinking whom she could ask the probing and extraordinary questions she needed to in order to learn about Cecil Crostwick, Creighton Foxley, and Ernest Halversgate. She had decided that the latter might not be as harmless and, frankly, as dull as he seemed.

In the end, she could think of no way to go about it but downright lies. She hated deceiving others, but she could do it without flinching; if there was a hesitation in her voice or a shadow across her face, it passed unnoticed.

She had already tried her best to question a few women at the clinic but had learned very little. It occurred to her then to speak to one of the patrons of the clinic, an immensely wealthy man who had been somewhat dissolute in his youth and who now made amends the best he could by donating very generously, to the clinic and other charities. She disliked approaching him on this subject, but she knew of no alternative. She would lie only to save him from the difficult moral dilemma he would have faced were she to tell him the truth.

"I'm sorry to ask you, Mr. Davidson," she said seriously. They were seated in his very pleasant study with the winter sun shining low through the windows and picking out the colors of the cushions on the leather sofa.

"Not at all, Mrs. Burroughs," he replied warmly. "Christmas is an excellent time to give to those in trouble."

"This isn't about money," she said hastily. "I have a friend whose son has lately become very close to a group of young gentlemen, and since then his habits and, to be honest, his character seem to have changed for the worse. I wondered if you could tell me, in confidence, if you have heard anything of these young men. Is their influence as she fears, or is she merely grasping for an excuse for her son's behavior?"

He frowned. "I'm afraid young men don't need much leading to go astray, if they are so inclined," he said ruefully. "I need only my own memory to remind me of that. Who are these young men?"

"Cecil Crostwick and Creighton Foxley," she replied. "Ernest Halversgate I am less certain of."

He pursed his lips. "Powerful families," he said quietly. "I have heard rumors that are less than flattering. Do you wish me to inquire?"

She drew in her breath to say that she did not wish it if it would be a cause of embarrassment to him, then she changed her mind and bit back the words.

"I would appreciate it profoundly," she answered. "I should not ask if the matter were not serious."

"I'm sure," he said with a smile. He spoke gently, and there was humor in his eyes.

She felt a flush of shame rise up her cheeks. She liked Arthur Davidson. There was an integrity in him that made him the last person she would willingly have deceived. He was gentle, and he never made excuses.

"Thank you," she answered gravely. "It is . . . it is very important to me." Claudine rose to her feet, embarrassed now that she had committed herself so openly. "Would it be too indelicate to ask that I might know before it is . . ." She stopped, unable to finish the request acceptably.

"I understand." He rose to his feet also.

He did not understand at all, but she could not tell him so. She regretted that far more than she had expected to.

While she was waiting for his reply, she made very unaccustomed morning social calls on people who used to be friends in the most casual sense but who actually bored her intensely, and whose acquaintance she had let slip since working at the clinic. Fortunately, Christmas was the perfect time to renew friendships, possibly with a small gift of chocolate or candied fruit, and to swap gossip.

It was not difficult to ask about parties, courtships, and who might be on the brink of marrying whom.

"A very nice young woman, Alphonsine Gifford is," one of her friends assured her. "My daughter is friendly with her. Less so, of course, since she has been courting young Halversgate." She smiled indulgently. "I know she has my daughter make a few excuses for her now and then, as girls will do, so that she can see him rather more often than she lets on. Of course, all the girls are willing to tell a little white lie for each other, now and then." She smiled fondly, and Claudine nodded, trying not to let her frustration show. All of this was familiar, understandable, and of no help at all.

*I*t was toward the late afternoon of the following day when Claudine was at the clinic checking on various supplies, that Squeaky Robinson found her in the small room where they kept the medicines. He came in and closed the door behind him. She turned around in surprise, at first not knowing who it was. She saw the weariness in his face, even beyond his usual rather haggard looks, and also what appeared to be very mixed emotions.

"I done a lot of asking," he said without preamble. "You want it straight? 'Cos that's about the only way I can tell it."

She put down the paper and pencil with which she had been making a list. She stood a little straighter, bracing herself. He was going to tell her Dai Tregarron was guilty.

"Yes, certainly," she agreed. "If you please."

"Tregarron drinks more than your average fish, enough so he should be as soused as a herring half his life," he said. "Takes his women where he finds them. Some o' the stories I heard I can't repeat to you. You pass out, I can't pick you up off the floor! He knew Winnie Briggs, all right. Liked 'er. Went both ways, from the sound of it. But she was a long way from being the only one."

He waited for her to argue, all but daring her to.

"Is that all?" she said a little shakily. She had been half expecting this, trying to prepare herself. It should not come as a surprise. It was exactly what Wallace had said, not to mention the Foxleys and the Crostwicks.

"No, o' course it's not all," he said irritably. "I just wanted to make certain you got that. But I ain't telling you any more o' the details because it's the kind o' thing ladies like you shouldn't hear."

She was surprised, and in spite of herself a little touched, that he was protecting her. She had heard enough tales from street women here to think there was not much left that would shock her. But all the same, she did not want to hear them about Tregarron.

"Thank you," she said, being careful not to smile, in case it hurt his feelings.

He went on. "I can't find 'ide nor 'air of the stupid sod, which means the police probably can't either. So he's likely run for the hills. But I don't think he done what they're saying. He's a drunk, but I couldn't find nobody who'd say he was vicious, like. He'd fight a man, if he were pushed to it, and pretty likely knock 'im senseless—unless he fell over hisself first. Which has happened. But nobody ever saw him hit a woman. Use them, make love to them, then throw them away, surely!

89

But when I say 'make love,' that's what I mean. Lot of talk, lot of courting them like he actually cared."

Squeaky shrugged, his expression mystified. "Maybe he did fall in love, or kid himself as he did. Every time! God help us. New one every few days."

Claudine was not quite sure what she felt—relief, confusion—and she was completely at a loss to know what to do next.

"But all three of the other young men said he did it," she pointed out.

"Whose side are you on?" Squeaky demanded indignantly.

This time she was obliged to smile, in spite of the bittersweet quality of it. "I'm sorry," she said. "I think I'm on Mr. Tregarron's. And it sounds as if you are now, too."

His face was twisted with emotion from somewhere deep inside himself. "I don't go for hitting women, 'less they really asked for it. But if there's anything I hate like poison, it's some bleedin' wealthy little sod committing a crime and then blaming someone else for it, someone who can't defend himself, while he plays all righteous and walks away with his skin untouched."

"What do you think happened?" she asked, suddenly finding she respected him. In spite of his lurid past, he had a code of ethics, and he despised those who trespassed across it.

"I think those three little bleeders were playing with her, and when she couldn't take them all on, one o' them lost his temper an' hit her," Squeaky replied. "'Cos she was ill, like, she took it harder than he meant. He got scared an' thought he'd really finished her. But she were still alive, and he panicked. Then he had to do her in for real. I think Tregarron tried to stop him, and all three o' them set on her an' beat the hell out of her and then blamed him for killing her. They're all out o' the same box, so they stuck by each other. Poor bastard doesn't have a chance against them, and they know that."

It was hideous, but it fell into place, fitting exactly. Claudine could see it again in her mind's eye: Dai bent over Winnie, the bruises on her face and the blood, the stiffness with which he had at last risen. Maybe his injuries were not from Winnie fighting against him but from the other three as he tried to defend her?

"How can we prove it?" she said aloud.

"God knows," he replied in sudden defeat.

"They'll all have bruises," she went on, thinking about it. "We've got to get evidence of that before they're healed."

"No point," Squeaky told her. "They'll all agree that they fought. But they'll say *they* were the ones defending her."

"Three against one?" She struggled for a different truth. "They couldn't beat him?"

"He's used to brawls," he pointed out. "He's been in enough of them. It could take three fancy pansies like that to take him. I'd believe that."

"Then why was he bending over the girl to see if she was all right, not one of them?" she demanded.

He smiled very slowly. "That's a good one. But it won't make no difference, 'cos they're gentlemen with society on their side, an' there's three of 'em. But it does make you wonder, don't it?"

"Then we have to find more." She stated it as if it were self-evident. "If they attacked Winnie, it won't be the first time they ever took a prostitute. There'll be history somewhere."

Squeaky's eyebrows shot up. "You think anybody's going to tell you that? What world are you dreaming of?"

"The one we both know, albeit from slightly different angles," she replied.

"I like your idea of 'slightly,'" he said with a wry twist of his mouth.

"All right, very different," she conceded. "I have made inquiries. I just don't have an answer yet."

"I'll look some more then, in the places I know," he said grimly. "See if there's a girl willing to talk."

"If you learn anything new, leave me a message," she said. "I'll do the same if I find something."

He nodded.

Claudine began again the very next day. With Christmas fast approaching, time was too short to waste, even if it meant forcing the issue in a manner she would never have done in normal circumstances.

She contrived to get herself more or less invited to an afternoon party at a large house because she knew Eppy Crostwick was bound to be there also. She wore one of the new afternoon gowns that Wallace had suggested she purchase. She had seen it at the dressmaker's, and it had required only minimal alteration to fit her really very well. It had most attractive sleeves, lending her broader shoulders than she possessed by nature. Both that and the unusually warm color of it were quite flattering.

She arrived at the party to the poorly disguised surprise of several of the other people present, but she was made welcome enough not to feel uncomfortable. Not that discomfort would have prevented her remaining. She had nothing else to go on, especially considering Arthur Davidson might find nothing of value; worse than that, he might have agreed to assist her only to be civil, and actually have no intention of telling her anything.

Within moments she was drawn into the buzz of conversation. Gossip was cheerfully exchanged, and for the first time in a long time she listened with genuine attention. One never knew what one might hear; any small piece of information might inadvertently fit into the puzzle of Winnie's death.

It was almost an hour before she managed to speak to Eppy alone and not obviously be overheard.

"What an unusual pleasure to see you here," Eppy said with undisguised curiosity. "I can't imagine you are going to find many donations to your clinic, though. We are all too involved in preparations for Christmas. It always costs more than you think it will, don't you find?" It was a rather heavy-handed warning that she did not intend to contribute to the clinic and would not appreciate being placed in the position of having to refuse.

Claudine smiled back at her with a warmth she did not feel. "Actually, we are doing quite well, thank you.

Many people have already thought of the less fortunate and given. A beautiful part of the true spirit of Christmas, don't you agree?"

Eppy's smile froze. "Of course. And how nice that you are not in the position of having people dread seeing you approach, in case you ask for something they cannot give."

"Exactly," Claudine agreed. "I would hate to embarrass someone who was in . . . straitened circumstances."

Eppy's smile turned to ice. A few yards from them, a woman in a silk gown whose cost would have fed a family for a year smiled happily and swept past to greet someone.

Claudine reminded herself why she was here and returned the warmth to her voice.

"But you are quite right," she said gently. "This is a time of year for enjoying all the blessings we have and being grateful for them. One can hardly do that with a long face or by thinking only of misfortunes. I do hope Oona Gifford does not feel crushed by that wretched event at her party. Until that moment, which no forethought could have prevented, it was completely delightful."

Eppy looked startled but hastily agreed. "I'm sure she will forget it in a while, especially if we do not keep reminding her." She met Claudine's eyes. "I imagine that wretched man will be caught sooner or later."

"He may have left the country." Claudine referred back to the remark at the theater. "That could be best for all of us, don't you think?"

Eppy thought in silence for a moment.

"I'm sure Cecil would rather not have to go to court to testify as to exactly what happened," Claudine went on. "Apart from anything else, when you have an interesting, busy life—as I'm sure he does—it gets harder to remember things as time goes by. There are so many other parties, other occasions."

"Yes," Eppy agreed. "Yes, of course. But I'm sure Cecil would remember. It's not every day you see some . . . some madman kill a woman in front of you." She shivered.

"Oh dear," Claudine said with commiseration. "Was that really what happened? Poor Cecil."

"Of course it was!" Eppy looked startled at Claudine's slowness of wits. "Tregarron brought the woman, and then when she refused to do what he wished, he struck her. Right across the face, Cecil said. He was horrified. He said that at first he was too appalled to do anything at all. Then when Tregarron struck her again, even harder, Cecil stepped forward and told him in no uncertain way that if he did it again, then he would be obliged to strike him back."

"Thank goodness he was there," Claudine said warmly. "What did the others do? Surely they were appalled as well?"

"Oh, yes, of course," Eppy agreed. "Cecil said Creighton Foxley was absolutely incensed. He tried to drag the wretched man off her, but apparently he had completely lost his head. Of course, he was out of his mind with drink. It took both of them—I mean all three of them—to drag Tregarron off. But by that time the poor girl was unconscious on the ground. Obviously that was all after you spoke with the man. Why did you go out to the terrace, anyway?" She looked at Claudine curiously.

"I went for a breath of air. It is actually a very pleasant space," Claudine explained. Nearly the truth. There was no need to say that the conversation had bored her and made her feel hemmed in by trivialities. That would be unnecessarily rude. Perhaps others felt as she did but had better manners than to let it be known.

"And you were the first one out after the . . . the tragedy," Eppy noted. "I expect Cecil was trying to revive her, when you found them."

"Actually . . . ," Claudine began then suddenly changed her mind. "They were all crowded near her when I got there. Poor Cecil, what a distress for him it must've been when she did not stir."

"Terrible," Eppy agreed. "I don't know how you think he could forget it in a few days, or even weeks."

"I'm sorry," Claudine lied. "I hadn't thought about it that way. Well, that testimony should be plain enough for there to be no defense for Tregarron."

"None at all," Eppy agreed.

"I imagine Creighton and Ernest Halversgate will say the same. They'd all be there to support one another . . . over the distress of it all, I mean."

"I imagine so," Eppy agreed. "And wouldn't you have to testify if that awful man is arrested? I mean, mightn't you have to?"

"Yes," Claudine said very soberly, "I would have to." She gulped air, and it caught in her throat, almost choking her. What Eppy had described was not at all what she had seen. But if all three of the boys swore to the same circumstance, would her word be enough against theirs? She doubted it. "Of course," she added when she had regained her composure.

*T*he day after that she decided to pursue another tack. She did not know Alphonsine Gifford well. However, on the occasions when they had met she had found her a very pleasant young woman and of an independent mind, which showed a degree of courage as well as intelligence. She decided to visit her and congratulate her on her prospective engagement to Ernest Halversgate.

They were sitting in the withdrawing room. It was the appropriate place to receive calls, traditionally known as "morning calls," although the visits actually took place in the afternoon. The fire was roaring up the chimney, in spite of the still unusually clement weather. The mantel was decked with garlands, as were many of the doors and archways. It all looked most welcoming. It took an effort of will to recall that only just over a week ago a tragedy had taken place in this house.

Alphonsine was dressed in an afternoon gown of rich burgundy, which was startlingly attractive against her warm coloring. Claudine would have expected the shade to be overpowering, but on the contrary, it seemed perfectly natural on Alphonsine.

"Thank you," the young woman said demurely when Claudine offered her congratulations. "I'm sure I shall be very happy." She looked down at her hands, avoiding Claudine's eyes.

With a jolt of memory Claudine thought of herself thirty years ago, sitting just like that, receiving someone's well-meant congratulations on becoming engaged to Wallace. What her visitor had implied was that a girl as plain as Claudine was lucky to receive an offer of marriage from a man as decent and promising as Wallace. Someone safe, comfortable, and assured of respectability. And in truth, it was much more than some women could look forward to. Heaven knew, she had ministered to hundreds who would have given everything they possessed to change places with her. A roof over their heads, warmth, food, and nice clothes were dreams that barely flickered in their imaginations.

Poor Winnie Briggs had been one of them.

That thought jerked Claudine back to her reason for being here, which had nothing to do with the fresh hot tea, cakes and tiny pies of pastry, and rich fruit that were before her on the table.

"I hope you will be," she said. "Of course, much of happiness is what we make of it. But I believe you are a woman of courage. You will embrace life. You will not expect it always to be gentle with you, or even fair."

Alphonsine's head came up sharply, and she met Claudine's eyes. "What . . . what do you mean? And don't tell me you don't mean anything. I know you better than that, Mrs. Burroughs. You are not one of the usual society women who goes from party to party, giving a little charity here and there and saying all sorts of things they don't mean. You work at the clinic in Portpool Lane, don't you?"

Claudine was surprised. "Yes. It means a great deal to me. Why do you ask?"

"Do you have women there like the one who died here the other evening?"

"Yes. Many exactly like her. We do manage to save most of them, and at least to give a little comfort to those we can't save. But if you're worried about Mr. Halversgate's part in all this, there's no need to be—I'm sure he did all he could to save her."

Alphonsine's eyes lowered again. "Of course. It was . . . dreadful." Suddenly she looked intently at Claudine. "Will he have to testify in court, if they find Mr.

Tregarron? Do you think they will? If . . . if they find him guilty, they'll hang him, won't they?"

In spite of the fire and the hot tea, Claudine was chilled. She remembered Lambert Foxley's words about assuring that the young men would not have to appear in court and therefore would avoid being cross-questioned by a lawyer for the defense. Was it because he wanted to spare them the ordeal of a trial, or because he wanted to ensure they would not be caught in a lie? Apparently, Alphonsine did not question the story Ernest and his friends had offered. Claudine doubted the young woman would be able to sit calmly on a sofa if she thought her soon-to-be fiancé was guilty of such a crime and that it was possible an innocent man could be hanged for something he did not do.

"Yes," she said decisively. "They will hang him, if they believe he deliberately beat her. But Mr. Halversgate was there. He must know what happened, and he will be able to testify to it."

Alphonsine stared at her. "Yes . . ." She swallowed. "He will. But of course he was not the only one who was there. Cecil Crostwick and Creighton Foxley were as well. Perhaps one of them testifying will be enough . . . do you think?"

"No, I'm afraid I don't think so at all." Claudine had no compunction in being blunt with her. "If you were the person defending Mr. Tregarron, wouldn't you wish to question them all, to make sure their accounts were exactly the same?"

"I suppose I would." Alphonsine gave a very slight smile. "Don't you think they will make sure that it is? If Mr. Tregarron is caught, of course?"

Claudine thought for a moment before she answered. "But, of course, they would have been standing in different places and therefore seen things slightly differently. So their accounts might be a bit varied."

Alphonsine was very pale, even in the gaslight. "I . . . yes, of course they would. I hadn't thought of that."

"It would probably be best if they each described exactly what they saw. One would wish to be as natural sounding as possible, should it come to anything, which of course it may not."

A succession of emotions crossed Alphonsine's face: relief, disappointment, then misery. "Yes, you are quite right," she agreed. "Perhaps he will never be caught, and they won't have to say anything at all."

In the hansom cab on her way home, Claudine considered all the bits of information she had gathered.

Only one struck her as very slightly incongruous now, after talking to Alphonsine—the fact that the girl was having her friends tell what amounted to lies, even if very conventional ones, so that she might spend more time with Ernest Halversgate. The girl didn't seem particularly besotted, though happy enough. It appeared to be a relationship of convenience . . . So, surely the ordinary social arrangements were more than sufficient? It was a small thing, but it nagged at her. She decided then that she had no choice but to call again on Arthur Davidson.

*S*he hated doing it. She was actually trembling as she stood at the front door and reached for the brass-headed bell pull, but she could not afford to wait any longer. If Arthur Davidson preferred not to answer her request, then better that she know it now. She was aware that by returning to press him for more information, she might also make him less likely to contribute to the clinic in the future. That would be a heavy blow. He had been generous.

The footman opened the door and recognized her immediately. A few minutes later she was in the withdrawing room in front of the fire, Davidson standing to receive her. She had always seen him in his study before, or at the clinic. However, there was no time to appreciate the glass-paned bookcase or the slightly mismatched furniture, evidence that he cared for comfort rather than for appearances. She wondered what his wife was like. He had never spoken of her.

Claudine forced herself to address the subject immediately.

"I apologize, but I must ask you if you have learned anything about the three young men we recently spoke about." She swallowed. Her mouth was dry. "I am afraid the matter grows urgent."

His mouth pulled a little tighter, and there was a sadness in his eyes. "I have. None of it particularly surprising. Halversgate is, as you implied, a follower rather than a leader. Crostwick and Foxley are another matter. In better society, they are merely a trifle daring. More privately, they indulge in excess of drink in very dubious places, which increasingly often descends to violence. I wish I could tell you otherwise." A faint humor touched his mouth. "I would advise your friend, if she exists, to counsel her son most strongly not to associate with them. They may never be caught doing anything wrong, but they are a malign influence."

Claudine felt the color burn up her face. She was clearly far more transparent than she had intended.

"Thank you," she said awkwardly. She could not tell him the real reason for her inquiries, but she made no more pretense at excuses. She was too embarrassed to accept any hospitality, even though she would have enjoyed conversing with him on other matters. After wishing him a happy Christmas, she excused herself and left.

The next morning Claudine told Squeaky Robinson what she had learned. They were in his office with the door closed. The rest of the clinic was busy preparing for Christmas—trying to bring as much cheer as possible to those who had nowhere else to go, or whose sickness and injuries made them unable to care for themselves.

Squeaky was impressed with her account, although he did his best not to show it.

"Good," he said a trifle sententiously. "It's a start. So Halversgate's a follower."

"Apparently. This is information, but I'm afraid it is not proof," she warned.

Squeaky pulled his face into an expression of disgust. "I know that! But don't underestimate it. It'll give you a lever to use with him."

"Me?" She was startled. "How?"

He squinted at her. "He doesn't know you don't have proof. We can't neither of us find anything much about Winnie Briggs, poor little cow. Nothing different from thousands of others, just unlucky. An' so far I still haven't found any sign of Tregarron, just a lot of stories, most of 'em lies, far as I can tell. But it only needs one nasty bastard rubbed the wrong way, an' someone'll nab him. So you'd better get about it, seeing as I can't hardly go, and put a flea in Mr. Halversgate's tail. You'll think of something."

Claudine did not find this task easy. She hated not so much actually telling a lie, but rather implying one and allowing it to be understood. Ordinary tact in talking about things that did not matter greatly was a social skill everyone was expected to possess. But deception came hard to her. Social exchange was a web of small flatteries and of compromises that entangled them all. It was one of the reasons she found it difficult.

Nevertheless, she needed to speak honestly with Ernest Halversgate.

While ostensibly calling on Tolly Halversgate, she actually met with Ernest in the large garden room overlooking their paved terrace and the rather fine balustrade, which gave the illusion that the lawn was bigger than it actually was. It was a clever piece of design, and she admired it.

"Thank you," Ernest said a little stiffly. "My grandfather had it put in. It was rather dull before. I'm so sorry Mama is not here, Mrs. Burroughs. I don't expect her for another half hour or so." He was a very correct young man and at the moment clearly embarrassed.

Claudine smiled at him. "I'm sure it is my fault. I must have written down the wrong time. Or else I have it confused with another date. If I improved my handwriting, instead of scribbling when I am in a hurry, I would save myself from inconveniencing other people. It's I who must apologize."

"Not at all," he said a trifle automatically.

"You're very kind." She looked through the windows at the lawn and the carefully planned curved walk, which appeared to lead to spaces beyond but in reality probably doubled back on itself. "It does not look too windy out there, and it certainly is not raining. Would you be gracious enough to show me around the garden?

I think it has a remarkable art to it, which I find most pleasing."

He could hardly refuse. "Of course," he said reluctantly. His body was tense and his hands oddly stiff as he walked over to the door and opened it for her.

As they crossed the terrace and went down the steps, she began the conversation for which she had come.

"I recently had a most delightful visit with Alphonsine Gifford, and she told me of your forthcoming engagement. May I congratulate you? She is in every way a charming young woman."

"Thank you." The shadow of a smile softened his face, but he did not turn his head or meet her eyes.

"It will be good to have someone to stand by you and be of support should this wretched business of Tregarron come to trial," she went on. "It cannot be pleasant to have to testify to such a distressing incident."

He stopped on the edge of the grass. "I don't think I shall have to do that. Surely the evidence is perfectly plain? I . . . I didn't really do anything."

"All the more reason why you should testify, if he is found," she said gently. "You will have had a clearer view and, I daresay, a clearer head. You seemed to me to be a little more . . . sober . . . than the others."

He gasped, and she realized that perhaps he had forgotten for a moment that she had been there, moments after the incident, when Tregarron was still attempting to revive Winnie and the other three young men were standing close by.

She waited for him to continue. The silence was heavy and awkward.

He started to speak and then changed his mind.

She was acutely aware of his difficulty, but she could not afford to break the silence or change the subject, as she would have at any other time.

"It was all . . . ridiculous and unpleasant," he said at last. "Tregarron should never have been invited. He's a complete outsider . . . appalling man. Creighton can't possibly have known how he would behave, or he wouldn't have had anything to do with him."

"Creighton Foxley invited him?" She affected surprise. She really only wanted to get a response from him.

"Well . . . I . . ." He trailed off unhappily.

"You are very loyal." The remark was not complimentary. Her voice held a shadow of the contempt she felt for his seeming emotional indifference to the tragedy of a young woman's death and the fact that neither he nor his friends had done anything effective to prevent it.

Ernest blushed hotly. "Yes, I am, Mrs. Burroughs. I have no intention of discussing the matter unless I am forced to. But of course I will testify against Tregarron, if they call me. I'm angry that the man was allowed onto the premises, especially into Miss Gifford's home. But when we are married I shall make certain that such a thing doesn't happen again."

"Of course," Claudine agreed, her heart sinking as she pictured a long and fiercely protected life stretching ahead for Alphonsine. Was it what she wanted? Or what she believed it wise to settle for? Perhaps there were sides to Ernest Halversgate that Claudine had failed to see. "I'm sure you will find it distasteful to stand in court and tell the public exactly what happened," she said more soothingly than she felt. "Any of us would. But you are, above all, a man of honor, so that is what you will do. I am so sorry any of this happened."

He managed a bleak smile then moved forward and pointed out a particularly fine holly bush that was brilliant with berries.

"Superb," she murmured politely but quite honestly. "Holly is such good value, I think. It provides color, shape, and interest in a garden when there is so little else at this time of year."

They made meaningless conversation around the rest of the garden, which was not nearly as large as clever optical illusion had suggested.

At last they reached the door to the withdrawing room again. Tolly Halversgate was standing just inside, controlling her expression of annoyance with some difficulty.

"I'm so sorry," she said coolly. "I thought I had made my arrangement clear, but apparently I was remiss. I hope Ernest kept you entertained." There was no lift in her voice to make it a question. She was expressing criticism, not concern. She glanced at her son with anxiety. He met her eyes then looked away.

"He was charming," Claudine said with warmth. "What a perfectly delightful garden you have. In this mild weather he was kind enough to show me some of its very best aspects. It seems his grandfather had a gift for design that I very much admire."

Tolly's eyebrows rose in something that looked like disbelief. "I had no idea you were interested in garden design."

"Surely anything that creates beauty is interesting?" Claudine countered.

"Tea?" Tolly asked. Then before Claudine could reply, she turned to her son. "Thank you, Ernest. Please feel now that you may leave to continue with your own business. I'm sure Mrs. Burroughs will excuse you, and I am most obliged for your courtesy."

"Thank you for your company, and your conversation, Mr. Halversgate," Claudine said courteously.

"My pleasure." He bowed in a stiff and rather old-fashioned manner for such a young man. Then, without adding anything further, he left the room.

"What an agreeable and sensitive person he is," Claudine said approvingly as she sat down in the chair by the fire, opposite the one nearest Tolly. "So much more mature than others I meet who are his age."

Tolly stared at her.

Claudine continued to smile, feeling as if she were baring her teeth. "Miss Gifford must be very happy, and quite confident in her future."

"We have not announced their engagement yet," Tolly said a trifle sharply. However, her shoulders were relaxing a little, and there was a hint of satisfaction in her voice.

"Alphonsine told me herself." Claudine stretched the truth considerably. "Of course it is very difficult for a

ANNE PERRY

young woman to keep such secrets, especially when we
are all involved in this other most unhappy matter." It
was clumsy, but she could not think of a more tactful
way to introduce the subject.

Tolly did not need to ask to which matter Claudine
was referring. "I have no idea what you mean," she said
coldly. "Ernest is not involved in it at all. He simply was
unfortunate enough to have been close by, and he very
naturally tried to restrain Tregarron. Heaven only
knows what the other two were doing, inviting that man
to the house in the first place. But if you had really
thought about it, you would have realized that yourself." She looked at Claudine directly. "Naturally you
were upset, having arrived at the scene before anyone
else. Anybody would be. But if you look at it with hind-
sight, it is perfectly apparent what occurred."

Claudine looked at her with interest. Her mind was
whirling, and there was a prickle of excitement stirring
inside her: fear mixed with the scent of the hunt. She
felt there was suddenly a glimpse of truth to be found
here, beyond the carefully prepared words that had
been there before.

"Yes. I am still thinking back over everything I saw,"
she answered, her own gaze not wavering from Tolly's.

114

"How wise of you," Tolly replied. "I can see that you are weighing your position very cautiously. After all, a word misplaced can do a lot of damage."

"It often can," Claudine agreed. "And once spoken, be very difficult to retract." She wondered if Tolly was merely concerned about her son's forthcoming engagement, which might be jeopardized if he appeared to be too closely involved with Tregarron. Or of the considerable unpleasantness if he were to testify in a way that reflected badly on Creighton Foxley and Cecil Crostwick, who were unquestionably leaders in their social set. Or possibly of the damage to Alphonsine's value if someone were to suggest, even obliquely, that Forbes Gifford's parties were of a character where men and women such as Tregarron and Winnie Briggs were often found.

Tolly smiled. "I see you understand exactly." Her voice was cold and careful. "I'm sure you will do the right thing. Alphonsine is a lovely young woman. My son is very fortunate. He will be marrying into a family who will take the greatest care of their daughter's reputation so neither of them will ever have cause for embarrassment. I'm certain, had you a son, you would wish the same for him." Her smile grew wider, easier. "You understand the nuances precisely. Now, may I offer you tea? I'm sure after your walk you would like some refreshment."

"How kind of you," Claudine accepted, her mind racing to weigh all that Tolly's remarks were intended to mean. The Giffords were powerful, wealthy, quite capable either of helping Wallace in his climb to success or of hurting him. It would depend on Claudine's behavior regarding the situation and the reputations of everyone involved—not only Alphonsine's but, by implication, that of the young man she was going to marry. If Claudine were to cause any kind of embarrassment, Tolly Halversgate would make very sure that she paid for it dearly.

Did that mean that there was some way in which Ernest Halversgate needed protection? Surely it did. Tolly was worried, and Ernest himself was afraid, afraid of his new friends, the circle of which he was on the edge and so badly wanted to be within. What price would he pay for that privilege? Telling lies as to who was responsible for Winnie Briggs's death? Would he let an innocent man hang for it?

If that was the case, Claudine must find a way to make sure he understood that price and that he would ultimately find it more than he was willing to pay.

Could she use Alphonsine somehow? How much of the truth did the girl know, or guess? Did Ernest know the answer to that, and did he care?

She could not yet answer those questions. Maybe it depended on whether Squeaky could confirm in any detail what Arthur Davidson had told her.

She remained talking idle nonsense to Tolly Halversgate until good manners were satisfied then took her leave.

Outside in the fresh air she walked briskly, her mind crowded with thoughts. The police might catch Dai Tregarron any day, unless of course he had left the country and gone overseas. The thought of him in another country, no matter how civilized or how beautiful, made her sad. She pictured an exile's loneliness, the rootless unbelonging of a man whose art was inspired by the land he loved.

She shook herself out of such useless speculation. She had spoken to him exactly twice, but his bruised and troubled face haunted her mind, making her behave like a stupid girl. She still hadn't confirmed that he wasn't guilty, and she needed to remember that and conduct her inquiries accordingly. Collect the facts, then deduce a theory to fit them—don't invent your theory then select your facts to suit. Hopefully, Squeaky could locate Tregarron and hear his side of the events. In the meantime, she must work with what she had. Begin again at the beginning.

*S*he was obliged to find Oona Gifford at an early evening soirée. An exceptionally large soprano was giving a recital of songs celebrating Christmas in different languages. Donations were to be given to charities in aid of the unfortunate.

She had not intended to attend; it was a last resort in order to find Oona. As such, Claudine arrived late and was obliged to sit in the back row. That turned out to be a blessing, since from there she could see everyone else, and in the intermission Oona would be obliged to pass by her if she wished to leave for the refreshments. Considering the seriousness and the monotony of the songs, that was extremely likely. Claudine herself would certainly leave and do everything within her power to avoid being invited to meet the hostess, or anyone else for whom she would have to invent a flattering opinion. It would be comparatively easier to part with a suitable financial offering.

In the end, Oona saw Claudine before Claudine saw her.

"Thank goodness!" Oona said with intense relief. "Please say you have something urgent to discuss with me and we must do it alone, because it would be most ill-mannered to disturb other people's listening enjoyment by making a noise. We must find somewhere private . . . as soon as possible. My head is ringing from these high notes. I'm not sure I shall ever hear a top C again without ducking in case the chandeliers shatter in pieces."

Claudine did not bother to hide her pleasure, even if she made a rather poor attempt to disguise it as surprise.

"How fortunate I am to see you," she said, quite seriously. "I'm afraid I must ask you to interrupt your enjoyment and spare me time to speak with you a little more privately. Most inconsiderate of me, I know, but it really does matter."

Oona looked taken aback. She searched Claudine's face for sarcasm and found none.

"I'm perfectly serious," Claudine assured her. "Seeing you is actually the reason I came. You didn't think I came for the music, did you?" She made the tone light and her smile a little rueful. She liked Oona, and being candid was not difficult, only a little uncomfortable in that she did not wish to hurt her.

Oona held out her hand in a gesture of invitation. "Then let us find somewhere uninterrupted and discuss whatever it is you wish." She turned and led the way out of the gallery and up a flight of steps to a landing out of sight from the main hall.

"What's happened?" she asked when they faced each other. "Not something more to do with Tregarron, is it? I really don't know who invited him. It certainly was not I. I suspect it might have been Creighton Foxley."

"It is to do with Tregarron, one way or another," Claudine admitted, trying to get her thoughts in order. She had expected to have to work her way toward candor, not be pitched headfirst into it at the moment of meeting. Now her careful plans were completely overturned. "I had a delightful meeting with Alphonsine the other day," she continued after a pause. "She told me she is shortly to become engaged to Ernest Halversgate." She let the statement hang in the air as if it were a question. She studied Oona's face as she framed her

120

reply. She saw anxiety in it and a degree of uncertainty. It mirrored her own feelings exactly.

Oona was extraordinarily candid, more than any other woman in Claudine's acquaintance would have been. "Do you know something about Ernest Halversgate that you think perhaps I don't?" she asked.

Claudine replied with another question. She was surprised how much she cared that Oona should think well of her, or at the very least know that she spoke out of honesty and concern, not unkindness.

"Do you know Mr. Halversgate very well?"

"No. Alphonsine is my stepdaughter. This arrangement has been made by her father, and I do not believe it is my place to question his judgment—even had I any cause to." She frowned, the concern in her face deepening. "Are you suggesting that there is some reason why I should?"

"I know nothing ill of him," Claudine assured her. "Except perhaps he is a tad unwise in the company he keeps. But it might be prudent to delay the announcement until there is more of a resolution to the death of that unfortunate young woman. I . . . I appreciate that it would be loyal to express your confidence in him, publicly, but perhaps be certain beforehand that that is what Alphonsine herself wishes. I may be speaking quite out of turn." She felt the hot color burn up her face. It was more than out of turn; it was meddlesome and possibly quite unjust. But Mr. Davidson's information was too serious to ignore, for Alphonsine's sake, quite apart from the need to know the truth about Winnie Briggs's death.

Oona was regarding her intently. "Are you carefully avoiding saying that you think there is something in Ernest Halversgate's behavior that we would find more than youthful indiscretion? Please be honest. Alphonsine is not my daughter, but I love her as dearly as if she were." She took a deep breath. "Ernest is not my choice, he is her father's, made with every consideration for her happiness. Ernest has an excellent reputation, both for sobriety and for wisdom, and the considerable ability to handle money well. Alphonsine will have a very large inheritance, eventually. She is an only child, and my husband loves her deeply."

"I can understand that it is a fundamental consideration that she marry a man who is both honest and prudent," Claudine agreed. The fact that Wallace Burroughs was both these things loomed in her mind.

"I hear no enthusiasm in your voice," Oona said unhappily. "Alphonsine is being very . . . awkward about it herself. I had attributed it to the fact that Ernest is—to put it frankly—dull. When we are young we look for romance, excitement, even a little danger. Only when we have tasted those qualities and find they leave a bitter taste, do we see the beauty of reliability, and of kindness, if you like."

Claudine closed her eyes for a moment, swallowing hard, then opened them again. "The voice of wisdom," she said in little more than a whisper. "But I notice you make kindness important. Real kindness has its roots in strength, don't you think? Without it, and courage, when would his apparent kindness become merely good intentions, which at the slightest chill can wither into nothing?"

Oona blinked several times, her face bleak with anxiety.

"I have the strongest feeling that you are trying to warn me against something, but I cannot see what. I know already that Alphonsine does not love Ernest, and I am not at all sure whether he loves her or not. But at twenty who knows the difference between love and infatuation? I have been infatuated a few times, haven't you?"

"Yes," Claudine agreed ruefully. The memory brought sudden pain, not of grief but of embarrassment.

Oona was smiling. "I see your choices were no wiser than mine. My parents decided my first marriage, and I know they meant well. He was much older than I, and he died quite early, leaving me free to choose my own second marriage. I am fortunate enough to be very happy in that. Enough that I will not impose my advice over his when it comes to a husband for his daughter, even if I might find poor Ernest both pompous and with little passion or humor." She gave a slight shrug. "But then, I liked Mr. Tregarron, so what does that say for my judgment?"

"I liked him, too," Claudine admitted. "But I would not let my daughter marry him, had I a daughter."

"Would you let her marry Ernest Halversgate? And please, do answer that honestly, or not at all."

"Not until the death of Winnie Briggs has been resolved more fully," Claudine said gravely.

"I see." Oona nodded. "Yes, I think I do see. Perhaps Alphonsine's reluctance to obey her father's wish in the matter should be considered more seriously. She loves him very much and would not be awkward just on a whim. I think I shall try to persuade him that after this recent unpleasantness, she should be given rather more time. He thinks women are fragile." She smiled with a sudden bright tenderness. "Which is utter nonsense, of course, but on this occasion I might pretend that I agree with him. Thank you. This cannot have been easy for you to say."

Claudine smiled back at her. "Easier than listening to the rest of the songs," she said lightly. They both laughed with fellowship, and there was a sudden easing of the tension.

Claudine went to the clinic the next day, determined to coerce Squeaky into further action regarding Winnie Briggs, even if it meant taking over some of the bookkeeping herself. The weather was still mild, but it was raining. She was glad to be inside where she could take off her wet boots and put on dry ones.

She intended to remain only until she could speak with Squeaky and find out if he had learned anything further. Regardless of what he said, she must tell him of her growing conviction that Ernest Halversgate was lying about something, and perhaps Alphonsine was, too. Might he even have confided in her? Or possibly she had guessed as much from his manner, or a slip of the tongue?

Claudine worked for nearly two hours, mostly on arrangements to provide a really good Christmas dinner for any patients who were resident in the clinic or who might come in longing for a dry bed and a warm roof over their heads on the days that were set aside to celebrate the birth of Christ, and the charity that went with that event. Efforts to ease the longing for a sign there was an eternity beyond the grief of this world, where so many had so little chance of happiness.

It was almost midday when Squeaky staggered in, disheveled and bleary-eyed. He led the way to his office and sat down heavily in his chair. Claudine looked at him. Both compassion and practicality sent her away immediately to fetch him a pot of tea and several slices of toast. She set them down in front of him and then took the chair opposite the desk and demanded his attention.

"Take your breakfast," she ordered him brusquely. "Eat the toast, whether you feel like it or not, and drink two cups of tea. I shall tell you what I have learned. Then, when you have finished and feel fit to conduct yourself like a man, you will tell me what you have learned."

For once he did not argue. It was only too clear that he had spent a long and supremely testing night, and much of it had been unpleasant. She wished to know exactly where he had been and what he had learned and did not intend to allow him to evade answering.

Carefully she recounted to him whom she had seen and all that had been said that mattered. She had brought two cups on the tray, and had tea herself, then wished she had also brought more toast. He ate all five slices himself, with butter and marmalade.

"Well?" she said impatiently when he had swallowed the last mouthful.

He shook his head slowly, pursing his lips. "Foxley and Crostwick are two very self-indulgent young men," he said, framing the words carefully, his eyes on hers to watch her reaction.

"Self-indulgent," she repeated. "Don't wrap it up, Squeaky. We don't have time."

"Couple o' drunken sods." He relaxed a little. "Bullies, lechers, arrogant bastards, but with enough money, and charm when they need it, so's they get away with it. You won't get anybody to swear to it—not that they'd be believed anyway. Can see how they get along with Dai Tregarron. Natural companion, you might say. Except that he can hold his drink better, and charm the women so as he don't have to pay nobody."

"But not Ernest Halversgate?" she pressed. Squeaky had confirmed what Arthur Davidson had said.

"Not him." Squeaky lifted his shoulders exaggeratedly. "Much too tight-collared and stiff-necked to do that sort of thing. Wants to be one of the boys, but only to be included, not for its own sake. Too careful, too clean." He raised his hands dramatically, the gesture losing something because of the ink stains on his fingers.

"By nature or out of fear?" she asked.

"Ah," he sighed. "Clever. I don't know. Does she have a lot of money, this Miss Gifford?"

"She will do," Claudine answered. "Why? Do you think he's careful because he wants to be master of that? Forbes Gifford has a deep affection for his daughter. And so, actually, does her stepmother. If anything really unsavory were known about Ernest, I am sure the engagement would not go ahead. Actually—" She stopped, not sure what she wanted to say, or if it should be said to Squeaky Robinson.

"What?" he demanded.

She should trust him. She had asked for his help without offering any reward to him for his trouble, only perhaps discomfort, even danger.

128

"I think Alphonsine herself is not entirely happy with the prospect of marrying Ernest Halversgate," she answered. "But I don't know the reason. Possibly she has learned something that her parents don't know, but she might not be able to prove it . . . Or maybe she heard it in confidence and cannot repeat it without betraying whoever it is that told her."

Squeaky shook his head. "Comes of having nothing else to worry about," he observed.

"What does?" She was confused.

"Gentry," he replied patiently. "Makes life a whole lot more complicated than it has to be. Don't just marry someone you want to marry, follow all these complicated rules—it's like learning the steps of a dance. Never go to anything in a straight line, stop and twirl and twiddle all over the place before you finally get where you're trying to go, when a plain man would've simply taken a couple of strides, following his nose. Still, got to have something to do with your time, I s'pose."

"It's not to do with time, Squeaky," she said. "It's to do with separating the best people from the second best."

"Best?" he retorted indignantly. "In whose eyes?"

"Their own, of course. Do you think they even know

129

there is anybody else?" She smiled as she said it, but there was a hard, sad honesty underneath the humor.

He stared at her. "You're an odd one, Mrs. B. Lot more to you than meets the eye, an' that's the truth."

"I think I had better see Alphonsine again," she said. "What will you do?"

"Balance the bleedin' books," Squeaky said tartly. "Then maybe I'll go and look some more for Tregarron." Suddenly he was deeply serious. "If I find him, do you think I should tell him to get the hell out of England? They'll hang him, you know."

"Yes, of course I do." She heard her own voice tight and hard in her throat. "I don't know the answer. If he goes, he'll never face trial, so in other people's eyes he'll always be guilty. It'll mean he can't ever come home again. That would matter more to him than to some men."

Squeaky raised his eyebrows.

"I've read some of his poetry," she said abruptly. "And that's another thing. His life as a poet, and his reputation, matter to him."

"Well. If I tell 'im to stay, you'd better be right," he said grimly. "There isn't going to be no second shots at it!"

"I know. If you do find him, speak to him honestly."
She took a deep breath. "And we should face the possibility that he really did kill her, even if he didn't
mean to."

He grunted. "Judge ain't going to make no distinction," he pointed out. "If he were Cecil Crostwick, for
instance, the judge might say it was all an unfortunate
accident, and we'll treat it like a brawl that went wrong.
But the powers that be'll make damn sure with Dai
Tregarron that they swing him by the neck. He in't one
of *them*. In fact, he's rather gone out of his way, one time
and another, to make a point of that."

"I know. You might remind him of that, too, if you do
find him."

Squeaky shrugged and picked up the teapot to see if
there was anything left in it. He put it down again, disappointed. "Not much chance of it. If he's any sense,
he'll be in Timbuktu by now." He frowned. "I s'pose I
get to go back out again!"

"We also need to find a connection between Briggs
and Foxley or Crostwick," she pointed out.

He glared at her and sighed heavily, but stood up
again and pulled his coat back onto his shoulders.

*A*gain it required a little engineering and quite a lot of duplicity from Claudine to arrange to meet with Alphonsine alone.

She regretted it, but time was short. If Claudine was right about the boys being guilty, then Alphonsine might suffer dearly in the years to come through her marriage to Ernest. And Dai Tregarron might pay with his life.

Was she fueled by a need for justice, righteous indignation, or just plain, ordinary anger? She did not yet have an answer for that question.

The place she expected to encounter Alphonsine was an exhibition of archaeological pieces recently found in Asia Minor. She was beginning to think all her elaborate plotting was for nothing when she finally saw the young woman standing alone in front of a display of glass jewelry, seeming to be deep in thought.

Claudine knew she was intruding. It made her hesitate a moment and then carry on regardless. An afternoon's unwelcome clumsiness was little enough compared with the misery that would follow if she was right, and did nothing.

"How pleasant to see you, Miss Gifford," Claudine said warmly, even though she kept her voice low. "This display gives one a whole new perception of the period, doesn't it?"

Alphonsine was startled, and she did not have the presence of mind to keep her dismay from her face.

Claudine decided for complete candor, then. "I am aware that I am interrupting you when you would prefer to be alone," she admitted. "If the matter could have waited, I assure you, I would have left you in peace. My interest in history is not so obsessive as to compel me to share it with someone. I am much more concerned with the recent past, and the near future."

Alphonsine scrambled to be courteous. "I don't think I understand you, Mrs. Burroughs. But it is most pleasant to see you. If I looked otherwise, it was merely because I was startled out of my reverie."

"You are very generous," Claudine responded. "But I can see that you are troubled and wish to be left in peace. Unfortunately, time and events will not wait for us."

Alphonsine pretended for a moment that she did not understand. Then, meeting Claudine's eyes, she knew that the struggle was destined to fail.

"Earlier you seemed confident that Mr. Halversgate did not have anything to do with the death of Winnie Briggs. That it was simply a case of being at the wrong place at the crucial time," Claudine began.

"Yes, yes, that's quite right," Alphonsine agreed quickly. "He tried to help, but as we all know, it was too late by then." She looked away.

Claudine thought of the lies Alphonsine had purportedly connived at in order to spend more time with Ernest.

"You care for him very much . . . ," she said aloud.

Alphonsine looked confused. For a moment her face betrayed the absurdity of the idea, then she masked it quickly.

"Of course," she replied.

"No one has been very clear as to how it began," Claudine went on. She kept her voice low and quite casual, as if she were actually discussing the old, rather dented beads in front of them, which might have been worn by a woman three thousand years ago, under a hot Middle Eastern sun. And here were they, two English

134

women with fair skins wrapped up against the English winter, staring at them and talking about anger, fear, and murder.

"How little changes," she said aloud.

Alphonsine turned toward her, the question in her face.

"The necklace," Claudine replied, glancing at the beads. "I wonder what she was like, the woman who wore those. Who gave them to her? More important, I wonder if he loved her." Claudine voiced her thoughts. She had never been beautiful—she had known that from the start—but she would like to have been loved, above all things. She would have to settle for being liked, perhaps for being trusted, respected. Best of all would have been to have had the courage to stand up for herself and fight for what she believed in.

Alphonsine was looking at the beads again. "I wonder if she was happy."

Claudine heard the pain in her voice—or perhaps "wistfulness" would be a more accurate word—and knew with sudden clarity that Alphonsine's stolen time was not spent with Ernest Halversgate. She was reveling in her freedom, while she still had it. Maybe she had come here to be alone, to indulge in her dreams while she could, before they were marred by an inner sense of having betrayed herself.

Claudine tried to put her own feelings aside. "There are many kinds of happiness, some of them within our reach, regardless of circumstances," she said. "How much of the truth do you know of that evening, Alphonsine? Was it really Dai Tregarron who beat Winnie Briggs? Or was it a more general fight that simply got out of hand?"

Alphonsine looked away. "Why do you think I know?"

"Because of what you have already told me," Claudine replied. "You are afraid that if Ernest Halversgate is called to testify, he will say something that shouldn't be said. I don't know whether that is because he will tell some truth that is inconsistent with what has been told to the police, or if you are afraid that he will lie, and very possibly be caught in that lie, becoming a suspect himself." She saw the fear crystallize in Alphonsine's eyes. "Or else that he will not be caught," she added, "but will cause the blame to fall on someone else, and in so doing see an innocent man hanged, and the rest of your own lives are then destroyed from within. And they will be. Never doubt that."

Alphonsine's eyes brimmed with tears.

"You have the chance to act now," Claudine said gently. "Perhaps you are wise enough to imagine what the future will be, whereas the young men concerned are not. They are afraid. That is easy to understand. So are you. It is there, very easy to read in your eyes. If they have neither the courage nor the honor to act for themselves, then you must do it for Tregarron. If you don't, and he is hanged wrongly, do you not think you will be haunted by his face and theirs, and imagine a rope around your own neck every time you lie alone in the dark, for the rest of your life?"

Alphonsine said nothing for a long time. Then at last she spoke.

"It was all fairly good-natured to begin with," she said quietly. "Then they got a bit insistent, demanding that Winnie . . . do more and more. She refused. It got a bit rough. I don't remember who it was. There's no good pushing me because I didn't see. She slapped him. He lost his temper. Then it got really rough. Someone hit her, and she fell against Ernest. I saw that."

"They were all on the terrace?" Claudine interrupted, trying to visualize it in her mind.

"Yes. Tregarron was a bit apart from the others, a bit farther away. They were moving about, pushing and shoving, you know?"

"I can picture it. Then what happened?"

"Ernest . . . Ernest was angry. I think someone must've broken a glass and spilled their drink over him."

"You smelled it . . . afterward?" Claudine interrupted quickly.

Alphonsine turned away again. "Yes."

"Then what?"

"I . . . I didn't see clearly. There was more pushing and a few blows. Someone shoved Winnie very hard, and she fell down completely. She was angry then, and when she got up she lashed back at someone. I only saw her arm swing. And there was blood. I mean, I don't know who she struck. But whoever it was, he struck back very hard. That was when I saw Dai Tregarron lunge forward at him and punch him, but he missed his face and caught his shoulder. The two of them fought, just a few blows. Tregarron staggered against the pillar. I think it was then that they realized Winnie was on the ground, and she wasn't moving."

"Who had hit her, Alphonsine?"

"I don't know. Except it wasn't Mr. Tregarron. Then he was bent over trying to get his breath, leaning against the pillar, when he saw she was on the ground, just lying there. He tried to help her. That was when you came in."

Claudine stared at her, stunned, her mind racing.

"I swear, that is the truth," Alphonsine said urgently.

"Part of it, anyway," Claudine agreed. "You don't know who it was who hit Winnie Briggs hard enough to kill her, when she fell and her head struck the ground. But you do know it wasn't Dai Tregarron. You know that if they catch him they will try him for murder, and if they find him guilty—and without your story there is no reason why they wouldn't—then they will hang him?"

Alphonsine gulped air and nearly choked. "Yes . . ." It was a whisper. "But I can't prove it, and they will only say that I'm lying. I—I can't prove it . . . I really can't!"

"You were there!" Claudine protested.

Alphonsine stared at her. Claudine thought back to the night: the terrace, Winnie lying on the stones, her face white, not moving. She remembered Dai Tregarron's black head bent as he tried to revive her, and Cecil Crostwick, Creighton Foxley, and Ernest Halversgate standing pale and shivering nearby. She did not remember seeing Alphonsine anywhere.

And yet Alphonsine had just described the incident in some detail, exactly as if she had seen it: confusion, anger, stupidity, and a fatal mistake.

"Where were you?" Claudine asked quietly.

"I . . . I was in the morning room. It looks out onto the terrace."

"I see. Thank you." Claudine smiled. "I'm sorry to have been so persistent."

Alphonsine relaxed a little and looked away. "It's all right. I understand."

Claudine took her leave and caught a hansom toward her home again. She relaxed against the cushion, tired and relieved, thinking over what Alphonsine had said. Her testimony, however reluctantly given, would show Tregarron's innocence. Should she have asked the girl what she had been doing in the morning room, or was that irrelevant? Speaking to someone? Avoiding someone! Staring out of the window at the terrace? And why had she been so slow to come forward? Because it implicated Halversgate; that was the obvious answer. Then Claudine had a cold thought: perhaps because it was less than the whole truth, after all?

With a weariness that reached her very bones, Claudine leaned forward and very unwillingly instructed the driver to take her to the Giffords' house. At this time of the day, it was quite possible no one would be at home. It should not be too difficult to gain a few moments alone in the morning room. The servants would merely think her very eccentric. Perhaps they did anyway. It was not an excuse to avoid doing what she must.

❀

Half an hour later she returned to the exhibition. She walked all the way through it until she came to the tearoom and found Alphonsine sitting at one of the small tables with a friend. She glanced up and saw Claudine. Her hand froze in the air, her cup halfway to her lips.

Claudine stopped, still gazing at Alphonsine.

Alphonsine lowered her cup and rose to her feet. She said something to her friend then walked over toward Claudine.

"Please . . . not here . . . ," she pleaded earnestly. Her eyes were wide, filled with fear.

"You were not in the morning room," Claudine said

very quietly. "If what you said you saw is the truth—and I believe it is—then you must have been much farther around the terrace. You must've been in the house next door. That was how you saw what happened, but only partially. And that was why none of them saw you."

Alphonsine was very pale. She was trembling.

At last the pieces fell into place, and Claudine understood.

"This is why you do not wish to marry Ernest Halversgate, isn't it?" she asked. "It has to be. There is someone else."

The tears slid down Alphonsine's cheeks. "My father won't ever permit it. He wouldn't even consider it."

"I assume he is unsuitable?" Claudine understood perfectly. They belonged to the same world. If it was a young man with no prospects, or perhaps a youngest son, he would be unacceptable, neighbor or not. Claudine had once dreamed a similar dream and then given it up to obey her father's wishes. She had no idea whether it would ever have worked well, or even at all. At her father's insistence, the young man had never given her the chance to accept, or himself the chance to be refused.

She had not remembered it so vividly for years. Now she understood far better than Alphonsine could imagine.

142

"It's hard, I know," she said gently. "But what happiness is there for you if you do not tell the truth about this? You can convince your parents, or the police, that you do not know what happened. But can you lie to yourself? You could avoid going to Tregarron's trial, quite easily. In fact, it would be more difficult for you to go than not to. But is that who you wish to be?"

"I can't tell them!" Alphonsine said desperately. "It was an—an assignation! If he knew of it, Ernest would never have me! I didn't . . ." She blushed scarlet.

"Of course you didn't," Claudine agreed. "But you saw this young man alone, romantically, when you were supposed to be in your own house and engaged, at least in understanding, to Ernest. I do appreciate your situation. He is somewhat straitlaced, to put it kindly."

Alphonsine swallowed hard. "Very kindly. He bores me till I could weep!"

Claudine smiled at her with intense gentleness. "My dear, I do understand. Believe me, I do. But if they arrest Mr. Tregarron and charge him with murder, then you must speak. You have no choice."

"Please . . ."

"I will say nothing, unless I have to," Claudine promised. "But I will not let them blame an innocent man, or let go one who is guilty."

"I don't know which one of them is guilty! I really don't!"

"I know. But maybe we will be able to find out or prove it some other way."

"Do you think so?" Hope flared in Alphonsine's eyes.

"No," Claudine said honestly, "I don't."

$\mathcal{W}$allace Burroughs was in a good mood that evening over dinner. They had barely begun the soup when he told her the reason.

"The police have caught Tregarron," he said, smiling at her over the gleaming silver cruet sets and the sparkle of glasses.

Claudine put her soupspoon back down in the plate. Her hand was shaking so much that he would have noticed.

"Really?" Her mouth was dry. The word sounded

forced. "That was very efficient of them." She swallowed. "Where?"

"In Dover. Trying to escape, I suppose. I'm glad you're taking it so sensibly," he observed. "I was afraid you might be upset."

He seemed to be waiting for her to say something.

"Were you?" she replied. "I think it was inevitable, wasn't it?"

"Of course, since he left too late. He could have gone earlier. People like him always think they're invulnerable."

"People like him?" she questioned then instantly wished she had not. It would only provoke a quarrel. She did not want to hear his opinion of Tregarron, and she had just been stupid enough to invite it.

"Drunkards," he replied. "Lechers, men who imagine that whatever talent they possess puts them above the laws that apply to ordinary people. Well, he'll discover he's wrong. Thank heaven it happened before Christmas, and it won't cloud the whole season for us. You should be glad it's over with."

"It isn't 'over with,'" she argued instantly. "They'll have to try him. We can't execute people just because we don't approve of them, or because they drink too much. Fortunately for a great many in our aristocratic class, drinking to excess is not a crime at all, let alone a capital one."

"Gentlemen know how to hold their drink," he said tartly.

"Oh, Wallace, don't be absurd!" she said with something close to a guffaw. "We just pretend we haven't noticed when they can't. I've picked up my skirts and walked around enough 'gentlemen' lying in the gutter not to have many illusions left."

He glared at her. "They may not stay upright on their feet, but they do not murder harlots on the terrace, Claudine. There is a difference."

She raised her eyebrows.

"A difference between the terrace and some back alley? A geographical one. It seems to be a distinction rather than a difference. I'm sure the harlot would rather prefer not to be attacked at all. The location of it probably matters very little to her."

"Claudine, your language has become very coarse lately. I don't care for the effect on you that working at the clinic seems to be having. Perhaps it would be better if you were to desist for a while. A year or two, maybe."

She did not retreat as usual, even though she knew she was losing, and would continue to do so. She looked at him inquiringly. "Is 'harlot' an unfortunate word? I learned it from you, Wallace. You used it just now, at the dinner table. I assure you I did not hear it at the clinic. It is not a term we use there. It is unnecessarily insulting."

His face burned hot, but with anger rather than embarrassment. "Well, did you learn your insolence there? I assure you that you did not get that from me," he snapped back, mimicking her tone.

"Of course not," she agreed. "You have no one to be insolent toward. Just as your employees dare not be insolent to you, out of fear of losing their positions, you are not insolent to your superiors, or you would lose yours."

He pushed his soup plate away from him, empty. He had not stopped eating while speaking to her. "They will try Tregarron in the New Year," he said, ignoring her statement. "I imagine he will be hanged before the end of January. Damn good thing, too. He is a bad influence all round."

"I agree with you." She pushed her plate away also, although it was barely touched. "He seems to have had a profound effect on Creighton Foxley and on Cecil

Crostwick. How sad that they will have to find harlots on their own now. Oh, I'm sorry. You don't like that word. I'm not sure I can think of another that quite fits the circumstances."

"Was there wine in the soup?" he said patronizingly.

"I have no idea. Do you wish for some?"

"It seems you have had more than enough. Did you already know that Tregarron had been arrested?"

"No. I had no idea. And I have had no wine at all. Would you be kind enough to ring the bell for the butler? I have eaten sufficiently. Perhaps he would bring the next course."

From there, the evening became worse, as she had known it would.

"hey won't try Tregarron over Christmas, but they'll likely do it straight afterward. If only to get it out of the way." Squeaky sat across from her at his desk in the clinic, gritting his teeth. It was now five days before Christmas. The weather was still mild. There was no frost in the air, no ice on the ground. "I wish the stupid

148

sod had left the country." He gave a grunt of annoyance. "I should've found him. Got him to go. I'm no bloody use at all—I've lost my touch. That's respectability for you!"

His voice was so full of self-disgust that Claudine was momentarily sorry for him. "You learned quite a bit about his life," she pointed out.

He gave a bitter look. "That he wasn't seen hitting women. What good is that? You never thought he was guilty anyway."

"I didn't think so because I didn't want to," she said with rather more honesty than she had intended. She had not meant him to know that. "Now I know because of a pattern of behavior you have traced."

"Yeah? And what difference does that make? Who's going to believe the likes of you or me?"

Claudine was taken aback by the idea that her word was of no more credibility than that of an ex–brothel keeper, but Squeaky was probably right.

"Then we have to get Alphonsine to testify," she said firmly. She did not know what Squeaky would make of what she was about to tell him. "But it will be difficult, because she'll have to say where she was."

"What do you mean?" he demanded.

"She saw the whole thing. She knows that it wasn't

149

Dai Tregarron who hit Winnie Briggs—but she doesn't know which of the young men it was."

He blinked. "How's that?"

"From where she was standing, she could see Tregarron; he was farther down the terrace, and when Winnie was hit, when he realized it had become ugly, he moved to stop it. But she was already down before he could do anything."

Squeaky was silent as he weighed her words. "You're certain?" he said finally.

"Yes, I am," Claudine assured him.

Squeaky nodded slowly. "That's a big step forward," he conceded with respect. "Now can we get her to admit that to the police? To say it in court, if it comes to that?"

"That might be difficult. You see, Alphonsine couldn't distinguish the other young men clearly, and none of them could see her, because she was across the terrace behind the windows of another house," she explained. "The lights on the terrace made them visible to her."

"Was she standing in the dark, then?"

"Yes. It . . . it was an assignation. She wasn't alone."

Squeaky turned that over in his mind for several moments. "Couldn't she just say that she was alone?"

Claudine looked at him witheringly. "Doing what?"

150

"What?" he asked.

"Why on earth would she be standing alone in the dark in a neighbor's house, staring out of the window at the terrace of her own house?" she said with as much patience as she could manage, which was very little indeed. Her voice sounded thin and tense.

He took the point and did not bother to say so. "And what would happen if she just plain told the truth?" he asked.

"It would jeopardize her engagement to Ernest Halversgate, because he would know that at the very best she did not love him, and at worst that she was actually involved with someone else. Knowing about it would be bad enough, but everyone else knowing would be unendurable. The arrangement would be ended."

"Didn't you say it hadn't even begun yet?" Squeaky looked at her sideways.

"Not formally," she agreed. "Informally, it is as if it were carved in stone."

"So he'll break it off—because she's betrayed him?" The ways of society still annoyed him. "Doesn't he love her?"

"I doubt it. But she will inherit a great deal of money, in due course."

ANNE PERRY

"Well that's better than love. If he's got any bloody brains at all, he'll forgive her, from a great height, and keep the engagement," Squeaky said with conviction. "By the way—not that it matters, I suppose—but who *does* she love? Or would she rather not have either of them?"

"I think she would rather have the other one, but he has no money," Claudine replied.

"Is he any good?" He looked at her curiously.

"I don't know. Perhaps I should find out. But it will all depend upon her father anyway."

"Are you sure she's telling the truth?" He squinted at her a little sideways.

She was surprised. "Do you doubt it?"

"Well, she's kind of cornered, ain't she?" he pointed out. "Her father's got her into this arrangement, which she doesn't like, but she can't see her way out of it. Now suddenly she's got the chance to play a real blinder by saying she was with another man an' she saw this fight clearly enough to say Dai Tregarron wasn't guilty. And on her conscience she has to come forward and say so, even though it'll make her unwanted fiancé unwant her a great deal more. He'll break it off, and there'll be nothing she can do about it. Maybe she'll find that the

152

only man who'll have her now is the one she wants anyway."

Claudine stared at him in growing horror.

"Better than that," Squeaky went on, "she can even realize, right at the last minute when she's been persuaded enough, that it were actually her fiancé that hit poor Winnie Briggs, and much as she hates doing it, honor forces her to testify to it."

It was a hideous scenario, and one that had not even occurred to Claudine. She struggled against it, trying to find even one reason why it could not be true. She failed. It could be exactly as Squeaky suggested.

In fact, the more she thought of it, the more she realized that Ernest Halversgate was going to be in trouble regardless, because he had clearly told the police that Winnie's assailant was Dai Tregarron. He had lied, either because he himself was actually involved or because he was prepared to send an innocent man to the gallows to save one of his guilty friends. That was, morally at least, also a kind of murder.

Squeaky was watching her, seeing in her face the thoughts reflected as they unfolded.

"Sorry," he said with a sudden gentleness. Then he looked away quickly.

Another, even worse thought occurred to her. What if, with her persistence, Claudine had unintentionally pushed Alphonsine into lying in the first place? Maybe Dai Tregarron was guilty, and by going on and on, insisting that there must be some other solution, she had maneuvered Alphonsine into this edifice of lies from which none of them would escape? What had her meddling done?

Wallace was right: She should have let the law take its course and kept well out of it. She had no skill, no knowledge, and very little sense. Suddenly, she was consumed with shame.

Squeaky was still watching her.

"What are you going to do?" he asked. It had clearly not occurred to him that she might do nothing.

"I don't know," she admitted.

"Well, you can't just sit there!" he exclaimed. "You done this—you'd better undo it."

She glared at him. She knew the truth; she did not need a semi-reformed brothel keeper, of all people, to tell her such things. Then she saw the concern in his face, which he probably had no idea he was betraying so openly; it caught her unawares, and she was quite painfully moved by it. He actually cared. It was an odd friendship—awkward, grown slowly from beginnings of mutual contempt—but it was real nonetheless.

She would not embarrass him by acknowledging it.

"I will go and face Alphonsine," she answered, "and persuade her to admit the truth, whatever that is. Perhaps we can even get this other young man to testify . . ."

The shadow cleared from Squeaky's face. "Well, you'd better get on then, hadn't you!" he said gruffly. "I got things to do, even if you haven't. I s'pose you haven't forgotten, but just in case you have, it's nearly Christmas."

*A*lphonsine did not seem surprised to see Claudine again. She arrived on what was ostensibly a Christmas call of general well-wishing, but both knew why she was truly there. They sat together in the morning room, as neither of them wished to be interrupted by others who might call. It was also a time of day when Oona would be out making her own visits.

"You will know that Mr. Tregarron has been arrested." Claudine did not waste time or stretch the tension unnecessarily by making light conversation about subjects neither of them cared about.

"Yes, my mother mentioned it," Alphonsine replied, looking down at the carpet. "I admit, I wondered if she knew anything about my . . . my knowledge of the incident. She brought it up most particularly."

"I daresay, she is anxious since the tragedy happened here at your house, and she can hardly be uninterested in the outcome," Claudine suggested.

"He'll be found guilty, and hanged," Alphonsine whispered. "You told me that. Unless I tell the police, and perhaps the court, that I saw what really happened and it was not Mr. Tregarron." She looked at Claudine like someone drowning and already beyond reach of the shore.

"I'm afraid that as far as I can see, that is the truth," Claudine replied. "I wish I could think of an alternative, and I have tried."

"My father will be furious." Alphonsine still struggled. "He has been friends with the Halversgates for years."

"Yes, so I believe." Claudine made no allowances because of that fact. "I imagine he would not have liked

you to marry into a family he did not know, and trust."
She hoped Alphonsine would pick up the argument, if in
fact she believed it could have been Ernest who struck
Winnie. She searched Alphonsine's face to see if there
was the duplicity in it that Squeaky had imagined possible. She saw nothing but desperation for an escape,
and rising panic.

"He'll despise me," Alphonsine whispered.

"Your father or Ernest?" Claudine asked her. It was
important that she did not misunderstand.

"Both . . . ," Alphonsine replied.

"Perhaps. But you surely know that above whatever
may happen, your father loves you. And while Ernest
may not love you, you might also consider that he was
there on the terrace at the time. He knows it was not
Dai Tregarron who killed Winnie, and yet he is willing
to allow him to be tried and hanged for the crime. Is
that because he is guilty himself and wants to escape
the consequences? Or does he wish to protect one of his
friends, friends who seem to matter more to him than
honor or justice? Or is he afraid that if he speaks the
truth, then there will be some price for him to pay in
popularity? Does he fear for his safety, that if he speaks
the truth, his friends will attack him and make him suf-

fer for it in more personal and immediate ways? No matter which it is, does that seem like a man your father would wish you to marry and into whose hands he would place your future?"

"No! No, of course not." Alphonsine gave a bleak little smile. "But there are two things you have forgotten. One is that I was in the house next door with John before I knew of Ernest's weakness." She winced. And clearly not for the first time. "The other is that quite possibly no one will believe me, anyway. Creighton, Cecil, and Ernest will all say it was Tregarron in order to save themselves. And it is what everyone else will want to believe. It removes the matter from any of our hands. And can't you see what they will say of me? Isn't it obvious?"

Indeed it was obvious, and Claudine had already considered it. She knew what she was asking of Alphonsine. She would almost certainly lose the marriage prospect ahead of her. She would also gain the enmity of the Halversgates, not to mention the Foxleys and the Crostwicks, whose sons' reputations she would drag into question. All of them had lied, but they would fight very hard to prove that it was Alphonsine who was the liar. They would paint her to be a loose and immoral young woman whose virtue was far from what she had claimed for it.

Silence would be so much easier. Everybody would approve of her. She would have a safe and prosperous marriage, her parents would be well satisfied, social events would proceed as before with nothing but an unpleasant incident clouding a few days before the Christmas celebrations wiped it away.

They would not even know what Alphonsine had done for them, because the young men did not know she had witnessed the tragedy.

Even Dai Tregarron would not know that she could perhaps have saved him. He would not blame her.

Claudine herself would find it easier, in a way, to keep quiet. It would be more comfortable. Otherwise the young men's families would hate her, too, perhaps blame her the more, thinking her older and better able to foresee the grief Alphonsine's testimony would bring upon all of them. Wallace would be revoltingly self-satisfied. She could hear his voice in her head: *I told you Tregarron was guilty! Why couldn't you see it, like everyone else?*

Claudine looked again at the girl's face, the pain and the indecision in it, the increasing understanding of what speaking out would cost her. And she saw also a growing appreciation of what her silence would cost. Perhaps she glimpsed the long years ahead, of looking at Ernest Halversgate and knowing what he had done, that he would lie for his own comfort and see someone else hang for it.

Would she ever feel safe again? Might she let slip one day that she had seen what had happened? What then?

"Alphonsine," Claudine said gently, "I cannot tell you what you must do, but I can warn you as clearly as I am able to of what the price will be, whatever course you take."

Alphonsine looked at her, fear in her eyes, waiting.

"If you are certain of what you saw, I think you have no choice but to tell it now," Claudine said. "Or be prepared to live with your silence, and whatever consequences might follow it, for the rest of your life. You will presumably marry Ernest Halversgate, knowing that he also knows the truth and that he chose to remain silent. You had better be very sure that you never tell him you also know. As it stands, he will have to testify under oath. No one will ask you to testify because they do not know you saw anything. Can you live with that silence, and do you trust the man you love, and who you were with, to keep that silence also? He knows you saw what happened. Possibly he saw it also. What manner of man is he?"

Alphonsine took a deep breath and let it out in a sigh. "He is an honest man," she whispered. "He will tell the truth. And he would despise me if I said nothing. The thought of that hurts more than I can bear. I have decided. Will you come with me?"

"Of course. Whom shall we see first?"

"John. His name is John Barton."

*I*t was not quite so easy to arrange a meeting between Alphonsine and John Barton, with Claudine present. It required a degree of subterfuge and rather a lot of hansom cab rides to one place and then another. Claudine did not dare take her own carriage. If Wallace were to ask the coachman where he had been all day that the horses were in such a lather, the reply would cause a good deal more trouble. Fortunately, she had funds to afford cab fares for both herself and Alphonsine.

Thus it was that late that evening they met with

John Barton. He had excused himself from a dinner with his friends on the pretext of urgent business, the nature of which was private.

They found themselves walking in the rain along the Mall, passing numbers of other people who were laughing and joking, putting up umbrellas and trying to keep them steady in the breeze.

"I'm sorry," Claudine said to John Barton, who was a very agreeable young man. He was not exactly handsome, but perhaps better than that—he had a face that showed both good humor and openness, coupled with a considerable intelligence. Had she been Alphonsine's age, Claudine had no doubt at all that she would have chosen him above Ernest Halversgate, whatever their difference in expectations or suitability.

But then Claudine was older and wiser. She had tasted years of pedestrian marriage that had now settled into a pattern of mutual dislike. If she had known then what she knew now, she would have taken the risks, sacrificed the parties, the balls, the theaters, the carriages, and the servants, in favor of a little hardship as the price of laughter and affection.

Not that she valued comfort lightly. It was easy to become used to, even to take for granted in a surprisingly short time. It was just that things had a different value when you were older and had lost the chance to make your decisions again.

"Mr. Barton," Claudine began as they moved down an empty pathway, the trees sheltering them from most of the damp. It was possible here to furl the umbrella again and speak more easily.

He turned to pay her his full attention.

Briefly she told him of their current situation regarding the struggle and death of Winnie Briggs and the fact that Tregarron was now in custody and due to be charged.

"I believe you and Alphonsine were in a situation where you witnessed at least a part of these unpleasant events." She made it more of a statement than a question, but she watched him carefully to see his response.

He understood with dawning gravity. "You mean, the young men lied?" he said, stopping on the sandy gravel.

"Yes. If what Alphonsine says is correct, and it was not Dai Tregarron who struck the young woman."

"It was not," he said, shooting a glance at Alphonsine then back again to Claudine. "I was witness also. I don't know who did strike her. I am not acquainted with the

163

young men to know one from another. But Tregarron is older, and quite distinctive. He was standing apart from them, and it was not he."

Claudine drew in a deep breath. She did not dare to look at Alphonsine, whom she was about to embarrass profoundly, but there was no alternative to it.

"Mr. Barton, I wonder if you have considered fully the consequences if you and Alphonsine were to tell the truth?"

"I know that they will fight against us, Mrs. Burroughs. In fact, they will do all they can to discredit us and prove that we are wrong. I don't know what motive they could ascribe to us. But Mr. Tregarron will lose his life if we say nothing, and that is not an acceptable bargain. No honest man would allow such a thing. I have only been quiet for this long because of Alphonsine." There was no pomposity in his voice. He was not proclaiming his virtue, simply stating what he believed to be a fact.

"Indeed. And *have* you considered what Miss Gifford may lose?" Claudine said as softly as she could in the breeze and above the sound of their footsteps in the gravel and the gentle swishing of skirts.

John Barton was embarrassed and for the first time unable to find easy and passionate words.

Claudine said it for him. "Mr. Halversgate will not marry her."

"Well, it seems unavoidably true that either he knew who killed that poor woman—and he lied to protect his friend and thus blamed an innocent man—or else he killed her himself, possibly not intending to," Barton responded. "I hardly think her father would permit the marriage after that, whatever proves to be true."

Alphonsine turned away, hiding her face from them both.

"You have not taken my point, Mr. Barton," Claudine said, hating doing it. "Mr. Halversgate will not marry her because she was keeping a tryst with another man, even if nobody believes you and he emerges with his reputation intact—and Mr. Tregarron hangs. Alphonsine's testimony will ruin her reputation, whatever happens."

Barton looked as if she had punched him in the stomach, knocking the breath out of his lungs. He stood still, not even fighting for words.

"It is likely no one else will marry her, after such a

scandal," Claudine added. Would he accept this? Did he love her as much as apparently she loved him?

Barton looked ashen-faced, but there was no time for pity now. She stood her ground and waited.

"I would marry her the day she would have me, Mrs. Burroughs," John Barton said at last. "But her father would not permit it. He has already said so."

"If you testify against Cecil Crostwick, Creighton Foxley, and Ernest Halversgate, his opinion may change," Claudine replied. "He may no longer have a more acceptable choice." She drew in her breath to add that she hoped passionately that that had not been their intention from the beginning, then thought better of it. The thought was too ugly to bear. Instead, she added further weight to the other side. "And of course the families of the three young men, who have considerable power in both business and society, will not forgive you. You may pay a very heavy price for your honesty, Mr. Barton. I don't know what your ambitions are, but it might spell the end of them."

"Are you trying to dissuade me, Mrs. Burroughs?" he asked, his voice tight in his throat.

"No, Mr. Barton, I am trying to be fair."

"You have been fair, Mrs. Burroughs," he said

gravely. "Now let us go and do what we have to. Whatever it proves, I believe the cost of silence would be greater, not only to Mr. Tregarron but to me."

Claudine hoped profoundly that he was right, but she did not say so. She simply nodded fractionally and smiled at him then looked at Alphonsine.

Alphonsine gulped. "I'm ready," she said huskily.

$\mathcal{A}$n hour later, damp and beginning to get a little chilled, the three of them sat in front of Oona Gifford. They were stiff with apprehension, struggling to keep their courage high.

"I think you had better explain to me," Oona said quietly after the maid brought in high tea and fresh toasted crumpets then departed. It was dark and late, far too late for such refreshments, but none of them had eaten since luncheon, and it was now past dinner.

Alphonsine looked at the man she loved, then at her mother, and finally at Claudine.

"One of you, please," Oona requested.

It seemed to fall naturally to Claudine to explain.

She did so as briefly as was possible, detailing all the facts and what she believed was likely to happen as a result of both Alphonsine and John Barton going to the police and telling the truth, or their remaining silent and saying nothing. She left out none of the consequences, good or bad, certain or problematical. No one interrupted her.

"I see," Oona said at last.

Alphonsine stared at her. She looked lonely, frightened, and very young. It occurred to Claudine to wonder how long she had been without a mother since her own mother died, and then her father had met and married Oona. Perhaps too long for her to retain the power to believe that she would not be left inexplicably alone again.

Oona smiled. She reached out her hand and put it very gently over Alphonsine's where it lay on her skirt.

"You seem to have thought this over very carefully. Are you certain that it is what you want to do, even knowing the inevitable consequences? I think Claudine is right and they will be exactly as she says. Innocent or guilty, and whether he loves you or not, I don't think Ernest Halversgate will marry you when he knows this. Even if he wished to, I doubt his mother would permit it." A very slight smile touched the corner of her mouth then vanished again. In that instant Claudine knew that Oona was entirely on her stepdaughter's side, perhaps with more understanding than her own mother might have had. Maybe the fear for her was less. She had not loved her as a child and so did not in any sense still see her as one.

It was Barton who spoke. "I have already met Mr. Gifford, ma'am," he said gently. "He is aware of my feelings for Alphonsine, and he made it politely but very definitely clear to me that I am not suitable as a husband for her. I'm . . . sorry."

"That was then," Oona told him. "It looks as if circumstances are about to change rather dramatically. I shall speak to him. You will remain here in the withdrawing room. Finish the tea and the crumpets. Claudine and I shall go and discuss the issues and what may be done."

Claudine was startled. She was not a family friend and had no standing in the matter at all. Was Oona about to tell her so and dismiss her with all the outrage she had so carefully concealed until now?

As she followed Oona across the hall and along a wide passage to the door of Forbes Gifford's study, Claudine found her head spinning. She was afraid for a moment that the sheer tension of it would make her trip, even faint.

Oona knocked on the door. Without waiting for an answer, she turned the handle and went in.

Forbes Gifford was sitting by the fire with a book in his hands. The room was warm both in temperature and in the rich leather and velvet of its furnishings, the polished wood and the glowing carpet.

He looked up and saw his wife with pleasure. Then, the moment after, he realized she was not alone and rose to his feet, his face grave with concern. "Has something happened?" he asked.

As soon as Claudine was inside with her, Oona closed the door.

"Yes, my dear, I'm afraid it has. I could explain it to you, but I might do so a good deal less lucidly than Claudine will, if you will permit it? I'm afraid it cannot wait until a more convenient time."

"Very well, if this is necessary, then we had better proceed. May we offer you some refreshment, Mrs. Burroughs? You seem . . . a little damp. Are you chilled? Would you like the seat nearest the fire?"

Claudine accepted it. To tell the truth, she felt shivery. It was not the temperature in the house, it was her own nerves. At Forbes Gifford's insistence, she again told the story of the attack on Winnie Briggs and exactly what Alphonsine had told her. As she did so, Forbes's face darkened. Every so often he glanced at Oona, and she affirmed what Claudine said.

When she had finished, Claudine sat motionless, waiting for the storm to break.

"And do you believe him?" Forbes asked, looking at her through narrowed eyes.

She considered for a moment evading the answer but knew it would be futile. She knew exactly what he meant, and he would not appreciate prevarication.

"I do," she answered. "Of course, I wondered if it might be an elaborate piece of opportunism he had seized so that he could sabotage Alphonsine's chance to marry Ernest Halversgate, or anyone else of suitable expectations. But I believe that Alphonsine really did see the incident and that it was not Tregarron who instigated it or indeed struck the woman at all."

"And do you believe that my daughter was keeping an assignation with John Barton when the attack took place?" he pressed. "Have you any means at all of proving that she was there, and not somewhere else, where she should have been, entertaining our guests?"

"I have not tried to find proof," she admitted. "But I am sure you could question your own staff, if you wished to. What Alphonsine described to me was exactly what she would have seen from the neighbor's windows onto the terrace. I saw the same myself, from the other side, when I went out there a few moments after the attack. Mr. Tregarron had moved forward from the place Alphonsine saw him, in order to try to save the woman who was lying on the stones. Everyone else was exactly where she described them. Tell me, Mr. Forbes—you have known Alphonsine all her life—do you believe her to be capable of creating such a story in order to free a man she knows might be guilty of murder and condemn to scandal at least, the gallows at worst, three young men whose families are friends—all in order to ruin herself socially and marry a young man who has no money and few prospects that are of the order she is accustomed to?"

"I think she is young and in love and has no idea of the realities of life," he replied guardedly. "She has always been very comfortable, having all the clothes and parties she desires, all the friends, opportunities to do whatever she wishes. She can have no idea what it will be like to lose those."

Claudine drew in a deep breath and let it out softly. Now was the time to speak, however shaming, however difficult. She did it for Alphonsine as she might have done for a daughter of her own.

"Mr. Gifford, we all like certain luxuries. They are things we enjoy but could actually survive without. Most people do. One of the happiest women I know is married to a man who earned very little, in their earlier years together. She came from a good home where she could have married money, but she chose a man with a difficult past and a very doubtful future, because she loved him, and I think she was as certain as one ever can be that he loved her. They are now more than ten years after that decision, and I don't think she has regretted a day of it. She runs a clinic for street women, where I work quite often, and for which I am always seeking funding. That work brings me the greatest happiness I have."

Forbes Gifford stared at her, his attention total, although there were questions in his eyes that he was too sensitive to ask.

Claudine knew it was necessary she answer them anyway. It was difficult. She was ashamed to admit the truth, especially to people whose good opinion she would like to have had.

"I married a man who was suitable," she said quietly, "in my parents' view, after considerable thought. He appeared to be sober, honest, hardworking, talented, and likely to be faithful to me. He was all these things . . . I shouldn't speak in the past—he still is."

Forbes Gifford looked even more puzzled. She seemed to be making the exact point that he had, and the opposite of what she had implied.

She drew in her breath, let it out slowly, and tried to compose herself. Even so, when she began again, her voice was husky.

"He is also unkind," she told him. "He seldom criticized me openly to begin with, but it was always there in a remoteness, the praise of others in comparison with me, the condescending explanations of things I did not immediately grasp, and then afterward the reminder that he had taught me. I grew to despise myself and believe that I was displeasing to him, possibly to most people."

Forbes Gifford frowned but not at her. His eyes remained gentle and increasingly distressed by the story she was telling. She saw that there was no need to explain further.

"He did not love me," she said simply. "Nor did I love him. It is a long time since we shared anything with pleasure, or even with kindness. We do not laugh at the same things or admire the same moments of beauty. I wish him no harm, but I am happier when I do not have to see him or speak to him. I think it is possible he feels the same of me. Perhaps I am not even the quality of person I could have been, had I believed in myself and my own worth. Humility is a sweet virtue in anyone, but to be without faith or hope only destroys. It is much harder to find when you are unhappy."

She could see plainly in his face that she need say little more.

"Alphonsine is a lovely young woman, and I refer not to her face, which we can all see, but to her spirit. Please do not crowd her into doing something that she knows to be bitterly wrong in order to cement a marriage with a man who does not love her, nor does she love him. And if you are still intending to, believing it in her best interest for the future, consider that if he would lie and let an innocent man hang for a crime his friends committed, how well will he care for his wife, if it should in some way inconvenience him?"

"You have said enough," Forbes interrupted her. "It will be most unpleasant to do as you say, but there is no alternative that is acceptable. I thank you for your honesty. It cannot have been easy. Your own example makes the best argument you could for virtue over expediency." He glanced at Oona then back at Claudine. "Thank you. It shall be done as you suggest."

Claudine was too choked with relief, gratitude, a strange sense of freedom, to answer him.

"*W*ell then, you'd better get on and deal with the rest of it, hadn't you!" Squeaky said when she told him the next morning.

"The rest of it?" She was at a loss. "Alphonsine will tell the police—Sergeant Green, or whatever his name is—and they will withdraw the charges against Mr. Tregarron."

"If they believe her," he said dubiously, pulling his face into an expression of tortured doubt.

"We'll have to make it so that they do," she said, not quite sure what she meant. She could not bear to have come this far, and at such cost, and give up now. Was she absolutely sure it was the truth, sure enough to swear on oath? Sure beyond any doubt at all?

"Right!" Squeaky agreed. "Why should they?"

She lost her temper with him. She was tired and had been bitterly embarrassed telling Forbes Gifford so much that was painful in her own life. She had never put it into words before, and it had hurt more than she had expected. It was a story of absolute failure. Now Squeaky was doubting her, too, and in the place where she felt safer than anywhere else, even her own home.

"If you don't believe it, then I had better continue without you," she said angrily, starting to rise to her feet.

"Wait!" he said abruptly. "Don't go all soft on me now! I believe you, but you need the police to. I only want you to think about how you're going to make that happen." He looked at her with a slight squint. "What's the matter with you? You seem all . . . pushed out of shape."

He was more perceptive than she had foreseen, but she did not want to tell him all she had revealed to Forbes Gifford about her personal circumstances. "I don't know how to make the police believe me, except that Alphonsine and Mr. Barton say the same thing about where people were, and it fits in with what I saw."

"Then you'd better go and see if Tregarron says the same," Squeaky said flatly. "I'll arrange it."

She was incredulous. "How are you going to do that? I'm hardly family. They wouldn't admit me to his cell. And for goodness' sake be careful what you say. Don't you—"

He froze her with an indignant glare. Slowly he rose to his feet. "Where'll I find you when I've done it?" he inquired with raised eyebrows. "And don't ask any questions you don't want the answers to."

It was arranged the following day. Claudine was let into the prison and conducted to the cell where she would be allowed fifteen minutes with Dai Tregarron.

She had rehearsed in her mind several times what she would say to him. Each time it was different, and nothing was satisfactory, let alone good. She was so nervous her fingers were stiff. Her legs were a little wobbly, and she did not feel as if she could draw sufficient breath.

When Tregarron came in, he looked smaller than she remembered him, and somehow faded, as if dust and the harsh light had robbed him of luster. Above all, he looked appallingly tired, the lines in his face deep and the vitality drained away from him.

He stood in the doorway, unwilling to come in, and she knew he was embarrassed in front of her.

She hesitated for a moment then began. "I have very little time, Mr. Tregarron. Please come in and sit down so I may speak to you without having to raise my voice, and perhaps be overheard."

"If you are sorry for me, you don't need to be," he said, moving forward only a few steps. "And if you've come to save my soul—"

"I haven't," she said sharply. "If you want your soul saved, you will have to do it yourself. Of more immediate concern to me is saving your neck. That is, if you did not strike Winnie Briggs so hard that she died of the blow."

"I didn't," he said, taking another step toward her and putting his hands on the back of the wooden chair. "But nobody's going to believe that. It's either me or one of those fancy young gentlemen from well-bred and well-heeled families. Who do you think they're going to believe? For that matter, who do you think they can afford to disbelieve?" He pursed his lips. "Sorry, Olwen, you're off in some dream of your own."

"I haven't time to argue with you," she said impatiently. "Please sit down. You are making me stare up at you, and it is uncomfortable. I need to know exactly what happened. And, please, be precise."

179

"Why? It makes no difference now." He looked desperately tired, as if he had worn himself out thinking, struggling to untangle in his mind a knot that may only be pulled forever more tightly.

"There are two witnesses," she told him. "If what you say is the same as they do, then you will be believed. Now stop wasting what little time we have, and tell me." She did not add that neither Alphonsine nor John Barton had seen who actually struck Winnie Briggs.

"Witnesses?" His eyes widened. Hope was naked in his face, and then the moment after, it turned to disbelief. "No there aren't. There was no one else on the terrace. If there had been, they'd have said something before now. There was nowhere they could have been. Someone's lying, for their own reasons. It won't hold up in court." His voice was edged with despair, which was the sharper for the brief flare of hope.

"They were behind a window, in a room where they should not have been. Now stop arguing and wasting what few minutes there are. Do you want to hang for this?" She was being brutal, but she was afraid the warden would return for her any moment and it would be too late. "What happened?"

He swallowed as if there were something solid stuck

in his throat. "I brought Winnie, because they wanted someone who'd be a bit fun," he began. "And honestly, I think they also wanted to shock a few people. They thought it would be amusing." He blushed very faintly; it was no more than a hint of color in his pallid cheeks. He caught her glance, both of disgust and of urgency. "We were laughing and generally behaving like fools. Winnie was good value. She had a sharp tongue, that one, and a ready wit. They liked her. Then Foxley wanted a bit more, wanted to kiss her, and she told him to wait. He thought she was putting him off, and he got more pushy. Crostwick stepped in, but he did it clumsily and it made things worse. Foxley was in a bad temper anyway, and then he thought Crostwick was above himself so he shoved him away, quite hard. That was when Halversgate got involved as well. And the wineglass broke. The shards like daggers."

His voice dropped.

"I told Winnie to get out of it, and she tried to, but Foxley caught hold of her. She pushed him away. I think she was scared by this time. Foxley lost his temper and slashed out at her. He caught her hard with one of the shards, maybe harder than he meant to, and she went down. She hit her head, and she didn't move again. At first no one took any notice. They were busy getting angrier with each other. I tried to pull them off and get to her, but Crostwick hit me, pretty hard. Halversgate was terrified out of his wits and tried to do something, but Foxley hit him, too, and he staggered back."

He looked at Claudine with haunted eyes. "That gave me a chance to get to Winnie. I thought she'd just passed out, but when I tried to find a pulse, I couldn't. I think I was too scared to try properly. My hands were shaking like I had the ague myself. That was when you came out—so you know what happened after that."

"Thank you," she said with a warmth of relief surging through her. "That matches what the witnesses say they saw. You are perfectly certain that it was Creighton Foxley who hit her?"

"Yes."

"Have you already said so to Sergeant Green?"

"There didn't seem to be a point. They all said it was me."

"Well, I suppose they wouldn't admit it was them, would they?" She rose to her feet. "Thank you. I will find out exactly how we should proceed now. Keep hope, Mr. Tregarron."

"Flowers, white flowers," he said softly.

182

She turned at the door to stare at him. "What white flowers? What are you talking about?"

He smiled. "Where Olwen walks, white flowers spring up in the earth behind her."

Her eyes filled with sudden tears, and she banged on the door for the warden to let her out. She did not want Tregarron to meet her eyes again, in case he saw far too much in them. She was behaving like a fool.

$\mathcal{W}$allace was outraged. He stood in the middle of the rug in front of the fire and stared at Claudine as if he could hardly believe what she had said to him.

"It is absolutely out of the question! Have you taken leave of your senses?" he demanded. "Have you even the faintest idea what it will do to our reputation if you launch on such a preposterous course? I don't know how you can be so totally unreasonable. Who have you spoken to about this? You make it sound as if you have been telling half of London."

"Forbes Gifford and Oona," she replied lamely. She, too, was standing, and she would not sit down as long as

183

he was lecturing her as if she were some obtuse school-girl. "I had no choice in that, since Alphonsine is the witness who saw what actually happened."

Wallace dismissed this with an abrupt jerk of his hand. "For heaven's sake, Claudine, she's a girl of—what is she, nineteen? She knows nothing. That's obvious by the fact she is prepared to throw away a perfectly good future with everything she could wish for, because she fancies she is in love with some young nobody who hasn't a penny to his name, but no doubt has a very ready eye on her fortune. Such a stupid girl is hardly worth listening to about anything."

"She is quite capable of recounting honestly and lucidly what she saw, as is Mr. Barton," Claudine said coldly. "As am I. What they describe is exactly what I found when I reached the scene. And it is, detail for detail, what Mr. Tregarron described."

"Indeed! And how do you know that?" he inquired, his eyes brilliant, challenging.

She had trapped herself. There was no escape, so she answered his question without excuse or evasion. "Because I asked him. There would be no point in speaking to the police if his account were different."

"You did what?" Wallace was aghast.

184

"I asked him," she repeated. "Is that not what you expected me to say?"

"I hoped I was wrong, that there was some other explanation." He shook his head as he spoke. "You seem to have lost whatever little sense you had. Do you even begin to grasp what you have done?"

It seemed to be a question to which he was expecting an answer, so she offered one, knowing it would be unsatisfactory. "I have given the police the evidence they need to clear an innocent man, and possibly charge those who are guilty."

"Don't be idiotic!" Wallace said furiously, his face purpling with anger. "You have meddled in matters that are none of your concern, and as a result you will ruin your own reputation and, more importantly, mine as well. And you will destroy young Foxley's life. He might have the friends and the influence to protect himself, but that remains to be seen."

He drew in his breath and continued. "You will, of course, also seriously damage Cecil Crostwick, and therefore his family, by implying that he lied in order either to cover his own part in the woman's death or to protect his friends. It will end Alphonsine Gifford's chance of a fortunate marriage. Halversgate can hardly offer for her now, when she has, by her own admission, had an indecent assignation with another man. In fact, no one of any standing will offer for her."

"It wasn't an indecent assignation," Claudine corrected him. "It was simply a meeting. The indecency is in your imagination. But I agree: Halversgate will not offer for her, because he now knows that he would not be accepted. He is both a liar and a coward, and Forbes Gifford would not have him for his daughter. Whether anyone else would offer remains to be seen; very probably not. But then, I think, she will be perfectly happy to accept Mr. Barton."

"Who has no means and no prospects," he said derisively.

"Perhaps it has slipped your mind that it is she who has the money, anyway," she said pointedly.

He sneered. "I am sure it has not slipped young Mr. Barton's mind!"

"He did not expect to marry her," she pointed out. "Or are you suggesting that this whole affair of inviting a street woman to the party and having Creighton Foxley lose his temper and beat her to death and Ernest Halversgate lie to protect him was entered into so Mr. Barton and Alphonsine could be conveniently placed to witness it? It was all a plot he invented for the purpose of creating a scandal from which they could benefit? Well, if Mr. Barton is clever enough to do that, then he should run for political office. He may well have ahead of him a bright future."

Wallace's face burned a deep plum red. "You have become absurd," he snarled. "I shall consult a doctor regarding the health of your mind. And I forbid you to attend Mrs. Monk's clinic anymore. The place and its occupants have obviously affected your wits."

She had nothing left to lose. "Why? Is it really your judgment, Wallace, that if Tregarron drank too much and lost his temper with a street woman and hit her hard enough to kill her, then he should hang, but if, on the other hand, the exact same actions, in the same circumstances, were committed by Creighton Foxley, then that young man should be permitted to blame someone else? See another man hang in his place and walk away unscathed? That is your idea of what is just, and best for society? Would you also lie to ensure that this is what would happen? Or at the very best, turn a blind eye and pretend that you didn't know the truth? You sound like Ernest Halversgate: both a liar and a coward."

He swayed on his feet, his face mottled red.

"Please tell me that is not so," she continued. "I know we have little enough in common, less even than I used to believe, but still, I always knew you to have a sense of what was honorable. Am I wrong in that, too?"

He did not answer.

If she was going to add what was sharp in the forefront of her mind, then there would never be a better time than now. In fact, there might not be another time at all. So she burned the last of her bridges.

"You wanted a peaceful, comfortable Christmas, with all reminders of poverty, injustice, or other people's griefs well out of sight, so as not to disturb your pleasure. That isn't what Christmas is about, Wallace. Christmas is about offering hope to all people, not just those like ourselves. Christmas is about everyone: rich or poor, friend or stranger. The moment you exclude anyone, you exclude yourself." She was standing now. "I am going to visit Tolly Halversgate to see if she will help me persuade Ernest to face his responsibilities."

She walked out of the room, passing him without looking back. In the hall she told the footman to fetch her carriage and have it waiting for her in a quarter of an hour. She was quite aware of the lateness of the evening, and she did not care. Tomorrow morning would not be suitable to call upon anyone, and tomorrow after-noon would be too late. The family might be out now, but they would come home sometime. Claudine was pre-pared to wait.

She was fortunate, though. Tolly had decided to spend the evening at home, making her last-minute preparations for Christmas. She intended the dinner to be one the family would remember, including the vari-ous uncles, aunts, and cousins she had invited. She was startled and put to some discomfiture to see Claudine, but she could not think of any excuse not to receive her.

The dining room was already decked with garlands of holly and ivy and dark green pine. There were silver-tipped cones in a woven basket, dried flowers, and well-preserved shining autumn leaves in two huge vases. A pleasant perfume of cinnamon mixed with other spices hung in the air. The fire was burning, but low, because the weather was still absurdly clement.

Claudine was intruding almost unpardonably, but al-though it embarrassed her, it did not cause her to hesi-tate for a second, much less to change her mind.

"I am sorry," she said as soon as the door was closed and the footman's steps had retreated across the par-quet floor of the hall.

Tolly forced a smile. "I'm sure you would not have come at such an hour without a good reason," she remarked.

"I'm afraid the reason is very good indeed, and urgent," Claudine responded, walking over to the other chair near the fire. She sat down without waiting to be invited.

Tolly followed because she had little choice. "What is it?" she said coolly, folding her hands in her lap.

"I will be brief. The very unfortunate quarrel on the terrace at the Giffords' party, in which the young woman, Winnie Briggs, was fatally struck, was witnessed from the window of another house. That has only just come to light, but now it is known exactly what happened."

Tolly's eyebrows rose in amazement. "My dear, Claudine, I really don't care! I cannot imagine why you should think I do, let alone at this time of the evening, three days before Christmas. If you think it is of concern to me, a letter would have been more than adequate." She gathered her skirts as if to rise.

"That would hardly be the act of a friend," Claudine said, remaining in her seat. "Or even of an honest person. You see, Ernest's account is quite seriously in error . . ."

Tolly froze, her body stiffening.

"I think it only fair to give him the opportunity to go to the police himself and correct it, rather than allow them to charge him with having given a false statement, which—as he has to be aware—will cause irreversible injustice."

This time Tolly did stand, her face white. "How dare you? What you are saying is preposterous! Who are these . . . witnesses? Why did they not come forward at the time? I don't believe you."

Claudine rose also. "Yes you do. Ernest was no doubt pressured into helping his friends, but he has been unhappy about it, because he is, for the most part, an honest man. If he goes on to lie under oath in court, he will have embarked on a path from which he cannot retreat. The guilt will be with him forever, corroding everything he touches from now on. He will have caused the appalling death of another man he knows is innocent. Will this not haunt him all the days of his life? If he marries and has children, what will he tell his family of this? Will he lie to them also? What will they think when they hear the truth?"

Tolly sidestepped the main issue. "Of course he will marry. He is shortly to become engaged to Alphonsine Gifford."

"She will not have him," Claudine replied. "Her father already knows that Ernest lied over who really struck the woman. And I doubt Ernest would want to have Alphonsine, when he hears that she is one of the witnesses."

Tolly stared at her, speechless.

"I'm sorry," Claudine said and was surprised by how seriously she meant it. She *was* sorry. Tolly had only the one son, and she loved him fiercely, if perhaps too protectively. Now just how vulnerable she was lay naked in her face.

"It is not too late to mend the situation," Claudine went on. "Ernest is at the point of a great decision in his life. Will he be the man he wishes to be, honorable and upright, even when being so costs a great deal of courage? It will not be easy, because I don't doubt the Foxleys will make this as difficult as possible."

"The Foxleys?" Tolly was not yet facing the inevitable.

"It was Creighton Foxley who struck her, albeit not intending to cause her death. But he will still have to pay the price for it," Claudine explained.

"It can't be!" Tolly shook her head. "What about that Tregarron man? He's a drunkard and a womanizer!"

192

"So is Creighton Foxley," Claudine replied. "A little less far along the road, perhaps, but with a more violent temper. Ask Ernest if that is not true."

Tolly was still hovering on the edge of decision.

"Virtue is not always an easy or a comfortable thing," Claudine continued. "Sometimes it comes at a high cost. Perhaps that is one of the reasons we admire it. If Ernest wishes to be what he seems on the outside—I hesitate to use the phrase 'pretends to be'—then he must do more than speak well. He must act well. Now, tonight, is the moment for him to decide whether he will speak the truth, even against his peers, or whether he will lie to cover their weaknesses. No—perhaps that is inaccurate. Alphonsine has had the courage to speak out, in spite of what it will cost her, as has the young man she loves. And I myself was there on the scene within moments of the incident. We will all speak as to what we saw. Ernest's deceit will become public knowledge. Knowing this, I'm sure you will do all you can to see that he does not make the choice to stay silent."

Tolly blinked and shivered, staring at Claudine. "I realize that I do not know you at all, Mrs. Burroughs. You are frightening."

"Life is frightening," Claudine corrected her. "And beautiful and full of strange and unexpected opportunities. This is one of them."

"I will speak to Ernest," Tolly said in little more than a whisper. "I expect him home within half an hour."

"Good." Claudine smiled. "I will wait with you." She returned to the chair by the fire and sat down again.

Ernest did not struggle against the inevitable for more than a moment or two. The weight of the evidence against him was overwhelming, and the chance to play a hero too great to forfeit. He conceded, shamefacedly, that the truth was exactly as Alphonsine had said. If the fact that she was in love with another man distressed him, he hid it. Claudine believed that it was a greater wound to his pride than his heart, but he bore it with more dignity than she had expected.

It would also be a blow to his financial expectations, but he did not mention that at all.

She was not sure, but she had a strange feeling that some small part of him would be relieved to escape the imprisonment of his friendship with Creighton and Cecil. They would hate him for what they might well see as a betrayal, but there would be those who would respect him. At the very least, he would be free to be his own man: less daring, less outrageous, but a good deal truer to the best in himself.

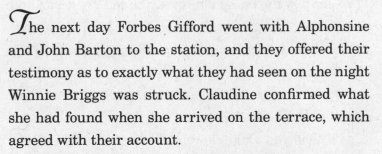

The next day Forbes Gifford went with Alphonsine and John Barton to the station, and they offered their testimony as to exactly what they had seen on the night Winnie Briggs was struck. Claudine confirmed what she had found when she arrived on the terrace, which agreed with their account.

Then in embarrassment and some shame, Ernest Halversgate asked if he might amend his previous account of the incident and confess to what had really happened. Sergeant Green allowed him to do so and then to sign his statement.

When it was over, the charges against Dai Tregarron were withdrawn, and he was set free. As he walked out of the prison doors he met Claudine, who was not willing to accept anything as accomplished until she had seen it for herself.

He stopped in front of her, blinking as if he had only just seen the sunlight.

"Thank you," he said simply. "You believed in me more than I believed in you. It's a long time since anything like that happened."

It occurred to her to say something a little humbling, in case he imagined his charm had inspired her to do it. Then she saw the pain in his eyes, the self-criticism, and changed her mind. He did not need that kind of cautioning. He was already more than sufficiently aware of his own weaknesses.

"Don't do it again," she said gently. "I think we had a good deal of luck this time."

"I'll send you white flowers, Olwen," he said quietly. Then with a nod of his head, he turned and walked out into the street.

She would tell Wallace in time, but first she would go to the clinic in Portpool Lane and tell Squeaky Robinson. He deserved that, and quite apart from his deserving it, she simply wanted to share the moment with him.

She walked into his office and found him sitting at his desk, sheets of paper with figures spread in front of him, his fingers stained with ink.

"Well, what now?" he asked as she closed the door behind her.

"I just thought I'd let you know," she replied. "We did

it. They withdrew the charges against Mr. Tregarron, and he is free."

Squeaky tried to keep a straight face, and failed. He could not keep the grin from spreading wide. He stood up and fetched a bottle of whiskey from the cupboard near the fireplace, and two mismatched glasses. He poured a good measure into each and passed one to her.

She did not even like whiskey, but she took it anyway.

"Here's to you," he said with a deep sigh. "You got no sense at all, but all the courage in the world. Saved a man's life, you did, and gave him the chance to save his soul. Let's hope he takes it."

"Nonsense," she said briskly, but she knew her face was coloring with pleasure. "But I have learned something good about myself. I can stand up to people who have more power than I do, and fight for what I believe in." She took a large mouthful of whiskey and winced as the fire of it slid down her throat. The taste was indeed unpleasant. "Here's to Christmas," she said a little hoarsely. "And to the rebirth of dreams."

Squeaky shook his head in amazement. "Here's to you, Mrs. B." He emptied the glass in one gulp, and it slid down his throat like silk.

A New York Christmas

To all the adventurers of the heart

*J*EMIMA STOOD AT THE RAILING ON THE UPPER DECK of the great ocean liner and gazed across the limitless sea. She had just turned twenty-three and was beginning what promised to be the first real adventure of her life.

It was December 1904, and she was crossing the Atlantic to New York, where she would stay for at least a month. Mr. Edward Cardew had invited her to travel as a companion to his daughter, Delphinia, who was to marry Brent Albright, the son of Rothwell Albright, Mr. Cardew's international business partner. It would be the society wedding of the year.

Phinnie had grown up in London, as Jemima had, but was only nineteen—so it was not at all suitable that she travel alone. Mr. Cardew was an invalid and thus unable to make the journey himself. Someone older and wiser was needed, a person who could be both friend and chaperone. So Jemima had a passage to New York, and an invitation to stay with the Albrights. She had heard that New York was almost as big as London, both raw and sophisticated, a city bursting with life and the expectation of all kinds of new experiences.

If she allowed herself to, Jemima might envy Phinnie her coming marriage, with its promise of happiness shared. Phinnie had met Brent Albright when he visited England the previous year. Within a month she was wildly in love. "He is handsome," she said, as she and Jemima sat together at afternoon tea. "And a great deal more than that. He makes me laugh. He knows about so many things, and yet he is kind. I feel wonderful just thinking of him." She was too discreet to mention that he was also very rich, so would not have courted Phinnie merely for her prospects.

Jemima's prospects were different, although she had to admit that was largely her own fault—or at least her own choice. Like her mother, Charlotte, she wanted adventure, interesting things to do, and, above all, love. She had no wish for a position in society. Perhaps, through tales here and there of her father's experiences and opinions, she had learned too much of its frailties, and she saw even the most powerful of men and the most elegant of women as no less vulnerable to the weaknesses of human nature than the footman or the parlor maid. Her father was Thomas Pitt, head of Special Branch in London. He had begun his career as an ordinary policeman, solving crimes that were often exceedingly grim. Her mother had sometimes helped him in that. Jemima could remember the excitement of it, and the heartbreak. Later, when he was head of Special Branch, his work became more concerned with official government secrets and was much more mysterious, at least to Jemima. That had not prevented Charlotte from participating, something Jemima had always admired about her mother.

In all the planning for this trip, no one had even mentioned Phinnie's mother. One allusion to her a few months ago had made Jemima think she had died when Phinnie was very young, not more than two or three years old. Nothing specific had been said, but the reference had been hurried past in such a manner that she felt it would be clumsy to speak of it again.

Phinnie must have missed her most of her life, but especially now. So Jemima was here to look after her, not only for the sake of propriety but also to be the friend and lookout her mother would have been. It was a trust she vowed to fulfill to the best of her ability. She would not let anything happen to Phinnie.

She smiled to herself, and turned away from the railing, and the wind. *Twenty-three, and I'm thinking like a policeman! You would be proud of me, Papa . . . and horrified!*

Shaking her head, she pulled up the collar of her coat and walked back toward the gangway down to the huge vestibule and the many formal rooms of the liner. She was passed by an elderly woman in a magnificent winter dress. The woman looked her up and down briefly, then nodded an acknowledgment. "Good afternoon, Miss Pitt," she said coolly.

Jemima was surprised that the woman knew her name, and not certain if that was a compliment or not. Then she realized it was actually Phinnie the woman knew. Jemima was merely "the companion." That was not an entirely pleasant thought.

"Good afternoon, Mrs. Weatherby," she replied, lifting her chin a trifle higher, and walking on without waiting to see if there would be a conversation.

She entered the cabin she and Phinnie shared, one of the more luxurious ones on the ship. It had both a bed-

room and a quite comfortable-sized sitting room—
Phinne was there, curled up in one of the chairs. She
was smaller than Jemima and just a trifle plumper, with
large, dark eyes—her best features—and thick hair, almost black, with a natural curl that Jemima envied.
Jemima's hair was a shining mahogany color, with
gleams of amber she did not much like. And it had to be
vigorously encouraged to have any curl at all.

Phinnie looked up as Jemima came in. She had just
finished writing in her diary, and now she carefully
closed it and snapped the tiny lock shut.

"I shall want to remember this," she said with a
smile. "I shall not be a single woman much longer. I may
forget what it feels like."

"I shall remind you," Jemima replied, closing the
door behind her and taking off her coat. She was glad to
be in the warmth again. The wind off the ocean had a
very sharp edge to it.

Phinnie gave a tiny shrug of one shoulder. "Oh, you
may not always be single," she said cheerfully. "You
really should turn your attention more fully to the subject. You do not need to be as fortunate as I am in order
to be well suited."

A blistering retort rose to Jemima's lips, but she bit

it back with difficulty. Phinnie's father was paying her fare, as she had been reminded twice already. She couldn't afford to alienate his daughter.

"Indeed, you are quite right," she said, walking across to the cupboard where she would hang up her coat. She kept her back to Phinnie so the younger woman would not see the expression on her face. "I would be content with far less," she added.

"That is very wise," Phinnie observed approvingly. "To know your own limits is halfway to happiness."

"What is the other half?" Jemima asked, hanging up her coat and turning round. "Knowing your husband's?"

Phinnie was momentarily taken aback.

"Perhaps it is knowing his limits but being careful not to tell him," Jemima said lightly. "Tact is a priceless virtue. It can cover a multitude of misfortunes, don't you think?"

"I don't know," Phinnie said instantly. "I don't have a multitude of misfortunes."

Jemima smiled. "Give it time. You are still very young."

Phinnie's smile vanished. Then with an effort she brought it back a trifle uncertainly. "You say that as if you think something awful is going to happen." There was a tiny whisper of fear in her voice.

Jemima felt guilty. She was having a wonderful trip at Mr. Cardew's expense, no luxury withheld.

"Of course not," she answered. "Nothing awful is going to happen." But she could not let it go entirely. "However, you would do well to learn a little tact. You are not the only one with feelings."

Phinnie bit her lip. "I'm so sorry. I didn't mean to insult you. I know I'm being selfish. I love Brent so much. I am incredibly fortunate that he loves me too."

"You will never please everybody; no one does," Jemima said more gently. "And it's wonderful that you have Brent. But you also need friends, Phinnie. We all do."

"Not everyone likes you," Phinnie pointed out. "You are very outspoken. Some people say you are opinionated."

"Indeed? And do they mean it as a compliment?" Jemima inquired with a slight edge to her voice.

"No, of course they don't."

"Then I am surprised that you wish to copy me," Jemima rejoined.

Phinnie drew in her breath sharply and could think of nothing with which to reply.

Jemima felt victorious, yet she had no pleasure in it. She went out of her way to be kinder to Phinnie that evening and listen to her without interrupting. She managed to sound impressed when Phinne was rambling on about the very considerable fortunes made by Albright and Cardew in their investments, and their climb from mere respectability to the pinnacle of power and influence in New York society.

"Everyone is in awe them," Phinnie said with admiration. "Brent says we shall carry on the family tradition in all kinds of ways. It will be marvelous, don't you think?"

Suddenly Phinnie looked chagrined, as if she had just realized that she was speaking of opportunities Jemima did not have. "I'm sorry," she said humbly. "I'm being thoughtless again, aren't I?"

"Not at all," Jemima replied generously. "In fact, I would love to hear about the charities they have endowed. I imagine you will one day guide some of these charities yourself."

"Do you think so?" Phinnie said eagerly, the warmth back in her eyes.

Jemima smiled. "I have no doubt."

Phinnie looked down, a slight flush in her cheeks. "As long as I please Brent, that's all I really care about."

That Jemima definitely envied her. She had met a considerable number of young men, and liked many of them well enough, but she had never really been in love. She had felt sparks, and excitement, but it had always been brief, and never accompanied by the deep liking that she had seen between her parents, the kind of friendship that strengthens with time and shared experience. She believed such friendship was the foundation of all the love that mattered.

Perhaps that was why she found it so difficult to meet someone she wished to marry. She could not settle for something that seemed far less than the love she had seen in her own family all her life.

"You'll find someone," Phinnie said with sudden gentleness. "I know it's taking rather long, but don't let that discourage you."

"I won't," Jemima promised, not because it was true but because she did not want to spoil Phinnie's happiness by selfishly indulging in her own feelings. What she meant, and intended to keep, was a promise to herself to look after Phinnie and make this adventure of hers as happy as it could possibly be.

Two days later the ship arrived in New York. From the deck of the liner, the city did not look so very different from London. But as soon as Jemima was ashore she heard the medley of different languages and saw Oriental faces and a good number of black ones, and others that were very fair, as if they were Scandinavian. Everyone was busy. There was an excitement, a tingle in the air, and she fully realized that she had come to a new place, even a new world, and, at least for the moment, alone.

It was overwhelming.

Phinnie clung to Jemima's arm as people eddied around them. Everyone else seemed to know where they were going.

Jemima felt a moment's panic. Then a slender brown-haired man was standing in front of them.

"Miss Cardew, Miss Pitt? My name is Farrell. I have come to take you home."

He gave orders that their luggage should be brought and conveyed to the carriage that was waiting for them. Discreetly he passed coins to the porters, and their obedience was immediate.

"If you will accompany me," he invited, "we shall go and take our places in the carriage so we may return home, where Mr. Brent is eager to see you."

Phinnie's eyes were bright with anticipation, and her cheeks flushed.

"Oh, yes," she agreed. "That would be very nice. It . . ." She took a deep breath. "It seems like ages since we last met."

"Much too long," Mr. Farrell agreed. "But then the Atlantic is very wide, as I am sure you are acutely aware at this moment. However, you are most welcome." He turned to Jemima. "And you also, Miss Pitt. You will find New York a marvelous city, full of life and adventure, a meeting place for the world." He followed the porter across the open space of the wharf toward the way out, and the road.

"Mr. Albright made sure that all the necessary paperwork was attended to," Farrell told them. "You will have nothing to do but show it to the officials as we leave."

Phinnie smiled. "I shall thank him. He is so very . . . thoughtful."

"That would be Mr. Rothwell Albright," Farrell corrected her gently. "He is a man of great influence here in New York. But there is no doubt you are already aware of that."

"Oh, yes." Phinnie nodded, covering her error easily. "My father speaks of him often, and with the greatest regard."

Farrell took her arm to help her up the steps, but he did not reply.

Jemima followed after them. Farrell did turn a couple of times to make certain she was not struggling, but the way was easy enough.

The ride from the dockside to the center of Manhattan, where the Albrights had their residence, was so fascinating that Jemima felt no wish to speak at all. Once they were off the main thoroughfare, she saw lots of shop signs not only in foreign languages but in lettering she did not recognize: Russian, perhaps? Or Hebrew? Some were undoubtedly Chinese.

But it was the people who held her attention. At a glance they were much like those of London. She was interested and somewhat comforted to observe the same fashions. At least she would not look as much a foreigner as she felt.

On the narrow pavements groups of young men walked with a little swagger, an air of confidence. They looked around them, surveying their territory, as it were. Was it out of nervousness, or was it the arrogance of those who feel they have destiny in their grasp?

It was too late in the year for open carriages, but there were plenty of horse-drawn vehicles about, especially the wagons of tradesmen. But she also saw more motor vehicles than she could remember having seen in London. Sputtering loudly, they moved at what she judged to be no more than ten miles an hour, not as fast as a good carriage horse.

"It is your first time to New York, Miss Pitt?" Farrell asked her.

Reluctantly she turned to reply. "Yes. I have been to Paris once, but never to America before."

He smiled. "And how do we compare with Paris?"

She smiled back at him. "I think my American will be better than my French," she replied.

He laughed outright. "I have never been outside America, but I hear Paris is marvelous."

"I think this will be marvelous too," she said warmly.

They were passing through a more affluent area now. The buildings were large and handsome, but newer than those she was used to at home, and taller. She counted one on Fifth Avenue that was at least twelve stories high. How odd that such fine streets should have numbers and not names!

They soon arrived at the Albright mansion. Jemima and Phinnie alighted from the carriage, staring for a moment at the gorgeous façade before following Farrell up the steps and into the entrance hall. The chandelier hanging from the high, arched ceiling was the largest Jemima had ever seen. She made an instant decision to be charming, complimentary, and unimpressed. She owed it to her national honor not to gawk as if such things were not common at home.

They were met by Miss Celia Albright, a rather thin lady of uncertain age, who was to be their hostess.

"Welcome, my dear Phinnie," Miss Albright said sweetly. "And to you, Miss Pitt. I hope you will be comfortable here. Mr. Cardew wrote to us to say how kind you had been in offering to accompany Phinnie so she would not have to travel alone." Her face was a trifle too bony to be handsome, and certainly neither her gaunt figure nor her rather ordinary clothes were those of a comely woman. Yet her thick, wavy hair was truly beautiful, and she moved her hands with grace. "I do hope you will enjoy your visit with us."

"I am sure I will," Jemima replied. Phinnie had told her little of Celia Albright, only that she was Mr. Rothwell Albright's unmarried sister. Meeting her, Jemima thought she seemed to lack the confidence that belonging to such a prominent family would confer.

Miss Albright turned again to Phinnie. "May I show you to your rooms? The footman will bring up your cases later. I hope you will find all that you need has been provided."

Phinnie followed Miss Albright up the wide, sweeping staircase. She looked very small behind the older, far taller woman. Jemima, a few steps behind, had the sudden impression that Phinnie was a lost child, far from home, seeking a new safety. It was ridiculous. Phinnie was going to marry a young man who loved her and was offering her a new and wonderful life, filled with every comfort she could wish. It was not as if she were among strangers. The Albrights and the Cardews had been in highly successful business together since long before

217

Phinnie was born. It was almost like a dynastic marriage within an extended family, aristocrats of the financial world.

Jemima was the stranger here, the daughter of a senior policeman but the granddaughter of a gamekeeper, for all that. Her mother was wellborn, but of gentry, certainly not either old wealth or nobility.

But none of that was supposed to matter, here in the New World where all men were equal, where it was the future that was important, not the past.

She drew in a deep breath and followed Phinnie and Miss Albright onto the landing and to the first bedroom, which was to be Phinnie's until the wedding.

When Phinnie was settled, Miss Albright took Jemima to another, smaller room farther along the passage. She opened the door and allowed Jemima to walk in past her.

The room was a surprise. It was dominated not by the charming dressing table but by a window that looked out to the branches of a bare tree. She imagined in the summer it would be gorgeous, but even in the winter its fretwork of dark limbs against the sky was of great beauty.

"I love it!" Jemima said in delight. "It's full of life!" She swung around to face Miss Albright, and was startled to see the emotion in the woman's face. "I know that's silly to say of a leafless tree," she went on, to cover what she thought was a moment of strange, deep sentiment in the other. "But I love bare branches. It is as if the tree is revealing its true self." She tried to think of further explanation, and saw in Miss Albright's face that it was unnecessary.

"I don't know Phinnie very well," Jemima, continued, picking her words carefully, "but I am very close to my own mother, and I cannot imagine how lonely I would be if I were to come to a new country, no matter that they spoke my language, without at least one person I could confide in." She smiled. "Even if it were only to tell them how happy I am, and for them to tell me when I don't look my best, or need advice. This is both a privilege and an adventure for me."

Miss Albright smiled with genuine affection. "I hope it will be both. If you wish to take a short rest before, dinner will be at eight o'clock. Betsy will unpack your cases for you. She is the lady's maid who will be looking after Miss Cardew. We dress formally for dinner, but

Betsy will advise you which of your gowns will be the most suitable. I daresay you would like a cup of tea?"

Jemima accepted with gratitude.

*T*he dinner was, as Miss Albright had said, very formal for a meal that involved no one outside the family except Jemima. She had accepted the advice of Betsy, who proved to be both efficient and knowledgeable, and had suggested a warm gown of dark green silk velvet with a wide skirt and a most flattering cut at the waist. Jemima was concerned that she might outshine Phinnie, but she need not have been. Phinnie came down the stairs in a gown of apricot silk, which murmured seductively as she walked, the warmth of its shading reflected on her skin, making her seem to glow with happiness.

Or perhaps she really did?

Brent Albright stood at the bottom of the wide staircase, watching her. A little farther back, his older brother, Harley, also waited as suited the occasion.

Harley was slightly taller than Brent, with thick fair

hair and a strong face that was not well-enough propor-
tioned to be handsome. Brent, on the other hand, was
almost as good-looking as Phinnie had claimed. His hair
was darker than Harley's, his eyes a deeper blue. But it
was his smile that was most engaging. He held out his
hand to Phinnie and she took his arm as she reached
the last step, brushing close to him for a moment. Then
she lifted her chin and sailed on to be presented to Mr.
Rothwell Albright, who stood underneath the magnificent chandelier, the light of it making his silver hair
into a kind of halo.

"Welcome to New York, my dear," he said to Phinnie.
"I wish your father could be here to join our celebrations, but I understand his reasons for remaining at
home. I hope he recovers fully and soon."

"Thank you, sir," Phinnie said modestly. "I am sure
he will. The doctors are hopeful."

Mr. Albright turned to Jemima and regarded her
with quite open interest. "And you are Miss Jemima
Pitt, I believe. I am told by Edward that your father is a
policeman of some considerable distinction. Is that
true?"

"Yes, sir, it is," Jemima said, and was about to add

more, but realized that it was not appropriate at the moment. This evening was in honor of Brent and Phinnie. "I am glad Mr. Cardew spoke so well of him," she added.

"Indeed. I have known Edward for more years than I care to recall. I trust him completely." He offered his arm. "Would you care to accompany me in to dinner, Miss Pitt?"

She accepted his offer and rested her hand on the fine wool cloth of his sleeve as he led the way into the richly decorated dining room.

Miss Celia Albright followed on Harley's arm, and Phinnie on Brent's.

Though Jemima was determined not to be impressed, she was unable to help it. The room was beautiful, in a way that far surpassed mere showiness. The silver on the table was old and had an elaborate "A" engraved on all the handles. The condiment sets matched. Nothing had the look of being new or unused. Contrary to her preconception, the Albrights clearly had generations of being elite behind them.

"I hope you had a pleasant voyage?" Miss Albright said to Phinnie. "The Atlantic can be a little rough at this time of year."

"Not enough to be uncomfortable, thank you," Phinnie replied.

It had been unpleasant at times, but of course Phinnie knew better than to say so. Jemima wondered if all their conversation was going to be so polite, and generally meaningless. She had a fear that some people's lives were like that: words skimming across the surface of reality, like birds over the waves, without ever getting wet.

"Our voyage to the Bahamas will be quite different," Brent promised with a smile at Phinnie. "We shall bask in the sun, as soon as we are far enough south. Have you ever seen a flying fish?"

Phinnie's eyes opened wide in amazement yet total belief. She would have accepted anything he said. "No, I haven't." She blushed. "I look forward to that."

Jemima thought for a moment how marvelous it would feel to be so much in love with someone. Then she wondered if she could ever feel that overwhelmed with emotion. Perhaps she was already too old for it, a little too realistic. Or too cynical? That was an ugly thought. After all, how could you find magic if you did not believe in it? She knew people who could look at the most amazing and beautiful things and not see them.

She must not turn into someone like that. In a way, such people were the walking dead, passing through life untouched by its joy.

She suddenly realized that Celia Albright was talking to her, and she had not heard what had been said.

"I'm so sorry," she apologized. "I was daydreaming." She should add some explanation. She smiled. "We have been looking forward to this for so long it hardly seems real now that we are here."

Phinnie shot her a smile.

"We will show you some of the sights of New York," Harley Albright offered, and there was no question in his voice. "Miss Cardew will have arrangements to make, and I daresay Celia will accompany her. She knows everyone. Perhaps you would allow me to take you to luncheon at Delmonico's, or the Hotel Astor? A walk in Central Park, if the weather remains clement?"

It seemed like a thoughtful offer, and it would be terrible to be here in this so very vital city and not see as much of it as possible.

"That is most kind of you," Jemima accepted. "I should be delighted." She knew Harley was several years older than Brent, but she had no idea if he worked in the family business or had as much leisure time as he wished. America was different. She had the idea that everyone was always busy, unlike half of London society, but that might be incorrect. "If I am not intruding?" she added, and then wished she had not. The look on his face was gentle but mildly patronizing.

"Not at all, Miss Pitt. You are our guest, and I should be delighted to show you something of our city, and perhaps a little of our history. There are parts that are very beautiful, others less so, but still of interest. We have just this year opened our subway, which is like your underground railway system. It has twenty-eight stations across town and has made an amazing difference. We really are one city now."

She saw the pride in his eyes, the absolute certainty, and knew that anything but acceptance would be discourteous.

"Then I am very happy to accept," she said cordially.

"We have so many people to meet." Brent took over the conversation, looking at Phinnie as he spoke. "I am looking forward to showing you off to my friends. I don't mean to rush you, but they are all so keen to make your acquaintance, and they are people we shall know for the rest of our lives." He let that observation hang in the air for a moment, so she might take the full meaning of it.

Phinnie lowered her eyes. "I look forward to it."

Jemima knew he was letting her know that all New York high society was to be their social circle, and first impressions mattered.

Miss Albright mentioned a few names, ones that Jemima had heard even in London, or at least read in the court and social columns of *The Times*. Harley added a few more, and Brent continued with details of who was married to whom.

The Albrights were letting them all know exactly where they fit in: at the top of the social hierarchy. It was a welcoming and conversational way of stating their family's position, and their thinly masked pride in it.

Jemima looked occasionally at Phinnie and tried to read her expression. After doing so the third time, she was satisfied that Phinnie was happy and excited, and very little awed by the prospect of living up to such distinction. Her eyes shone with trust as she looked at Brent, and there was a flush of joy in her cheeks. This evening she looked truly beautiful.

Did Jemima envy her? Perhaps.

Did Celia Albright envy her? That was a harder question to answer. Jemima looked across the table and caught the older woman's eye. There was humor in her, and a sadness. Had she ever found anyone she could have loved, and who had been equal to the Albright heritage and pride? Or had she loved and lost someone whose heart she had never touched?

As she sat at this family table, she suddenly felt keenly that she was the only stranger. The world she wanted was far bigger, more dangerous, and perhaps also lonelier. Might she end up like Celia, somewhat on the edge of things? And was it her own naïvety, looking for a love like that between her parents, that put her there?

"Do you have an opinion, Miss Pitt?" Mr. Albright was saying. It had been a political question about Europe and Jemima had caught only the end of it.

"Not yet," she replied with a smile. "I would like to learn a great deal more before I form one."

He looked impressed. "How wise of you," he said approvingly. "I should have known Mr. Cardew would pick a young woman of fine judgment to accompany his daughter on the way to her wedding, since—" He seemed about to add something more, then quite clearly changed his mind; it was obvious from the sudden si-

227

lence that followed. The thought of Phinnie's mother now hung in the air like a presence.

"Maria would be very proud of you, Phinnie," Celia said gently, breaking the awkwardness and yet somehow making it worse.

Mr. Albright almost smiled at some memory he did not offer to share.

Harley raised his eyebrows, and his voice when he spoke was chilly.

"Maria contributed nothing whatsoever to Phinnie's charm or spirit. They are entirely to Phinnie's own credit, as we all know. Even Maria would not claim to have had anything to do with it."

A dull stain of color marked Celia's face and she struggled for a moment to keep her temper.

"That may be so, Harley," she said. "But truly, any woman would be proud of such a daughter."

Jemima was acutely embarrassed, both for Celia, who had been so publicly criticized, and for Phinnie.

Brent reached out his hand and laid it over Phinnie's on top of the table, where the gesture would not be missed.

"You are about to become part of my family," he said

to her, but sufficiently loud for everyone to hear. "You will be mistress of the house, and mother to whatever children we may have. We shall all be proud of you." He looked at Harley, then at Mr. Albright. He did not look at Celia.

Jemima wished she were anywhere else. The reference to Maria Cardew—who, it seemed, was alive after all—had been turned from a passing remark into a painful issue, and poor Celia had been publicly and very sharply reminded that her own place as hostess in the Albright house was about to end. How long she had claimed that status Jemima was not sure. Presumably since Mrs. Albright had died, but she did not know when that was.

Was the title "Aunt" literal, in that she was Mr. Albright's sister, or was the truth that she was some more distant relative, perhaps a cousin? Did she even have another place to go? How many female relatives were used that way, as unpaid servants, and only until someone else took over?

Phinnie looked slightly uncomfortable, but her happiness was too intense to be seriously disturbed by Celia's predicament. "I can think of no greater honor," she said quietly. She turned for a moment to Brent, then away again, as if to ease the emotions that had been aroused and continue with the meal.

Jemima wanted to say something polite and meaningless that they could all grasp on to, but she felt that it was not her place. There was obviously some family issue to do with Maria Cardew that no one wished to address openly yet was always just under the surface. She wondered what it was.

They ate in silence for several minutes. Every touch of knife or fork to the plate was audible. Even the movement of fabric against the padded seats of the chairs could be heard.

"I imagine Christmas will be celebrated wonderfully in New York," Jemima said at length. "It is a time of new beginnings, and so is probably especially appreciated here."

Harley looked at her blankly. "I had always thought of Christmas as a time of tradition above everything else," he remarked. "It is nineteen hundred years old!"

"It is a time of rebirth of hope, and gratitude," she replied, remembering something from a sermon she had heard, under protest, a year ago. "I believe it carries the promise that we can start again, wherever we are." Her look challenged him to argue with her, if he dared refuse the olive branch she held out.

"Of course it is," Mr. Albright said firmly. He smiled very slightly, but with a flash of approval in his eyes, for her tact, and perhaps also for her theology.

"We celebrate it with bells and garlands and music, just as you do," Brent agreed. "And, of course, wonderful food. It is a time for families to be together and rejoice."

That was not what Jemima had meant, but she let it go. They spent the rest of the meal recounting Christmas experiences and traditions that were special to the Albright family. Maria Cardew was not mentioned again, although the late Mrs. Albright was remembered often. It seemed that Harley had been especially close to her, and clearly still missed her presence.

Jemima was sorry that Phinnie would not have an older woman to guide her around the pitfalls of society. She was profoundly grateful for her own mother's advice, and even more for that of her aunt Emily, who was less of a rebel than Charlotte. It was very good to know the rules, even if you did not intend to follow them.

Much later in the evening, when she had already bidden everyone good night and was crossing the upstairs landing on her way to bed, she met Celia Albright.

"Do you have everything you need, Miss Pitt?" Celia asked.

"Oh, yes, thank you," Jemima replied sincerely. "I'm sure I shall sleep very well. You have been most kind."

Celia did not move, as if there were something else she wished to say.

Jemima also hesitated. It would have been a dismissal to have left, and she already felt a sympathy with the older woman, even if it was for a situation she only imagined.

"If you are worried about Phinnie, she may be too excited to sleep, but she is very happy and well suited also," Jemima added.

Celia gave a tiny gesture of resignation. "I'm sure. She will not miss Maria because she never really knew her. A pity, because she was a beautiful woman. Oh, I don't mean her face, although that was lovely too. I mean her courage, her gentleness, her laughter. Whatever else you hear about her, Miss Pitt, don't judge her unkindly. Emotions can run"—she searched for the words—"in ugly paths sometimes. Assumptions are not always correct."

"Assumptions about Mrs. Cardew?"

"I haven't seen her or heard from her in many, many years, but I believe she was a good woman at heart, in spite of appearances." Celia bit her lip. "Sleep well." She turned away and hurried along the corridor and around the corner, her head high, her thin shoulders stiff.

Jemima went to her own room and closed the door. The curtains were drawn across the window, perhaps to keep out the cold on the glass as much as anything else, but she had liked the sight of the bare trees. It was something familiar and beautiful in a strange new place where she was very much alone.

She thought about Phinnie, madly in love with Brent and on the edge of a new life, with no one but Jemima here by her side. What on earth could have made Maria Cardew leave her only child, little more than a baby, and surely needing a mother desperately? Jemima could barely even imagine the loneliness of that child, the bewilderment, the confusion. Why would any woman do such a thing?

The only thing she was sure of was that, whatever happened, however much Phinnie irritated her, she must try harder to be the friend the girl needed now. She ought never to feel abandoned again.

$\mathcal{F}$or the next three days there were social events to attend where Phinnie was proudly introduced to some of the cream of New York society. There was a soiree with an excellent violinist, and of course the sort of pleasant conversation Jemima was used to from parties in London. It was like being on a most elegant stage, everyone acting as if he or she were the star, with polite laughter, sophisticated wit, calculated remarks. Jemima was both disappointed and relieved that it was so familiar, with no hint of adventure to be found. But she could see how well and how easily Phinnie would settle in, and that was all that truly mattered.

The weather was cold but still pleasant, and there were sightseeing trips around Central Park, which was quite attractive, rather different from the London parks. For a start, it was enormous, and far more naturally scenic in spite of being in the very middle of the city. There were no formal gardens such as Jemima was used to, but some very beautiful walks nonetheless.

There was also a visit to the Metropolitan Opera; very grand indeed, and the music was superb. On the fifth evening there was a ball, and for the first time Jemima was acutely envious of Phinnie. She radiated happiness and had acquired a polish to her beauty that turned more than just Brent Albright's head. Suddenly Jemima ached to have someone look at her the way Brent looked at Phinnie, to feel the safety and warmth of being so loved.

She forced these thoughts from her mind and smiled as if she were enjoying herself. She danced with whoever asked her, even though it was more out of courtesy than desire.

On the following morning, to her surprise, Harley caught up with her as she was crossing the hall to go back up the wide, sweeping staircase to her room.

"Miss Pitt," he said urgently, putting his hand on the carved newel post as if he intended to be there some minutes. "Are you engaged this morning?"

Surely he must know she was not? Celia Albright was taking Phinnie to a dressmaker to have further gowns made for her, with the winter season in mind. She had brought many with her, but one should not appear twice in the same outfit, if in company with people from another recent event. For Phinnie, the only child of a very wealthy man, cost was of no importance at all. Jemima herself had no need of more gowns, and while her family was now financially comfortable, it would remain so only if expenses were regarded with care.

"No," she replied to Harley. "I thought I would take the opportunity to write to my parents and tell them what an exciting city New York is, and that your family has been most kind to me."

"It is our pleasure," he answered, although his smile went no further than his lips. "I'm delighted you find New York so . . . invigorating. It is my city, and I admit I am proud of it. I would welcome the chance to show you some of the more colorful parts, such as Little Italy. You will be quite safe, and the food is excellent. Of course, it is best explored on foot. Or if you prefer, there is Battery Park, down by the water?"

It was a pleasant idea, and Jemima had no reason to refuse, although she admitted to herself that the invitation surprised her. She believed he made it more from good manners than from a desire for her company. Perhaps his father had suggested he do so.

"Thank you. If you are sure you can spare the time, I would love to see Little Italy. I daresay I may not have the chance again."

"It would be my pleasure," he assured her. "Shall we meet here in half an hour? Please wear your overcoat. The wind is chill."

Harley was quite right. As Jemima sat in the carriage beside him on the way toward Little Italy, the wind was indeed sharp. However, she was too interested in the sights of the bustling streets to mind. He was a good host, explaining the recent history of many of the neighborhoods (including those they would not visit, such as Hell's Kitchen, down by the river).

"Started when they put the tanneries there," he told her. "Made the river filthy, of course, but industry does. Lot of Irish immigrants, fleeing the Great Famine. After the Civil War the population got a whole lot larger, and gang warfare started."

Harley was more talkative than she had expected, and she enjoyed his stories of the city and its different areas. He loved the life, the variety and the courage of the people, and his face grew animated as he spoke. She caught a glimpse of a very different man from the rather stiff one who occupied the mansion. She wondered fleetingly what the arrangement would be when Harley married. He was the older brother, so would Brent then find his own home? Or would they all remain under one roof? The house was certainly large enough.

"This is Little Italy—Mulberry Street, to be exact. Would you like to walk a bit?" Harley invited as the carriage drew to the curb. "Perhaps we could have a hot cup of coffee? There is a place a couple of hundred yards away, not very glamorous, but the coffee is good."

Jemima accepted with pleasure, and fifteen minutes later they were seated in a crowded but most agreeable small restaurant. All around her people were speaking in Italian, a musical language, much of it loud. The walls were hung with pictures of Naples and Sicily, and there were Chianti bottles on the tables.

Harley leaned toward her. "Miss Pitt, may I confide in you? I am certain you have Delphinia's happiness very much at heart, as I have my brother's."

Suddenly she realized why he had brought her here. It was far more than a matter of hospitality, or even of pride in his city. He was deeply concerned about something and it showed clearly now in his face.

"Of course," she agreed, putting her coffee down and giving him her full attention.

He considered a moment before he spoke again, as if carefully formulating his words.

"I am not sure how much Phinnie knows about her mother, Maria Cardew, although that may not be her name now . . ."

Jemima was startled at the mention of Maria's name, especially coming from Harley. She had assumed none of the Albrights wished to speak about her.

Harley saw the expression and smiled bleakly.

"I'm sorry to raise the subject, but you seem by far the best person to turn to. You clearly care for Delphinia and are taking your role in her life most seriously. Your first concern is always her well-being."

Jemima felt herself blushing. He was praising her where she felt she had not yet deserved it sufficiently.

"You are modest," he said quickly. "But what I say is true. Also, if I have understood correctly, your father is a man of some wisdom and experience in matters of . . . I really don't know how to put this delicately . . . of criminal acts . . ." His phrasing was awkward, yet he did not look discomfited. She realized with a rush of very mixed emotions that he was too confident in himself to care what she thought of him.

"He is head of Special Branch," she said coolly. "They are responsible for any threat to the safety of the nation in a criminal or espionage kind of way."

He looked momentarily blank.

"Not military attack," she added for clarification. "Why do you mention my father? Do you think Maria Cardew is a danger to New York?"

This time it was he who blushed, and a flash of appreciation gleamed in his eyes for an instant.

"No, of course not," he answered. "She is simply a woman of poor judgment and even poorer morals. Despite her being absent for most of Delphinia's life, I am afraid that she may turn up at the wedding. If that happened, it would be in appalling taste and desperately embarrassing. And goodness only knows who she might bring with her. Some of her associates were . . ." He spread his hands in a gesture of hopelessness. "It might be better if I left it to your imagination. I don't wish to use language you would prefer not to hear."

Jemima's imagination was racing. What kind of woman was Maria Cardew? If she had been impossible to understand before, she was now also frightening.

Jemima could see in her mind's eye the vision of a cathedral wedding, the high-society guests in their gorgeous clothes, with their stiff faces and their polite laughter. And then suddenly Maria Cardew, perhaps drunk, loud-voiced, announcing that she was the mother of the bride. Phinnie would never live it down. Ruin had been brought about by less.

How could any woman twice so injure her own child?

"Is she mad?" she asked quite seriously.

Harley Albright looked at her with something close to gratitude.

"I see that you understand. Yes, I think perhaps she is, and more deserving of our pity than our anger. But the damage she would do to our family, especially Phinnie, who is about to become one of us . . ." He shrugged. "I don't need to describe it. Even the kindest people would find it impossible to forget. The less kind would make it their business to see that no one else ever did!"

Jemima winced at the thought of it.

He misunderstood. "Of course we have enemies, Miss

241

Pitt. It would be dangerously naïve to think that we didn't. We have wealth and power. My father is a generous and good man, but he has been highly successful in business, far more so than some of his acquaintances. My mother was beautiful. That alone can sow the seeds of envy. There are those who would rejoice at our downfall."

Jemima waited for him to continue. She sipped her coffee, but it had lost its flavor.

"That is why I ask you to help me," Harley said gently. "I believe you will, for Phinnie's sake, not mine."

She was puzzled. "What can I do? I can see perfectly how awful it would be if Mrs. Cardew were to turn up at the wedding, but what could any of us do to stop her?" She frowned. "Why do you think she even knows about it?"

"Ah . . ." He let out a sigh. "That is the crux of the whole situation. I am almost certain that she is in New York."

"In New York? That's terrible!" Now she could see the situation perfectly.

"Yes . . . yes it is," he agreed. "I suppose we should have foreseen it. After all, the marriage was announced as the wedding of the year. I imagine that even in other cities it will have been reported in the society columns of newspapers. If Mrs. Cardew read of it, she could be misguided enough to come."

"Surely she must see, after all these years, that she would not be welcome?" Jemima protested. "I don't know the circumstances of her leaving, but nothing alters the fact of it. Phinnie doesn't want to see her. How could she?"

"Exactly." Harley nodded grimly. "I am aware of the circumstances. My mother told me, shortly before she died. But I prefer not to discuss them. Suffice it to say that they could hardly be worse. Will you help me?"

"Of course. But I still don't understand what we can do."

"I have given it a great deal of thought," he replied earnestly. "I can think of nothing else but to find her, and persuade her that she would hurt Phinnie, perhaps irreparably, if she were to appear at the wedding. If she wishes to see her, which I suppose is possible, we could promise to arrange it, but privately." His face registered extreme distaste. "I would even be willing to pay her a certain amount, if she remains several miles away, perhaps even in another city, and never makes the relationship known. I hope that will not be necessary, but as a last resort—"

"Then she could extort money from you indefinitely," Jemima warned. The moment the words were out of her mouth, she wondered if she had been wise to say them.

Harley stared down at the table for several moments before meeting her eyes.

"I had thought of that, Miss Pitt. That is why I hope to persuade her of the unpleasantness of that course. She would earn Delphinia's undying contempt, to say the least. I don't know if it will work. I am unaware of what has become of her and what manner of person she is now."

"And what was she like before?" Jemima asked the question that she knew her father would have asked.

"At the time of her marriage to Cardew?" His eyes widened. "A pretty and ambitious young woman who had already had more than her share of romantic adventures, with all manner of men, but who knew how to please an upper-class Englishman in a foreign country, a man who had no idea such women even existed."

Jemima doubted very much that upper-class Englishmen were anything like as innocent as Harley Albright supposed, but this was not the time to say so.

"I see. Now we are twenty years later, her looks may

not be as attractive, nor her health as good," she pointed out.

His face tightened. He looked bleak and even a little frightened.

"Of course. You are quite right. We need to find her, then deal with her in whatever way seems best. I need you to help me, Miss Pitt. You seem to have just the right combination of common sense and imagination, which, coupled with my reputation and my knowledge of New York, should be sufficient."

She nodded. "I will do all that I can. Where shall we start?" New York was a teeming city full of all manner of people; this she knew after barely a week. Maria Cardew could be anywhere, and none of the Albrights had seen her for nearly two decades. She could have changed entirely since then.

"What would your father do?" Harley asked with perfect seriousness.

Pitt would have sent one of his men on the job, but she did not say that. It was certainly not the answer Harley Albright was looking for. She thought hard while the minutes ticked away, and he waited, watching her intently.

She must concentrate her mind, think logically. Most important of all, she must rescue Phinnie from a ruinous embarrassment. Her future life in New York, and with Brent, would depend upon Maria's not turning up and spoiling it all. Society here would be just like society in London: It would never forget a tragedy, still less a scandal.

Also, in a way, she was representing the intelligence and the standing of her own family.

"She will have found accommodation somewhere," she began thoughtfully. "Either she is staying with a friend, or she has a house or a room. She will be aware that she is not welcome at the Albright home—she will know where it is, but stay out of sight."

Harley nodded but did not interrupt.

"Before we begin to look for her, it would be good to make note of all we know about her. We will have to ask questions of people. The more precise they are, the less time we will waste."

He frowned. "She could be anywhere." His voice held a note of defeat.

"No," she answered, far more firmly than she felt. "There are many areas she will not be, and even among those where she might be, some will be more likely than others. In London I could tell you, but here you will have to think of it."

"What do you mean?" he asked.

"She will need to feel safe." Jemima had tested her ideas in her mind, and hoped she was as reasonable as she sounded. "If there is an area she stayed in before, she might choose it. We all prefer the known to the unknown. It is both easier and pleasanter. Also, she must be able to afford it. Do you know her circumstances? How does she support herself?" The moment the words were out of her mouth she regretted them. The answer was one she could guess, and preferred not to know. But, perhaps in her fifties, Maria had changed her ways. She might well be obliged to.

Harley pursed his lips in an expression of distaste. "She was always good at living off men, one way or another." His voice lifted. "But I see the point of your questions. That does narrow it down considerably. I shall think of them and give you answers. Is there anything else?"

"Yes. What does she look like? Some things don't change much. How tall is she? She may be gray-haired now, but eyes and skin tone do not change so much. What about her voice, her mannerisms? Where might she eat? Is there something she likes that would take her to a particular place?"

"Likes? To eat?" He looked uncertain.

"Yes. When you are far from home, in trouble of any kind, it is natural to turn to something familiar and pleasant. Chocolates? A special kind of tea? A place where you can be alone? A view that has meaning? A particular park to walk in, pictures in a museum, anything?"

He began to smile. "Yes, I see what you mean. You are a credit to your father, Miss Pitt. Would you like another cup of coffee, or shall we return home and begin our quest?"

She rose to her feet. "I think we should begin as soon as possible, Mr. Albright. We cannot afford otherwise."

For the first time in their acquaintance, he smiled at her with genuine warmth.

The next three days were exciting and of absorbing interest to Jemima. Harley came up with an account of all that he knew about Maria Cardew, which turned out to be a bit more than Jemima had expected.

"She was apparently a very vivacious woman," he began. "Pretty in her own way, and very fashionable.

Made herself most agreeable. I think she tried to keep her more eccentric opinions to herself, but she certainly did not always succeed."

"What opinions?" Jemima asked, then saw his expression and wished she had not.

"On racial matters, and people's position in society, property rights. Which is amusing in a dry way, considering she met Edward Cardew in our house, and was quick enough to accept his proposal of marriage."

"Are you saying she was a hypocrite?" Jemima asked as innocently as she could.

"Yes," he said quietly. "I suppose I am. Her subsequent history rather proves my point."

"Yet Miss Albright speaks well of her," Jemima pointed out.

Harley's expression was a mixture of anger and attempted patience.

"Celia likes anyone who likes her, and Maria knew that."

"I see," Jemima replied, forming a strange and not very pleasant picture in her head of a selfish and manipulative woman who had deeply hurt her husband and her only child.

Jemima was careful to say nothing to Phinnie about how she was spending her days. As far as everyone else was concerned, Harley was merely spending time with Jemima in order to show her around the city he knew and loved, and she was greatly enjoying it.

Soon the weather turned much colder. Jemima woke up on the third day of their quest to find everything mantled in white.

"I must show you Central Park in the snow!" Harley said at the breakfast table, a gleam of excitement in his eyes.

"Indeed," Mr. Albright agreed. "It is a wonderful sight. If it is deep enough, there will be people playing all manner of games. And if there is ice, there will be skating. I might come with you . . ."

"Thank you, Father," Harley said with a very slight drop in his voice. "But we will be fine. I'm sure you have matters that need your attention."

Brent stifled a smile; a complete misunderstanding, as Jemima knew. Harley had no interest in being alone in her company. What he had was an idea as to where they might find Maria Cardew. Something about the snow had clearly awakened a memory in him. She could not afford to pass up this chance. She bowed her head slightly as if both happy and self-conscious, and saw a fleeting look of alarm in Harley's eyes.

"Of course," Mr. Albright agreed, as if he understood perfectly, and it pleased him.

Jemima concentrated on the anticipation of discovering Maria Cardew.

She and Harley set out as early as they could without giving rise to more comment, which she thought he found even more uncomfortable than she did. The air was brisk and the wind had a bite to it, but he did not ask her if she still wished to go out. It would have been the courteous thing to do, even though he knew she would not refuse to go.

They took the carriage as far as Central Park, then dismissed the driver, saying that their plans were too open for them to estimate a time for him to return. He smiled and drove off.

Harley looked discomfited for a moment, then recovered himself.

"The snow this morning has reminded me of something Aunt Celia once told me, Miss Pitt. Maria Cardew used to enjoy such weather, most especially when the snow was newly fallen and still outlining the branches of the bare trees. If she is here in New York, as I am

ANNE PERRY

certain she is, she will be most likely to walk in the park this morning. Of course we could well miss her—it is a very large place—but I do know the best walks for such sights, and undoubtedly Maria does too. If you are willing to go at a brisk pace, we perhaps have a chance of spotting her. Together, we will not draw any unusual attention, and we may follow her to wherever she is staying."

"That is a good plan," she agreed, walking rapidly beside him. "And people will be going carefully, watching that they do not slip, so she will be less likely to notice that the same couple is behind her over a considerable distance."

"Yes," he agreed. "I had not thought of that." He offered her his arm.

She took it as if it was the most natural thing to do.

It was well into the afternoon and Jemima's feet were aching badly when finally, they spotted a woman of medium height standing on her own some thirty yards ahead of them. She turned to face their direction for a moment, staring up at the light through the snow-laden branches of the trees, her face filled with wonder.

Harley stiffened. His hand grasped Jemima's arm, so she stopped as well. Then, as the woman continued her

252

walk, he moved forward urgently. His pace increased so that gradually the distance between them closed.

"Is that her? Do you want to confront her here?" Jemima asked him breathlessly. "If she makes a scene, we will draw everyone's attention, and if she leaves, we may not be able to follow her to wherever she is lodging."

"I think it is her, but I can't be entirely sure." He let out his breath in annoyance, and slowed down again, allowing the woman in front to reach the edge of the park and walk along the pavement toward a crossing.

The traffic eased and they followed the woman to the other side. She continued along the footpath and they moved a little closer to her so as not to lose her in the general crowd as they went eastward.

"Have you thought what you will say to her?" Jemima asked, but she did not quite hear his reply amid the sounds of the street and the crunch of footsteps in the snow.

Once, she lost Harley in crossing a busy road whose name was merely a number, like most of the ones around them. A wave of panic swept over her. Then she remembered that she had money, she knew the address of the Albright mansion, and she was certainly capable of speaking the language and asking for assistance. There were public conveyances here, just as there were in London. She took a deep breath to calm herself.

The next moment, he was there beside her.

"You had better take my arm, Miss Pitt," he said a little sharply. "It would be disastrous if I were to lose you."

"It would be inconvenient," she corrected him. "I am afraid an elderly lady stepped between us and I could not move around her to keep up with you."

"It can't be helped. I lost the woman, but I am fairly certain it was Maria, and I believe I know the neighborhood where she went. We will go there tomorrow when we have prepared ourselves, and we shall find her exact rooms. Your assistance has been of the highest order, Miss Pitt, and our whole family owes you a considerable debt." He started to walk back the way they had come, automatically taking her with him. "Phinnie will never know of it. I am sure you have more grace and tact than to tell her, but I shall not forget what you have done. I am truly grateful. Now if you are ready, we shall find a cab and return home. It is getting dark, and I think it is very much colder."

Jemima was glad to agree.

*D*inner was full of conversation about the wedding: Were they sure the right flowers would be available? Was Aunt Mabel going to recover her health in time to attend? Was the cake perfectly iced yet? Jemima was asked politely about her day, but as soon as she had made clear that it had been enjoyable, and that she was impressed by the beauty of the park in its white covering, discussion returned to the wedding.

She felt a little left out; she didn't know most of the people referred to. But she reminded herself that she was here to look after Phinnie and see that it was truly the happiest day of her life. Above all, without Phinnie ever knowing, she must make certain that Maria Cardew did not get in the way.

She pictured the woman they had seen in the park. Her face, as she turned in wonder to gaze at the snow-mantled trees, had not looked dissipated, or even angry or tired. But Jemima had been some distance away. Closer up, it might have betrayed all kinds of weaknesses, even the beginnings of disease. As her mother was wont to say, "At twenty you have the face nature has given you; at fifty you have the face you deserve." Time has a way of carving your character into you so that all may see it at a glance. The lines of habit cut deep, for better or worse.

The next morning she set out with Harley to find and confront Maria Cardew. He assured her that he had decided exactly what to say to her, and a fall-back attitude to adopt if she should prove unreasonable. He was prepared to offer her money, in spite of Jemima's advice to the contrary.

They were in a coffee shop a block and a half from the building where he suspected Maria had gone on the previous evening when Harley spoke of his plan.

"I am fairly sure I know which building it is, but I don't know which rooms," he told her as they sat opposite each other, their hands around their hot mugs. "I will go and inquire. Perhaps it may be necessary to bribe someone to let me know exactly where she is. Also, of course, I don't know how she is satisfying the landlord regarding her rent," he went on. "It is not a seemly place for you to come, except when I have actually found her. I regret that I have to involve you at all, and I am still hesitant, now that I see the neighborhood in daylight. But I think you may be able to persuade her of the harm she would do Phinnie better than I can. I am ashamed to use your help, but I fear I cannot do without it."

"Mr. Albright," Jemima said urgently, "please don't apologize. We have come this far together, in a cause that is important to both of us. I am not afraid of a slight unpleasantness at the end. Let me know when you find her, and I shall come."

"I admire you, Miss Pitt, and I am most grateful," he replied. Then he ordered another cup of coffee for her, paid for it, and left to go out into the gently falling snow.

A full half hour later, he had still not returned. Wondering what could've kept him, Jemima decided to approach the building herself. If she did not see Harley, she could always return to the coffee shop.

She fastened her coat and went out into the snow. It took her seven or eight minutes walking into the wind before she reached the building. She went in at the entrance and found herself in a tired and rather grubby hall. She understood at once why Harley had not wanted her to come here without him. But what on Earth could've kept him for so long? Jemima walked the length of the hall, annoyed. After a few minutes, she decided it was best that she just return to the coffee shop. As she turned toward the door, a young boy came in.

257

"Excuse me," Jemima said impulsively. The boy turned toward her and smiled, showing beautiful teeth.

"Do you by chance know which rooms belong to Maria Cardew?" She did not believe he would know, but thought it was worth asking.

The boy nodded. "309, I think," he said, but with so strong an accent from somewhere in Eastern Europe that she took a moment to deduce what he said.

"Thank you!" Jemima gave him a nickel from her purse. He took it and hid it immediately, then gave her another smile and darted outside again.

It was a steep climb to the third floor, but in minutes she was at the top, looking at numbers on the doors. She found 309 at the far end and hesitated outside the door, wondering if she should go down and look for Harley. But perhaps Maria Cardew would be more inclined to listen to her, someone who had no history with the Albright and Cardew families, save being Phinnie's friend? She decided it was worth a try, and knocked on the scratched wooden door.

There was no answer. Actually, it was not completely shut. She gave it a push and it swung wider.

There was a slight rustling sound from inside.

"Mr. Albright?" Jemima called. She would have said "Mrs. Cardew," but she was not certain if that was the name Maria still used!

Again there was no answer, just a faint swish of movement, like the fabric of a long skirt over the floor.

She would have to use some name.

"Mrs. Cardew?" She tried again.

Nothing but the swish of fabric on the floor again. This was absurd. The door was unfastened; there must be someone inside. Jemima pushed the door open the rest of the way and went in, calling again for Mrs. Cardew.

The sitting room was pleasantly furnished but very shabby. One of the windows was open and a curtain blew in the wind, making a slight noise as it moved over the carpet and settled back. That was the sound she had heard.

She stared around her. There were plenty of signs of occupation: a number of books on the shelves, a bag with knitting needles and wool sitting neatly by one of the armchairs, a handmade rug for the knees folded up but within easy reach.

Another door was open and she could see that it led

to a tiny kitchen. Anyone inside would have been visible.

"Mrs. Cardew!" she called again, going to the door on the opposite side. She knocked on it and waited, then tried the handle. What could she possibly say in explanation if she intruded into someone's bedroom and found them there? She had no earthly excuse.

And yet she did it.

She saw the woman immediately. The bedroom was small and neat, with two single beds in it. One was neatly made and empty, as if it were not used. On the other a woman lay motionless. The skin of her face was bleached almost gray and her dark hair, streaked with white, was loose and tangled as if she had been moving restlessly only a short while ago. One thin, blue-veined hand rested on the covers.

Jemima felt a shock of grief. She knew the woman was dead, but what struck her most strongly was the difference between this half-sunken face, the life fled from it, and the one she had seen only yesterday, staring up at the snow-laden trees with such joy.

She stood looking at the woman until she heard a sound behind her and swung around, her throat tight with fear.

"Miss Pitt?" Harley's voice broke the trance. "Are you in here? A boy downstairs said he saw you . . . "

Harley appeared and relief overwhelmed her, then vanished again like a huge wave sucking back into itself.

"I think she's dead," she whispered. "Poor soul . . ."

"What!" Harley walked rapidly over to the bed and put his fingers to the skin of the woman's neck. He looked across at Jemima. "Yes, she is, but she is still warm. It can't have been long. Maybe only a few minutes."

She was amazed. "Just a few minutes? If we'd come sooner . . ."

Harley pulled the covers away from the woman's chin and shoulders. Suddenly all Jemima could see was scarlet blood, wide-spreading, wet, from a heart only just stopped beating. Dizziness overtook her and she had to fight to keep from fainting.

"We had better call the police," Harley said grimly, his voice catching in his throat. "It was not a natural death. She's been stabbed."

Jemima nodded. She tried to speak but no sound came.

"Come," Harley ordered. "There's nothing you can do for her now."

Jemima coughed and cleared her throat. "Is it . . . is it Maria Cardew? She looks so ill!"

"Yes, it's her. Come. We must go and call the police." He held out his hand and obediently she stumbled the few steps to reach him. He gripped her firmly and guided her to the door and out into the passageway. Almost as if it were an afterthought, he pulled the door closed, but she did not hear the latch turn.

They reached the bottom of the stairs and there was no one in sight. Harley went to the front door and out into the street. He looked one way, then the other, then came back to Jemima.

"I'm going to find the nearest policeman. I don't think anyone around here will have a telephone. It's not that sort of area. You stay here and don't speak to anyone. I'll be back as soon as I can."

"Can't I come with you?" she asked, then heard her own voice and wished she had not sounded so plaintive. No backbone! "No," she said before he could reply, although the refusal was in his face. "Of course not. You'll move far faster without me. I understand. Please go."

He looked immensely relieved and turned quickly, starting to run as soon as he was on the open sidewalk.

Jemima stood in the hallway for what seemed like

forever. A man came out of one of the ground-floor apartments and said something to her, but she did not hear the words, could not find her voice to reply. He went out the door and disappeared. Two more people went by.

Her mind was racing.

Who could have killed Maria Cardew, and why? Had some part of the evil life Harley had hinted at finally caught up with her? Where had Harley been? If he had arrived sooner, they might have saved her! Jemima should have felt outrage, even fear, but thinking of that ravaged face all she could summon was pity. She hoped Phinnie would not have to learn the whole truth. Was there any way they could keep it from her, at least until after the wedding?

She was still busy with that thought when Harley came back in through the front door, followed by a young man easily his height but dark-haired and with startlingly blue eyes. He introduced himself before Harley could do it.

"Miss Pitt? I'm Officer Patrick Flannery. Mr. Albright tells me that you discovered the body of a woman upstairs in apartment 309. Is that true?"

Jemima looked at him. His presence, his dark blue

uniform, made it all suddenly no longer a nightmare but a reality—official, ugly, and dangerous. How could they possibly keep Phinnie from knowing? If this young policeman had any brains at all, he would ask what Harley Albright was doing here in the first place. And she knew from her father's experience that lies only made everything worse. He had said more than once that the lies a person told gave away more than most truths.

"Yes, sir," she replied. Another thing her father had said was not to answer more questions than you were asked. It made you appear nervous.

Flannery nodded. "I see. Mr. Albright said that he found you inside the apartment, in the bedroom with the dead woman. Is that right?" He had a nice voice, with a lilt of the Irish in it. "Miss Pitt?" he prompted.

"Yes," she said quickly, trying to keep her composure. Of course Harley had had to say that. She was there already when he arrived. "I didn't touch her," she added, then wished she hadn't. Was she so rattled that she was going to forget all her father's advice already? If only he were here now!

"Mr. Albright says you're English. Is that right?" Flannery asked.

"Yes. I've been here just a few days. I came over for the wedding of a friend."

"I see. That would be Mr. Albright's brother's fiancée?"

Jemima nodded. "Yes, Phinnie—Delphinia—Cardew."

"And do you know the dead woman, Miss Pitt?"

"No. Mr. Albright says she is Maria Cardew."

Harley stiffened, but he did not interrupt.

"The mother of Mr. Brent Albright's fiancée," Flannery said. "He mentioned that. Perhaps we had better go up to see her. I've sent for the police surgeon to take a look at her." He glanced at Harley.

"The family asks for your discretion and will deeply appreciate it," Harley said. "I will personally pay for a decent burial for the woman."

"Yes, sir." Flannery nodded. "I'll do what I can. If you would lead the way upstairs, please . . . ?"

Harley moved, and Jemima followed him, with Officer Flannery after her. It was then that she realized how much the whole affair had distressed her. She had expected an unpleasant scene, but not death; certainly not violence, blood, then the police. And now there was the fear that she would not be able to protect Phinnie from a grief, or at least a shock, that would deeply overshadow all happiness at the prospect of her upcoming wedding day.

Harley pushed open the apartment door. The latch was broken and had not locked behind them.

"Did you find it like this, sir?" Flannery asked.

"Yes. Miss Pitt was already inside. I told you."

Flannery turned to Jemima, his black eyebrows raised.

Jemima felt a prickle of fear. "Yes. It was open when I pushed it."

"So you went in?"

"Yes."

Flannery looked unhappy. "Did you know Mrs. Cardew?"

"No. But I've known her daughter, Delphinia Cardew, for . . ." It was not so very long, but she must finish the train of thought. "I am here with her for the wedding, to look after her until then. She is only nineteen. Her father is ill and cannot travel. She is . . . estranged from Mrs. Cardew. She has no one else . . . except the Albright family, of course." Was she talking too much and making it even worse?

"So you were trying to bring about a reconciliation with her mother?" Flannery looked dubious. This was plainly at odds with what Harley had implied.

"No. I wished to persuade Mrs. Cardew . . ." She realized with horror what she was about to say, and how it would sound.

"Not to appear at the wedding and cause distress and embarrassment," Harley finished for her.

Flannery shot him a sharp look that was close to dislike, then turned back to Jemima.

"Is that correct, Miss Pitt?" he said gently.

There was no escape.

"Yes." Her voice was hollow, as if she had no air in her lungs. "We hoped she would realize that it would be far better, if she wished to meet with Phinnie again, to do it privately." Should she add that Harley had been willing to pay her not to cause a scandal? No. It sounded desperate.

Flannery nodded, then led the way to the bedroom. The dead woman was lying on the bed exactly as Jemima had left her, the sheet still pulled back to expose the terrible wound. She heard Flannery's sharp intake of breath. He must have seen dead bodies before, but there

ANNE PERRY

was something horribly tragic about this elderly woman,
so frail-looking, perhaps even dying anyway, who lay
alone, soaked in her own blood, her graying hair spread
across the pillow, her features etched with pain.

Flannery looked at her closely without touching her,
except to place one strong hand briefly on her pulse
point. He must have felt that she was still warm. He
turned to Jemima, his face filled with pity.

"Did you see any weapon, Miss Pitt? Did you move
it?"

"No! Of course not!"

"It would be a natural thing to do."

"My father is a policeman, Officer Flannery. In fact,
he is head of Special Branch in England. I know better
than to move a weapon from the scene of a death."

He looked grim. "So you know quite a lot about
crime?"

Another mistake. "No!" she said hotly. "Only what I
have overheard now and then. But if you think about it,
it's common sense." She must stop talking, stop telling
him too much. She sounded guilty, when really she was
only grieved and afraid for Phinnie.

"I see," he acknowledged. He appeared increasingly

unhappy. He looked back at Harley. "You said, sir, that you arrived here later than Miss Pitt and found her standing beside the body, which you identified as that of Mrs. Maria Cardew."

"Yes," Harley answered quietly. "I'm sorry, but that is so."

"Where were you, sir?" Flannery met his eyes squarely.

"I didn't see anyone come in here, if that's what you mean?" Harley replied.

"It's part of what I mean. If you weren't in the street outside, where were you?" Flannery insisted.

"Someone stopped me to ask directions, and I ended up having to take them part of the way," Harley replied a little sharply. "When Miss Pitt wasn't in the coffee shop where I left her, I assumed she must have come here. A boy on the street told me he had seen her, and that she had gone to room 309."

"When did you last see Mrs. Cardew alive, sir?"

"About twenty years ago, when she first met Mr. Cardew. It was through my family that they became acquainted. My father and Mr. Cardew are partners in business."

"Yes, sir, you mentioned that." Flannery's face was

pinched, his eyes bleak. It seemed he did not like Harley, for whatever reason. He looked at Jemima again. "Is this all true, Miss Pitt?"

Jemima realized with a chill that made her feel sick exactly how it looked. There was nothing she could deny.

"Yes . . ." she admitted.

Harley spoke before Flannery could. "Miss Pitt, if you moved the knife, however well you meant it, it would be a good thing if you told me. I know your devotion to Miss Cardew, but this is extremely serious. I will do my best to protect you, but really, only the truth will serve now."

He was making it worse, making it sound as if he thought she could have killed the poor woman! Why? It would hardly protect Phinnie. The scandal of having her mother turn up at the wedding would be small compared with that of a murder. Did he really think she was so stupid, so impetuous and hysterical as not to know that? She stared at him, and the answer was clear in the sad, puzzled expression in his eyes.

"I did not touch her!" Her voice sounded frightened, as if she were close to losing control. "I did not touch anything. I didn't even know for certain that she was Maria Cardew."

"Yes, you did," Harley contradicted her. "We saw her in Central Park yesterday evening. We followed her."

"We were fifty yards away!" she protested. "She looks quite different close-up."

"But it is the same woman, Mr. Albright?" Flannery said. "You are quite certain?"

"Yes," Harley said decisively. "There is no doubt. I'm sorry. I . . . I understand your devotion to Phinnie," he said to Jemima. "I believe you did this to protect her. It is my duty to my family now to see that you don't in any way suggest that she had any part in this. I know how intensely she is looking forward to—"

Flannery cut him off with a glance. "If you are looking to protect your family, sir, you would not serve that purpose by suggesting that anyone in your household had a part in this."

A dull color swept up Harley's face, but he did not answer.

Flannery turned to Jemima. "I'm sorry, Miss Pitt, but I have no choice but to take you to the station for further questions."

"But I have no blood on me!" Jemima protested. "I would have . . . if I had done that!" She indicated the body on the bed, but could scarcely look at it.

Flannery swiveled round to look at the kitchen, where the corner of a wet towel was visible in the sink. He looked back at Jemima.

"Please, Miss Pitt," Flannery said quietly as another policeman came in through the door, followed by a third.

"I'll do what I can," Harley said to Jemima, then turned on his heel and left without looking at Flannery or speaking to him.

*T*he next few hours passed in a daze of misery. Jemima was taken in a closed carriage, her hands manacled together, down to the center of the city, where she was asked questions about her identity, her nationality, and her purpose here in New York. She was finally charged with the murder of Maria Cardew, and her belongings were taken from her, except the clothes she stood up in, and a small handkerchief. She was then placed in a cell and left alone, trembling and queasy with fear and shock.

How could this have happened, in the space of a few

hours? It was the middle of the day, yet breakfast time seemed as if it had been in another era. Did Harley really imagine that she had killed Maria Cardew? With a knife from the kitchen? Did he think she was both stupid and cold-blooded enough to have committed murder rather than let Maria make a scene at the wedding?

Why? To protect Phinnie from embarrassment?

That was absurd, even insane.

Then, sitting on the hard bench that served as a bed, shuddering with cold in the bare, iron-barred cell, she knew the answer. Not to protect Phinnie from embarrassment at all, but to make certain that the wedding went ahead and Phinnie became part of the powerful Albright family, with its immense wealth. Harley had all but hinted as much to Officer Flannery. And then Phinnie would reward her appropriately.

That, of course, had assumed she would not be caught! Now all she would gain was a length of rope to hang her, or whatever they did with murderers in New York!

Would anyone tell her parents? Surely they would?

Then her father would come over and he would find the truth. He had no official status as a policeman, or anything else, here in America, but that would not prevent him. He would do anything to save her. She was not guilty of anything except . . . what? Foolishness? Placing her trust in the wrong person? Overconfidence in her own ability? Perhaps pride? It was a miserable thought.

She was given supper; by then she was hungry enough to eat the rough and tasteless stew. The bed was hard and lumpy and the whole cell was bitterly cold. She slept very badly and woke up so stiff she could not move without pain. And of course there were no clean clothes for her, nothing even to wash in except cold water.

About the middle of the morning, the woman in charge told her that she had a visitor, and to straighten herself up and prepare to be conducted to the room where she could speak to him. She did as she was told, wondering if it would be Harley Albright. What could she say to him? He had practically accused her of killing Maria Cardew in a secret agreement with Phinnie, to save her from any embarrassment in her new life. She hated him for that so much she felt as if she would choke on her words if she even tried to speak to him. He was the one who had asked for her help in finding Maria.

And yet, furious as she was, she also knew that he was trying to protect his family. That part she could believe, and even sympathize with.

But when she was conducted to the interview room, her hands again shackled behind her back, it was Mr. Rothwell Albright who stood up from the hard-backed wooden chair, not Harley. He looked tired and so pale it was as if the cold had seeped through everything he wore and reached into his bones. Was it the prospect of scandal that affected him so much?

He looked at her with distress. "Are you all right, Miss Pitt? Unhurt?"

"I am not physically anything worse than stiff and cold, thank you," she replied. She softened her voice. He had at least come to see her. She should be grateful for that. "Would you please contact my father to let him know what has happened to me? I have no way of doing so myself."

"Should it prove necessary, of course I will," he replied. His voice was gravelly, as if he had not slept either.

"It is necessary," she said, with rising panic very nearly breaking through. Had he no idea what was happening? "They have accused me of killing Mrs. Cardew!

I didn't even touch her! There was nothing I could do to help her."

"I am afraid it seems otherwise," he answered slowly. "Poor Maria. She did not deserve to die in such a way. She was a good woman . . . misguided, perhaps, but not evil."

There was real grief in his face, in his eyes. It seemed that he did not share Harley's view of Maria, whatever else he felt.

"Mr. Albright, I did not harm her in any way," Jemima said earnestly. "Mr. Harley asked me to help find Maria and persuade her not to attend the wedding and cause embarrassment. That was all I attempted to do. I never saw her at all except for a brief glimpse in the park, and then the next morning when she was dead. I have no idea who hurt her. Please . . . please tell Phinnie that . . ."

He avoided her eyes. "Delphinia is very distressed. She has now lost all possibility of reconciliation with her mother, and this terrible manner of her death has cast a dark shadow over her forthcoming wedding. I asked her if she wished to send any message to you, perhaps of comfort or support. She declined. I'm . . . sorry."

It was another blow. Maybe she should have expected it. Phinnie was as changeable as the spring weather at home. But this hurt. Surely Phinnie knew her better than to imagine she would have killed anyone, let alone a frail old woman she had never even met?

But of course Phinnie would not be thinking, only grieving, and fearing that the scandal of murder would affect the Albright family, and spoil the longed-for wedding to Brent.

"I shall contact the best lawyer I can afford, Miss Pitt, and perhaps this matter may be dealt with before your family has to be informed." Mr. Albright rose to his feet. "I am very sorry your visit to us has ended in this way."

She watched him go out the far door without turning back, his perfectly tailored shoulders stiff, his white hair gleaming in the light. He had said nothing about putting up bail to have her released. Perhaps, considering the charge, it was not possible anyway. She would stay here, hungry, aching, and cold to the bone. Christmas was ten days away—they might not bring her to trial before then. And when they did—then what? Oh, please heaven he would tell her father, and he would come and shatter this nightmare!

*O*fficer Flannery came to see Jemima late in the afternoon, as it was already getting dark. She saw him in the same bare interview room where she had been charged, sitting on the same wooden-backed chair.

He looked different without his police hat. He had thick dark hair with a heavy curl in it. He looked tired and cold.

"Are you all right?" He asked her the same question Mr. Albright had, and with something of the same anxiety.

"I cannot tell you anything further," she said more stiffly than she had meant to. It was her only defense against showing the fear and misery she felt. "I did not see Mrs. Cardew alive, except for a few moments in the park the previous afternoon, when she turned toward us and looked up at the snow on the branches. I would not even know it was the same woman if Harley had not told me. But he knew her; I did not."

"Are you certain that you didn't, Miss Pitt?" he said gravely.

"Yes, of course I am. I've only just arrived in New York." Surely he must know that?

"Actually, you arrived over a week ago," he pointed out. "At exactly the same time as Miss Cardew."

"I know that!" Then she felt the chill of a new apprehension. What did he mean? There was no accusation in his eyes, only sadness.

"Did Miss Cardew know that her mother was in the city?" he asked.

"Of course not!" Jemima protested. "That is what Harley and I were trying to do—stop Maria Cardew from turning up and creating a scene, upsetting Phinnie at the wedding. Didn't he tell you that?"

"He seems to now think that it is possible she *did* know," Flannery replied.

Jemima was astonished. Suddenly nothing made sense. "If she knows it is because *he* told her! But why would he do that?" She was utterly confused. "Harley wanted the whole wedding to be a high-society event, with no hint of scandal to mar it. He told me he was even willing to pay Maria Cardew to stay away."

"That would've been an extraordinarily foolish thing to do. If she was the kind of woman he said, then she could extort him for the rest of her life."

"I told him that!" She could feel fear sharpening her voice, building up inside her like a trapped thing, ready to lash out. "I said there would be no end of it!"

"I want to believe you, Miss Pitt," Flannery said gently, "but the only thing in your favor is that he says it is possible that Miss Cardew not only knew that her mother was in New York, but also knew where she was."

"If that is true then Harley told her," she said again desperately.

"Yes, maybe . . ."

"Are you sure you didn't tell her, even unintentionally?" There was an urgency in his voice, as if the grief of this tragedy touched him too. "Perhaps she would be able to piece it together from other things you said. Could she have guessed? Might she have known what you were doing anyway? If you mentioned where you had been that afternoon, could she have worked it out that her mother was there?" Flannery looked as if he wanted any of those options to be true almost as much as she did.

Jemima steadied herself with an effort. She must keep some control. Just at the moment it was her only chance to save herself.

"Even if she had worked that out from something I said, that doesn't explain how Harley knew that she knew."

"Perhaps he is trying to help you, Miss Pitt. It would

be in your interest if she did know. Then at least there is another person to suspect of having killed Maria Cardew." He looked at her steadily, his eyes intensely blue.

"Harley would never accuse Phinnie of such a thing. And Phinnie wouldn't do that," she said miserably. "And I'm not going to try to blame her. She can be selfish and a bit silly at times—she's terribly young—but she wouldn't stab anyone to death, let alone her own mother! She just wouldn't. Apart from anything else, she hasn't the courage or the emotional intensity."

He smiled a little ruefully.

"Honest, if not flattering," he said.

"I don't think I can afford to be anything but honest," she confessed. And then she wondered, for a moment, if perhaps Phinnie wanted the marriage to Brent Albright enough to have elicited the information from Harley, and then crept out to try to persuade her mother herself. Could she have offered to keep her in comfort for the rest of her life, if she just let the marriage take place without upsetting anything? Once married to Brent, Phinnie would have the means. If the marriage did not go ahead, then she wouldn't! If Maria Cardew was as greedy and ruthless as Harley had said, she would understand that.

Was that impossible?

She said all this to Flannery, stumbling over the words, hating the sound of them in her own ears.

He looked unhappy, but he did not argue.

She knew the inevitable ending to her train of thought. She gave it words before he could: "Even if all that was true, Phinnie had no reason to kill Mrs. Cardew. Why would she? She would just pay her off until such time as the Albrights could deal with her more effectively."

"Maybe she didn't want them to know?" he responded. Now he was arguing to defend Jemima!

She shook her head. Phinnie would never manage to keep something like this from Brent.

Officer Flannery pushed his hand through his hair in a gesture of exasperation. "I'm trying to help you!"

"Thank you," she said with a laugh that turned into a sob. "But are you sure you should be?"

"I don't think you killed her," he replied. "I just don't know who did."

"The door was open. Anyone could have gone in."

"Why would they? Nothing was taken. There wasn't much to take. No one else was seen. We spoke to all the other residents. No one saw anybody else."

"I didn't touch her," Jemima said yet again. "She was dead when I got there."

"Have you had anyone tell your family you're in trouble?" Flannery asked her.

"Mr. Albright said he would, if we couldn't sort it out quickly without their having to know. It would take my father a week or more to get here anyway. And what would he do?" That was a possibility she had not even thought about before, and in spite of her best effort she could feel the tears prickle behind her eyes, and the lump in her throat become almost too large to swallow.

Flannery stood up. He looked stiff and awkward.

"I'll sort it out before then," he promised, the color hot in his cheeks. "You won't need him to come."

*J*emima remembered those words all afternoon, sitting alone in her cell with its solitary window far above her eye level. She could hear other women prisoners shouting and sometimes even laughing, but it was a hard, raucous sound, totally without pleasure.

The white light, reflected off the snow, was beginning to fade. She was finding it very hard to keep hope when one of the guards returned, brandishing the keys.

"Your lucky day," he said without a smile. "Someone put up bail for you." He unlocked the door noisily and pulled it wide. "I guess that means we don't have to give you supper."

Mr. Albright? Harley, relenting? It was his testimony that had put her here, at least mostly. Or Phinnie? Maybe she had prevailed upon Brent to come?

"Thank you," she said to the guard, and went out through the iron-bar door as quickly as she could. "How do I get . . . ?" And then she wondered if she would be welcomed back into the Albright house. Perhaps not. Where could she stay? She couldn't leave the city because she was on bail, but she did not have sufficient money to pay for her own lodgings for as long as it might be before she came to trial. It was midwinter, nearly Christmas. She would freeze to death without shelter. The streets would be worse than jail.

The guard was looking at her. He sighed. "She's out there waiting for you. You'd better get out of here before she changes her mind."

Jemima's heart rose. It must be Phinnie after all. Phinnie, of all people, had realized that she could never have hurt Maria Cardew, let alone killed her.

"Thank you," she said hastily to the guard. Then she followed him along the stone passageway and, this time, out as far as the entrance.

But it was not Phinnie who stood waiting for her; it was Celia Albright. She was wearing a very ordinary dark cape over her dress and a hat that could have belonged to anyone. She seemed to have shrunken into herself, her shoulders hunched wearily. However, her face lit up with relief when she saw Jemima and she moved toward her quickly, searching her face.

"Are you all right? No one has hurt you?"

"I am perfectly well," Jemima answered as levelly as she could, but her voice was thick with emotion. "Just cold and . . . frightened."

"Of course you are," Celia agreed. "Come, we must get out of here as quickly as possible. It is a dreadful place. The carriage is waiting around the corner; there is no room for it here." She led the way at a brisk pace and, all but treading on her heels, Jemima followed. It was getting dark and the streetlights, less elegant in this part of the city, were beginning to glow brightly.

As soon as they were seated in the carriage, it moved away.

"Thank you," Jemima said again, meaning it with a depth of feeling she could not conceal.

Celia's face was unreadable in the shadows, but her voice was tense.

"I would be grateful if you did not mention it to Mr. Albright—in fact, to anyone in the family. It could lead to . . . unpleasantness."

Jemima was puzzled. "Did Mr. Albright not—"

"No," Celia cut her off. "I did it myself, with Farrell's help. Rothwell may guess that, but I would prefer that he did not know it. I doubt he will ask me."

Jemima was stunned. The family had been prepared to leave her in jail, perhaps even over Christmas! Fight for her, pay a lawyer, perhaps, but only because she was connected to them as Phinnie's friend.

"Did Phinnie ask you to?" she said impulsively.

Celia remained staring ahead. "No," she replied very quietly. Jemima had to strain to hear the words. "Please do not ask me any further questions, Miss Pitt. I prefer not to answer you. I do not know what happened to Mrs. Cardew, but I don't believe that you had anything to do with it, except unintentionally. But not everyone agrees with me."

Jemima took several moments to weigh what she had heard. Why would anyone imagine she could have so savagely killed Maria Cardew, a woman she had never met and who had nothing to do with her life? Could they really believe that Phinnie had asked her to do it and she had agreed? Whatever kind of person did they think Phinnie was? She was in love with Brent, certainly. Her only dream was to be his wife. Yes, she liked the wealth and the position in society, but the idea that she would kill for those things was absurd.

The murderer must have been someone from Maria's past life, whatever she had been doing over the years between leaving Mr. Cardew and finding herself in the cheapest of lodging houses in New York. It was just the most wretched of misfortunes that Harley and Jemima had found her on the day of her death. Such coincidences were rare, but of course they did happen.

What was it going to be like living in the Albright mansion from now until Christmas, and then the wedding, under the shadow of suspicion? She could hardly attend parties with people wondering if she had knifed a woman to death!

But would they know? What had the newspapers said? She needed to be aware of that before she arrived. She turned to Celia again.

"Miss Albright . . ."

"Yes?"

"What have the newspapers said? Did they name me?"

"No. Rothwell managed to prevent that. And of course Mrs. Cardew was not named either. And he simply told Phinnie the barest of facts, which was both a sadness to her and something of a relief. She no longer has to fear that her mother might turn up at the wedding, or one of the parties, and cause the most acute embarrassment."

Jemima tried to imagine it. "It would have been unfortunate," she agreed. "But not so terrible . . ."

"Phinnie has been told that Maria drank," Celia explained. "So far as I know, that is not true. She has also been told that her mother was of extremely loose morals with regard to men. That is . . . questionable. I would have said she had somewhat eccentric tastes, which is not at all the same as being loose."

Any further conversation was prevented by their arrival at the Albright mansion. It was completely dark. They were only a moment or two on the lighted front step, and then in the warmth of the bright hall. The butler greeted Celia with respect and Jemima with civility.

"I am sure you would like something hot to eat," Celia said as they crossed the hall under the blazing chandelier. "The family is dining out. I am not hungry, but you may have your food brought up to your room; or, if you prefer, you can eat in the kitchen. I do that myself occasionally, and it is very pleasant, and rather more comfortable than dining in a bedroom. I do not care for the odor of food remaining all night."

"Thank you," Jemima said, accepting. "The kitchen sounds a good idea, and will be less troublesome to the staff. You don't think they will mind my presence?"

For the first time, Celia smiled with genuine warmth. "You have been most courteous to them, my dear. They will not mind in the least." There was a wealth of implication hidden in her words, but Jemima did not pursue it, although the ideas whirled in her mind later as she sat at a bench in the kitchen and enjoyed one of the best meals she had eaten since leaving home. She could hear Lucy, the chambermaid, giggling in the pantry and every now and then the footman's voice singing a snatch from one of the latest musical shows—"Give my regards to Broadway, remember me to Herald Square . . ."

Cook was rolling her eyes and muttering, but nothing unkind. Violet, the scullery maid, was sweeping the floor, the broom making a swishing sound over the stones. Billy, the boot boy, was restoking the stove. It was warm and familiar in the way that well-used kitchens are.

The following morning at the breakfast table it was very different. Jemima arrived at the usual time that the meal was served. The last thing she wanted was to cause inconvenience by being either early or late. Everyone else was present. They all looked up as she came into the room and took the same chair as she had previously, the only one currently unoccupied.

"Good morning," she said quietly.

Mr. Albright looked up from his plate and replied politely but without expression.

"Good morning, Miss Pitt," Brent answered. He looked at her guardedly, his light eyes distant, as though she were the merest acquaintance. Perhaps he was withholding judgment, but certainly he had not acquitted her in his mind.

Harley glanced at her without speaking at all, and continued with his meal.

Phinnie was very smartly dressed in clothes Jemima knew she had not brought with her. They were the height of fashion, big-sleeved and wide-skirted, actually rather too old for her, dominating her youthful beauty.

"Good morning, Jemima," Phinnie said coolly, then searched for something else to say, and found nothing.

Only Celia addressed Jemima with warmth. "Good morning, Miss Pitt. I hope you slept well?"

Harley glared at her but she ignored him, continuing to speak to Jemima.

"I am going shopping in the middle of the day, and will take luncheon in town. Perhaps you would like to accompany me?"

"Is that wise, Aunt Celia?" Brent asked, frowning at her.

Celia's temper was raw and she clearly held it in with difficulty. "What are you suggesting, Brent? That we require Miss Pitt to spend the rest of her time as our guest sitting in her room? It is still nine days until Christmas, and two weeks until the wedding."

"I am aware what day it is," Brent replied. "It is the middle of winter and everything is covered with snow. It is not a great hardship to stay in a well-heated house with a library and a music room, and servants to bring you anything you might wish. Most people would count themselves very fortunate to enjoy such a life."

Phinnie looked at him, her eyes soft and bright, then back at Celia. "Brent is right. I'm sure Jemima will be very comfortable, and grateful for your hospitality." Her voice quivered a little on the last sentence, but it was impossible to tell what emotion moved her. It could have been pity, fear of the future, an ever-increasing devotion to Brent, or anxiety that he thought Jemima guilty of some kind of complicity in Maria's death. It might even have been grief. Even so, Jemima did not care for being spoken around, as if she were not present to answer for herself.

Harley looked at them one by one, and said nothing. He seemed to be watching, waiting for something.

Jemima looked at Celia. "Thank you," she said sincerely. "I would be delighted to come with you. To walk a little would be very pleasant, and I should enjoy your company."

Jemima was in the hall, with her overcoat on, waiting for Celia, when Phinnie came over to her. Her brows were drawn down and her expression was one of annoyance.

"Jemima, are you deliberately trying to spoil my wedding?" She said it quietly, so no nearby servant could overhear her, but with an edge of real anger in her tone. "Celia was just being pleasant to you! Can't you see that? The last thing she wants is to be seen with you in public. Mr. Albright paid to have you released because he is a good man. That doesn't mean anyone here thinks you are innocent!"

Jemima felt as if she had been slapped. No wonder Celia did not wish the rest of the family to know that it was she who had paid Jemima's bail, presumably with her own money!

"Indeed?" Jemima said coldly. "And does that include you?"

"What can I think?" Phinnie demanded. "That it was some lunatic off the street? Why? From what Harley said, she had nothing to steal. She was found in her own bed, stabbed to death."

"I know that!" Jemima snapped. "I was the one who found her, poor woman."

"She wasn't a 'poor woman,'" Phinnie said bitterly. "She had everything—a good and decent husband, kind, respected, and wealthy—and she left him . . . and me . . . to go back to a life on the streets. No one forced her to do that, she was just a . . . a whore! She chose that, no one made her. Some women have no choice; she had every choice in the world." Now tears were running down her face and her voice was all but choked.

Jemima felt the burning pain and injustice of the situation, and a terrible pity for Phinnie. Her own childhood was filled with memories of love, laughter, and adventures, long, lovely days spent mostly with her mother and her brother, Daniel, as well. Phinnie had had none of that.

But no matter what Maria Cardew had been, or what

she had done that was selfish, or even lewd or revolting, it didn't change the fact that Jemima had not hurt her.

"I did not kill her, Phinnie," she said firmly. "I have no idea who did. I just found her."

"Why?" Phinnie challenged. "Why were you even looking for her?"

"Because Harley asked me to help him."

Phinnie's eyebrows rose. "Why would Harley want to find her?"

"For heaven's sake!" Jemima said desperately. "To make sure she didn't interrupt your wedding and embarrass you! Or embarrass the family, of course," she added, remembering that Phinnie must know Harley as well as she did.

The color bleached out of Phinnie's face and she looked stunned. "Harley asked *you*? That's not what he said . . ."

"Really?" Jemima should not have been surprised. Except the thought that came fleetingly to her mind was whether it was Harley who was lying or Phinnie. "Think about it," she went on. "How would I even know that your mother was in New York, let alone where to look for her?"

"Then . . . then maybe it was Celia," Phinnie suggested. "She's known my mother for years. She pretends to have liked her, but she's very protective of the family. She would be; it's her family too."

"You aren't suggesting that Celia killed your mother, surely?" Jemima was aghast. It was a monstrous notion. "Why, for heaven's sake? That makes no sense at all!" And the moment the words were out of her mouth, she knew that it made very ugly sense, even though she could not believe it.

Phinnie met her eyes boldly. "Yes, it does. When I marry Brent, I will be mistress of this house. What will she be? I could understand it if she were not willing to see that happen."

Jemima looked at her icily. "Yes, I believe you could. You have the advantage of me. I hadn't even considered such a thing."

Phinnie's face tightened. She recognized the insult. "There's rather a lot you don't consider," she retaliated. "You'll probably end up like Celia, being hostess and housekeeper for your brother, if he marries and then loses his wife. Although of course he won't have the Albright power or influence. Hardly anybody else has."

"You really value that, don't you?" Jemima stared at Phinnie as if she had not truly seen her before. "How far would you go to make sure you get it? The police thought you might have done it yourself, you know? I told them that was impossible. That you were not the kind of person who would even think of such a thing. Perhaps I was wrong?"

Phinnie blushed scarlet. "You told them that?"

"Yes. And you're right, I am naïve," Jemima replied. "But perhaps they will discover that for themselves." She turned to walk away, but Phinnie grasped her arm and held her back.

"Jemima!" She gulped. "I'm sorry. I didn't mean it. I'm horribly confused. I hated my mother all my life, because she left me and my father. I know it hurt him too. He never even imagined loving anyone else. But now that she's dead, and in such an awful way, I'm sad that I'll never know her. I didn't think I wanted to, but I'm not sure." She gulped. "Above all, I love Brent so much it makes me sick to think that anything could go wrong with our wedding. I know what I said about the Albright name, but it really doesn't matter to me. In fact, at times I wish we were quite ordinary, then there wouldn't be all this pressure to do everything the right way all the time. It's like . . . like being royalty. I don't really want to be a princess. I just want to be with Brent."

Jemima smiled in spite of her own confusion of emotions. Did she believe Phinnie? Yes, at least in part. Everything she had said was true. But there was a lingering presence there of passion to succeed, at any cost. She had been so quick to blame Jemima. The kind of love she felt was like a fever. It overcame everything else and destroyed the restraints she might normally have exercised.

"Jemima!" Phinnie said urgently. "You must believe me!"

"Of course," Jemima agreed quietly, and it was almost true. Phinnie wouldn't let Jemima go to trial for a murder she had not committed—well, probably she wouldn't. Before Phinnie could see the doubt in her eyes, she turned and walked away. Phinnie called after her, but she pretended not to have heard. She was surprised by how hurt she felt, and by how frightened she was.

That night Jemima did not sleep well. She woke up often and, even though the room was well heated, she felt cold and stiff. There was no sound, not even that of the wind outside the window. She opened the curtains and saw everything cloaked with snow, the huge city lit as if it too were awake, but frozen into lifelessness. She had been here less than two weeks, but she had learned to like New York—the vitality, the strange mixture of peoples.

And yet she was terribly alone, and accused of a crime for which her life could be taken. And there was no one to help her but herself.

If she was her father's daughter, that should be enough. Thomas Pitt had been a regular policeman, solving murders just like this one, before he joined Special Branch.

She went back to bed and lay with the covers up to her chin, trying to get warm again, and concentrated her thoughts. What would he advise her to do? Certainly not give up and wait for help, or lie here feeling sorry for herself and hope that the police went on looking for the answer. Why should they not accept that the foreign young woman who had found the body was not as guilty as she seemed?

Patrick Flannery's strong face with its gentleness and humor came into her mind, and she forced herself to dismiss it.

Her only defense was to attack. In the morning she would get up early, have breakfast in the kitchen, and then go out and begin to look for the truth. Nothing had been stolen, Phinnie had said, and a glance at Maria's possessions and style of life would have been enough to know there was nothing worth taking. The knife, the violence of the wound that had killed her, made it clear that bringing about her death was the sole purpose of her assailant. So it was someone who knew her.

Then Jemima must learn to know her also. How long had Maria lived there? Who were her friends, and her enemies? Who might believe she had wronged them, or was a threat to them? And why? What could she know of anyone that was worth such a violent and terrible way of preventing her from telling it?

*B*y nine o'clock the next morning, Jemima was already at the apartment building where Maria Cardew had lived, blinking against the flat, white light reflected off the snow. She had chosen different clothes from the ones she'd had on when she was here with Harley, and she'd pinned her hair up in as different a style as it would take.

She had planned what to say. She was less than satisfied with it, but all the alternatives she could think of were even worse. It was always best to stick as close to the truth as possible. It was easier to remember, and one was less likely to make an irretrievable error. Apart from that, consistently lying took up a great deal of one's emotional energy, and that in itself often gave one away.

"Good morning," she said cheerfully to the first woman she met as she stood in the hallway. Of course the one thing she could not disguise was her English accent. Her voice would betray her every time.

"Mornin'," the woman replied, at first barely glancing at Jemima, then stopping and looking at her again more carefully.

Now was the time for the first invention. It might be passed around within hours, so she must be careful what she said. "I wonder if you can help me." She smiled tentatively. "The woman who died up on the third floor—"

The face of the woman in front of her hardened. "If you're from one o' those newspapers, you can just turn around and go right back where you came from!" she said tartly. "She were a good-livin' woman, an' I got nothin' to say." She started to move away.

"I'm not!" Jemima said sharply, taking a step after her. "She has English family. I want to be able to write to them and tell them that she was properly cared for, and there were people to speak well of her . . ."

The woman stopped and looked back. She surveyed Jemima up and down, and Jemima met her eyes with total innocence. So far what she had said was the truth.

"So what do you want to know, then?" the woman said cautiously. "She's gone, poor soul. Can't do nothin' for her now."

"I can speak well of her reputation," Jemima replied. "I think I would want that after my death, wouldn't you?"

"I s'pose," the woman conceded. "She deserved it, anyhow."

Jemima smiled. "It's a horribly cold morning. Would you like a cup of coffee? There's a place about two blocks away from here. I would be pleased if you would join me."

"There's a better one back there." The woman jerked her head, indicating the opposite direction.

"Excellent," Jemima said immediately. "Please lead the way."

"Don't look nothing from the outside," the woman warned.

"That hardly matters," Jemima replied. "Is it warm?"

The woman smiled. "You bet! My name's Ellie Shultz."

"Jemima Pitt. How do you do?" She held out her hand.

The woman looked puzzled.

"I'm English. That's the way we say hello."

The woman gave a little laugh and took Jemima's hand.

They spoke little on the journey over the freezing pavements. Ellie nodded to several people and called out greetings to others. She was right about the coffee shop. It was shabby, parts of the roof hung with icicles where the gutters had broken, but inside was warm and several people welcomed her. The black woman behind the counter gave them a brilliant smile and offered them coffee. At a corner table a man with a thick beard was speaking in Russian to his companion, and laughing jovially at her response.

Ellie gave Jemima a questioning glance, and Jemima smiled her approval. She found it exciting rather than strange, like several districts of London squashed into one.

The coffee smelled every bit as good as Ellie had said, and while it cooled Jemima asked about Maria Cardew.

"That place wasn't really hers," Ellie explained. "It was Sara Godwin's, but she was so sick, poor soul, she couldn't manage. Maria came to see her, and just stayed. Looked after her, she did. Couldn't have been better to her if they'd been sisters. Sat up with her all night sometimes, when she was really bad."

"Oh!" Jemima was surprised by this, but then remembered the empty bed in the flat. "So what happened to Sara Godwin?"

"She got a bit better," Ellie said cheerfully. She blew on her coffee, impatient to be able to drink it. "Last time I saw her she were up and walking. Maria cooked for her an' everything. Kept the place clean, washed the sheets and that sort of thing. Poor Sara was too sick to do it herself. Not that she wouldn't have. Just couldn't hardly move."

"But she got better?"

"Yeah. Don't know if it was for keeps, poor thing. But

cared for each other, those two. Sara's husband was gone. Died hard, she told me once."

She went on to tell stories of both women. The more Jemima heard, the deeper her sense of loss became. She could not help seeing Maria Cardew's face as she had looked up at the snow on the trees in Central Park, and the joy that had been in it.

"But where did Sara Godwin go?" she asked at length, when they had finished their third cup of the best coffee she had ever tasted.

Ellie shook her head. "I dunno. Some man was looking for her, last I heard. Didn't mean her any good, I'd bet. She must have gone to get away from him. Maybe she'll be back. She didn't take much with her."

"Did Maria tell you that?"

"She said somebody'd followed Sara. Wish I knew she were all right. Course, she'll be torn up to pieces about Maria." She sniffed. "A good few people will be." She looked hard at Jemima. "You see they speak right about her! I don't know who did that to her, and likely they'll never find out. Far as the police think, she was just another woman nobody wanted. But you can't help it if you lose your folks and there's no one to care. Woman on your own doesn't mean you're a whore!"

Jemima had a sudden vision of loneliness, poverty, always dealing with judgments based on ignorance and fighting for warmth and a place to belong. Why on earth had Maria Cardew left all the safety of an excellent marriage in England, and her own small child who desperately needed her, for such a life?

"Thank you," she said with a wave of feeling. "If she was kind to someone in need, that repays a multitude of past errors . . . if there were any."

"You'll say something good of her?"

"I will."

After leaving the coffee shop Jemima started to walk around the neighborhood, looking for the places where Maria might have shopped, eaten—specifically, bought food, or medicines for her friend Sara Godwin.

She moved slowly along the busy streets. In this poorer area they were far narrower than the avenues where the Albrights lived, but there was a variety in them that fascinated her. Strange foods were displayed like works of art—lots of pickles, cuts of meat she had never seen before, and every kind of sausage you could imagine, some with rich-colored skins. She knew enough to recognize some Italian names, and some German. Others she couldn't even attempt to pronounce.

She saw women with different clothes, concealing their hair, and wondered if they would look half so mysterious dressed like anyone else. Their manner of dress concentrated attention on their marvelous eyes, full of expression. She wondered what their thoughts were of her. With her fair skin and auburn-tinted hair, she probably looked Irish to them!

After some questions, and a little laughter at her accent, she found an apothecary shop that seemed to stock a rich variety of medicines, all known by their Latin names.

She was trying to describe Maria Cardew to the woman at the counter when she heard an Irish voice behind her. She swiveled around and saw Officer Patrick Flannery standing about a yard away. He was not surprised to see her, although he would hardly have recognized her from the back. He must have heard her voice.

"Are you ill?" he asked with some concern.

"No, not at all . . ." Then she realized that she had little option but to tell him the truth. It was going to come out anyway, as soon as he spoke to the woman behind the counter. She must remember what her father had said about lies revealing more about you than the truth would.

"I met a woman who knew Maria Cardew. I wanted to hear about her, so I asked. The woman said Maria looked after a sick friend, Sara Godwin. I thought Maria might have bought her medicines here."

"What difference would that make?"

"It would be a record of Maria Cardew looking after someone with considerable kindness. It would show she wasn't the kind of person Harley Albright said she was." Why did she have to explain that to him? Surely it was easy enough to understand. And why was she disappointed that he was so slow? She would probably never see him again, unless he came to arrest her!

"Does that matter to you, Miss Pitt?" His voice was still gentle.

"Yes." She thought of the face of the woman in the park. "Yes, it does. I saw her alive only once, but there was something good in her. I don't believe Phinnie hurt her mother, and I want her to have at least one pleasant memory of Maria. You can't discard parents, even if you want to. They are part of who you are."

For a moment there was raw emotion in Flannery's face also, a mixture of pity and joy. "No, surely you can't!" he agreed. "And it'd be the last thing I'd want.

My mother is the best woman I've ever known." Then, as if embarrassed by his feelings, he went on quickly, "But I doubt you'd persuade Miss Delphinia Cardew of that. She hasn't a nice thing to say about her mother."

"Don't take her too seriously," Jemima pleaded. "She's never known why Maria left her as a tiny child. It seems nobody knows. And now, when perhaps she could have met her and made some reconciliation, Maria is dead, and we'll never understand."

"She might have killed Maria herself, and yet you're out here in the snow, walking around the back streets trying to find out something positive to tell her?" he asked in amazement.

Now it was Jemima who felt embarrassed. "I have other reasons. Don't you think I killed Maria? Nobody seems to be doing anything to prove otherwise. I need to defend myself, and the only way I can do that is by finding out who really did kill her."

"So you're beginning by looking for every fine thing she did, any kindness, maybe every lame dog she helped over a stile?" he asked with a trace of humor.

"I'm trying to find out anything I can about her!" she said sharply. "She was stabbed to death with a knife, probably from her own kitchen—or actually Sara God-win's kitchen. Somebody must've hated her pretty badly. That's who I'm looking for. I haven't done very well so far, but then, I started only this morning."

It sounded ridiculous, put like that, and not only stupid but also hopeless. Suddenly she felt small and cold and very silly. She should never have left London, where she was safe and had her family to believe in her and help her.

She swallowed the lump in her throat and stared back at Officer Flannery. "Someone killed her, and whatever you think, I know it was not I!"

He looked at her as if she were a lost child. "I think here's a smart place to start," he said. He looked past her to the woman behind the counter. "What did you sell to Mrs. Cardew, please, ma'am? We need to find as many people she knew as we can, so we can learn a thing or two about her. Then we'll leave your shop, so you can be getting on with your business." He smiled at her, looking kind, but also large and stubborn and very official.

The woman pulled out her records and told him everything she knew. Maria Cardew had spent quite a lot of money on medicine for Sara.

"And did she happen to mention her friend's illness?" Flannery asked.

"Consumption," the woman answered. "The poor soul. No cure for that, but Mrs. Cardew made her life a lot easier. Had some real strong spells, she did."

"Thank you." Patrick Flannery smiled at her and the woman looked pleased.

Outside on the pavement he stopped, standing closer to the street than Jemima, protecting her from the splashes of passing vehicles.

"And what did you plan to do next?" he asked.

"Food shops," she answered. "She might have bought special items for Sara. There might even be a doctor . . ."

"Are you sure you want to do this?" he said doubtfully. "You might find she wasn't as nice as you think."

"Of course," Jemima said quickly. "I don't believe she was a saint. If she was, then why did someone kill her?"

"Well, I suppose there's the chance she knew something that was dangerous," he said. "She might unintentionally have witnessed an argument or a fight, someone making an illegal deal or . . ." He stopped abruptly, a faint color in his cheeks.

She laughed, then instantly wished she had not. It

would have been far more ladylike to have affected not to know what he meant. "I'm sorry," she said contritely.

He blinked and shook his head. "Don't apologize. Perhaps I shouldn't have said—"

"Of course you should. She may very easily have seen somebody where they should not have been, or with someone they should not have been with. But how do we find out what, if anything, she knew? And if it really mattered so much as to kill her for it."

"High society is very proper in New York," he told her quickly.

Jemima was taken aback. Did he consider her part of that high society and somehow worry that he had offended her by being so candid? How could she undo that impression?

"I know that," she said. "I am staying with the Albrights, remember? They are far more correct than anyone I know at home. But . . ."

"But what?" he asked, now watching her very carefully, although she did not know what the intensity in his face meant. She was beginning to feel self-conscious.

"But very often, the higher up in society you get, the less 'proper' you are," she answered. "My great-grandaunt Lady Narraway's father was an earl, and she is the most outrageous person I know. I think you would like her enormously, though that is a little presumptuous of me to say."

"Do you like her?" he asked with interest.

"As much as anyone I've ever known," she answered without hesitation. "When she was young she was said to be the most beautiful woman in Europe. Now she is far older, and I think she still is. But she is brave and funny and terribly wise, which is what matters."

"In what way is she wise?" He was asking because he wanted to know. There was no challenge in his voice, or in the expression in his eyes.

She thought for a moment. She wanted him to understand what she meant. It mattered to her, but she wanted to do Aunt Vespasia justice as well, and that was not easy.

"She knows what matters and what doesn't," she answered, choosing her words carefully. "She remembers what she receives, but never what she gives. She doesn't hold grudges, and if she thinks something is funny she will laugh, whether it is the 'done thing' or not. She loves the opera, and gorgeous clothes. She is honest

when it is fashionable not to be, but she is never unnecessarily unkind. And she will fight to the death for a
cause she believes in."

"Do you wish to be like her?" he said gravely.

She did not have to consider that. "Yes," she said
instantly. "Yes, I would like that more than anything
else."

His expression was hard to read, as if powerful emotions were in conflict inside him.

"Then please take care of yourself," he said softly,
"so that you may have the opportunity to do that. You've
given me many ideas about where to look for Maria
Cardew's killer. You need to be careful. Whoever it is
won't want to be found."

"Of course not," Jemima agreed. "And I am not at all
sure that the Albrights wish the matter given any more
coverage in the news than has already been given."

"Well, you are not going to wander around the streets
in a neighborhood like this, asking questions about a
murdered woman," he said sternly. "That is the perfect
way to get hurt."

"I'll be careful," she promised.

"No, you won't. You'll follow any clues you find and
walk all around here, up back alleys and into places

where you won't be welcome," he argued. "I can't let you do that."

"But you can let me be convicted of something horrible that I didn't do?"

His face looked pinched. She had hurt him.

"I'm not going to let that happen either," he said rashly. "I'm coming with you. I'll find whoever really killed her, and you'll be safe."

For a moment she saw in his eyes something beautiful, and then she looked away. She could not afford such thoughts. The New York police believed she had stuck a knife into the heart of Maria Cardew. If she were to survive, she must prove that she had not, and the only way to do that was to discover who had.

"Thank you," she acknowledged. "Where shall we begin?"

He made a sharp little sound that she thought was laughter.

"Continue," he corrected. "As you see very logically, it was a crime of deep emotion. Someone either hated her or was frightened of her. The only reason for fear of an elderly woman in her state of health must have been that she had knowledge that could have ruined someone."

"We don't know that she was ill; that was her friend Sara Godwin," Jemima pointed out. "Why can't we find her? Wouldn't she know who might have killed Maria?"

"We can look for her, but she might be anywhere. She could even be dead, given that she was so ill. She must have had a hard life. She probably worked too much and didn't eat very well." There was pity in his voice, and Jemima liked him for that. It made her think for a moment of her father. He was always sympathizing with the wrong people—at least, wrong as far as both the police and society were concerned.

Then she forced that thought out of her mind. If she were to think of home and family at the moment, she would dissolve in tears and that would be both embarrassing and useless.

They were sheltered where they stood, but it was time to move. For a start, walking would get the blood circulating again, and make them warm, even if it took them away from the narrow alley and into the broader, straighter streets, where the buildings on either side funneled the east wind off the water.

"Where are we going?" she asked after several minutes.

"Best local bakery," he answered. "Then the butcher.

316

She'll have made chicken soup, maybe got bits and pieces many folk don't want. My mother used to do that, when times were harder."

Jemima kept up with Flannery's pace with difficulty. He had not stopped to think that while she was tall for a woman, she was still several inches shorter than he, and wearing heeled boots and a heavy skirt. It was a kind of oblique compliment that she did not want to spoil by lagging behind.

She tried to think what kind of information Maria Cardew could have had that could be so dangerous. At her age it didn't seem likely that she was having inappropriate relations with anyone. And anyone important enough to matter would not be frequenting this area. The locals around here were immigrants, the hardworking poor.

They reached the poultry shop, and yes, the owner knew Maria quite well, kept good pieces for her and slipped them in with the other bits he sold her cheaply. He was distressed to hear of her death.

"She was a good woman," he said, pulling his mouth into an expression of disgust at such a tragedy. "Always had a pleasant word. I don't know what the world's coming to." He glared at Flannery. "And what are you doing about it, eh? Just one poor old woman, no money, no power, so what does it matter?" He sighed, shaking his head.

"We're going to find out who did it," Jemima said firmly. "But it isn't easy. For a start, why would anyone do that? She had nothing worth taking."

The butcher stared at her. "Who are you? You talk oddly."

"I'm English," she explained. "I know some of her family, and I liked her. I want to know what happened."

"She wasn't English. She was as American as anyone. She was born here!" He made it a challenge.

"I know. But she lived in England for a while. She was married to an Englishman."

"Oh?" He raised his eyebrows. "She didn't say anything about that. Only man I ever saw her with was black!"

There was a moment of silence, then Flannery spoke. "Black? Did you know him?"

The man shook his head. "Not from round here. But he spoke regular, so he could have been from anywhere. He didn't mean her harm. Spoke softly to her, and she to him."

"But she knew him?" Flannery said.

"Only saw him a couple of times. Like I said, not from round here."

Flannery leaned forward a little. "Help me to find who killed her, sir. I need to know about her for that. It wasn't any passing robbery. Whoever did it did it violently, and there was hatred in it."

The man winced. "You could try Dr. Vine, down the road a couple of blocks, number 416. His real name is something longer, Russian or Polish, that sort of thing. Everyone calls him Dr. Vine. She went to him for her friend."

"Thank you." Flannery accepted the advice and took Jemima by the arm, guiding her out into the windy street.

Dr. Vine was as much help as he could be. He too was distressed to hear of Maria Cardew's death.

"Can't tell you much, except that Sara Godwin could not have managed without Maria's care." He shook his head. "Great shame. Don't know how the poor soul will get on now. Have you seen her?"

"No," Flannery said quickly. "We thought she'd gone before Mrs. Cardew was killed." Now he looked anxious.

"There was no sign of her in the apartment, and she doesn't appear to have returned since. I've been keeping an eye on the place."

"Could be she died anyway, before Maria was killed," Dr. Vine said unhappily.

"I'll check the city records," Flannery promised. "If she died, somebody will know. Thank you, Dr. Vine."

But no city records of recent deaths showed any sign of Sara Godwin. The following day, Jemima and Officer Flannery looked at the residential records. The clerk stood beside the bench with the ledger in his arms.

"I don't know what you're trying to find," he said as if he were afraid of being overheard. "But you should be careful, sir." He spoke only to Flannery. "I suppose you already know it, but the woman who was murdered in that building was related to Miss Delphinia Cardew, her that's getting married to Mr. Brent Albright."

"Yes, I know," Flannery answered. "Nobody seems to know much about her."

"No, sir, I suppose they don't. But we know a lot about the Albright family, and most of us know enough not to upset them by asking a whole lot of personal questions. Do a very great deal for this city, they do. And doesn't do to fall out with people with that kind of power, if you get my meaning?"

Jemima started to speak, but Flannery put his hand on her arm, closing his grasp firmly enough for her to fall silent.

"Better to clear this up now, rather than later, don't you think?" he said politely to the clerk. "I'm sure Mr. Albright would like to have the matter settled, and then not raised again. Over with, if you see what I mean?"

"Ah!" The clerk nodded and a smile spread slowly across his face. He touched one finger to the side of his nose in a gesture of understanding. "Then I'll just leave these with you, sir." He looked at Jemima. "Ma'am."

Jemima realized with horror that the clerk thought Flannery was here to serve the Albright family, not Maria Cardew. He had assumed that even the police were bought, one way or another.

"Don't look like that!" Flannery let go of her arm. "Your face gives you away!"

She could not think of anything to say. He had read her thoughts perfectly, and it was at once frightening and comforting. She wanted him to understand her. It was the end of a kind of loneliness, and yet it was the beginning of a new experience that could be too enormous to handle.

She swallowed. "Are the Albrights really so important?"

"Yes. Didn't you know that?" He put his hand back on her arm, but this time lightly. She could see his fingers on her coat sleeve rather than feel them. "Albright and Cardew make millions of dollars. All the power rests in the two families. When the present generation dies, or retires, it will all pass to Mr. Albright's sons."

"And Phinnie," Jemima added. "I wonder why Maria Cardew came back to New York. Was it really to try to see her daughter? She must have known the Albrights would not want her here. Was she hiding so close to them with the hope that they would never look for her on their own doorstep?"

Patrick was looking through the ledger as he spoke. "Could be. America is a huge country, thousands of miles across. She could have gone West and disappeared if she had truly wanted to." He went on leafing through the pages.

"Then she had a reason to be here," Jemima concluded. "It must have been a very strong one, Officer Flannery . . ."

He looked up. "You are not under arrest, Jemima. Do you think you could call me Patrick?"

She felt the color burn up her face, but she liked the idea. In fact, it had been in her mind when she thought of him, and she had had to remind herself not to use it.

"Patrick," she began again, a little self-consciously. "She must have had a very important reason for coming back here."

"Perhaps she knew that Harley Albright would pay her well to stay away from the wedding."

"Then who killed her? Did he?" It seemed far-fetched, but it wasn't impossible. she asked him.

"Or Delphinia herself," he replied. "I know you hate the thought, but she's a healthy young woman. It wouldn't be out of the question for her to have driven that knife through her mother's chest, especially since she would be the last one Maria would suspect. Face it, Jemima, she had the best motive of all. She's in love with Brent. She might have convinced herself she was protecting him."

"If she were really protecting him, she would have told him about Maria and let him make his own decision," she said hotly. "Or had a smaller wedding pri-

323

vately somewhere where Maria wouldn't have known about it! I think she's in love with being in love!"

"Most of us would like to be in love," he said very gently. "Wouldn't you, one day?"

She did not dare meet his eyes in case she gave herself away. "Oh, I expect so," she said as lightly as she could. "But I hope it would never bring me to a point where I could consider doing something so . . ."

"Crazy?" he suggested. "Probably not. But love can be pretty overwhelming. It can make you take risks you wouldn't normally even think of." Then he looked a little uncomfortable, as if he had said more than he meant to. He turned away from her, facing along the street into the wind and snow.

For a wild moment Jemima wondered if the reason he was so determined to find Maria's killer and save her from suspicion was that he cared for her. Then she dismissed it as a daydream she couldn't afford to indulge. If they didn't find the real killer, then the police were left with her. She was the one who had found Maria's body, and she had been alone.

"Do you think it could've been the other way around? Brent killed her, out of love for Phinnie?" she asked as sensibly as she could.

"That is possible," he answered slowly, still facing down the street. "We need to know more about Maria. Her murder might be something to do with her own life, something we missed entirely. Maybe it is only chance that it happened now, so close to the wedding. Come on." He took her arm and started to walk along the pavement briskly, as if he had a specific destination in mind.

*J*emima spent the rest of the day with Patrick. They learned more about Maria Cardew, but it was incidental to their search for Sara Godwin. They met many people who knew Sara and spoke well of her. It seemed she was quiet and kept to herself, but was willing to help anyone. But her illness had steadily been getting worse. No one had seen her for several weeks, and frankly, they assumed she had died.

Jemima and Patrick arranged to meet next the morning at the coffee shop to which Ellie Shultz had taken Jemima the previous day. Then Jemima went back to the Albright house feeling both tired and disappointed.

She had not said so to Patrick—she had learned rather too quickly to be comfortable using his name—but she was very much aware that they had little time before she would be arrested again, and tried for murder. Only the closeness of Christmas had allowed her even this reprieve.

She hated going back to the Albright mansion, but she had nowhere else to stay. She certainly had not sufficient funds to find herself a room at a hotel of even modest comfort or safety. Added to which her bail was conditional upon her staying where the police could find her at any time.

She had taken off her heavy outdoor coat and was walking across the hall when one of the maids told her that Miss Celia would like to speak with her.

"Thank you," Jemima said with a sinking heart. She had intended to speak with Celia anyway. She owed it to her to keep her apprised of what she had learned, little as it may be. When she went over it in her mind, the information she and Patrick had gathered amounted to nothing that would help. Rather the opposite! Maria Cardew seemed to have been a good woman who was well liked, even respected. Only the Albright family, and Phinnie, had any reason to fear her. And now it looked as if Sara Godwin, the only person who might've been able to shed some light on the matter, was also dead.

She went upstairs to her bedroom, washed, put on dry boots, and then presented herself at Celia's sitting-room door.

The room was warm, both literally from the fire in the hearth and figuratively from the rich colors, the sheen on the polished wood of the furniture, and the wealth of books on the shelves. At any other time, Jemima would have taken great pleasure in being there.

Celia was sitting in one of the armchairs. A piece of embroidery, half finished, lay on top of a sewing basket next to her.

Celia smiled and gestured for her to sit. Jemima accepted gratefully, glad of the warmth, and also very happy to be still at last.

"How are you, Miss Pitt?" Celia said with apparent concern. "I hear from Farrell that you have been out all day. Is that so? The weather is bitter."

Jemima wanted to scream at the banality of the question, but she forced herself to keep calm and respond courteously. "Very well, thank you. I have been outside, but I am fine."

"Cold, tired, no doubt." Celia smiled. "I have sent for

tea. It should be here any moment. I shall not ask you where you went. It is possible I prefer not to know."

Jemima drew in her breath to say something, and no sensible answer occurred to her. She was saved from silence by the arrival of the maid with a heavy tray of tea, milk, hot water, and two plates of food: one of delicate savory sandwiches cut as fine as any she had seen in the high society of London; the other of little cakes of several sorts, some filled with whipped cream.

Celia thanked the maid and dismissed her, then without asking poured the tea for each of them.

Jemima accepted a sandwich, for the sake of good manners, and found it delicious. This whole performance was absurd, yet there was nothing remotely funny about it.

"I still can't believe Maria is gone," Celia said conversationally. "I was very fond of her."

"People speak well of her," Jemima replied. She wondered if Celia would tell her anything more about Maria, if she asked. Yet she could not work out if the woman had been completely honest with her or was playing some game of her own. Looking at her thin, intelligent face, with its almost hidden humor, she had an urgent feeling that it was the latter. But what was at the heart of it? Fear of losing her position in the Albright mansion? Jemima loved her brother, Daniel, but she had no intention whatever of being beholden to him for the rest of her life.

Celia was nodding. "They would do. She had a considerable charm."

What did that mean? Was "charm" a way of saying Maria was manipulative? Even dishonest?

"Did you know her well?" Jemima asked. What had she to lose? The police were going to charge her if they didn't have anyone else, no matter what Patrick did.

"I believed so," Celia answered. Now she was smiling sadly, her thoughts clearly turned inward.

Jemima could not afford diplomacy. "But you had cause to reverse your opinion?"

Celia gave a slight shrug of her thin shoulders. "I was surprised that she abandoned her husband and child. But I never had the opportunity to ask her why. How well does one ever know another person? You have to love without knowing, don't you think?" She looked at Jemima very directly, her gaze probing. "There are always things that are private, and should remain so." She was waiting for a reply.

"Yes, I suppose there are," Jemima agreed.

"When you are older, you will have secrets," Celia promised her. "That is one of the great burdens of a public life. Too many people know too much. One lives like a fish in an ornamental bowl."

"Goldfish . . ." Jemima was struggling to understand the obliqueness of the conversation. She took another sandwich to give herself time to think.

Celia moved the plate a little nearer her.

"It is the great drawback to political office, I think," she remarked.

Jemima was lost. "Political office? Has that something to do with Maria Cardew's death?"

Celia's eyes widened. "Oh my goodness, I hope not. I was merely making conversation. I wish I could offer you greater comfort. You came all this way from your own family, and now you seem to be caught up in our troubles, and I confess, I see no way out for you."

Jemima felt the panic well up inside her. She was stupid to have imagined Celia was going to be any help. The poor woman was facing the end of her own manner of living.

Jemima controlled herself with an effort. "I did not know Mrs. Cardew," she said levelly. "And she was already dead when I found her."

"Poor Maria," Celia murmured, pain quite naked in her voice. "She always struggled, but mostly for other people."

Jemima leaned forward. "Other people? What do you mean?"

"So very idealistic," Celia said, not looking at Jemima but at some indefinable point on the far wall.

"What kind of ideals?" Maybe if she pressed hard enough, Celia might tell her something useful. "It sounds like she was . . . admirable. Could she have angered someone, do you think? One person's ideals sometimes endanger someone else's privileges." She was grasping desperately at straws.

"Oh, indeed," Celia said heavily. "Harley, for example, would not agree with her ideals. But of course he was not yet born when she was fighting her big battles."

"What battles?" Jemima said a little huskily. Was this something real at last?

"Thirty years ago." Celia avoided Jemima's eyes.

Jemima's heart sank. For a moment she had felt hope surge up.

"Freedom for the slaves," Celia continued. "Real freedom, not just on a piece of paper. Even in the seventies and early eighties it was very hard for them. There was so much bitterness here in New York. Never knew what it was like farther south, except that it was so much worse."

"But surely Maria didn't ever have slaves!" Jemima protested.

"Oh, no, of course not," Celia agreed. "But she fought on their behalf. Ran herself into quite a lot of danger. I don't know a great deal about it, because my father was always very stern over such things. Just as my brother is, and Harley, of course. But you'll know that because of his political stance."

"Political?" Jemima was lost again.

"Oh! Has he not told you?" Celia seemed surprised. "Harley is expecting that President Roosevelt will appoint him, as soon as he starts his second term in the new year. I'm sure you know he won the election last month."

"Really? I had no idea."

Celia met her eyes, no amusement or deceit in them.

"Oh, yes, very really indeed. Never doubt it."

"How . . . interesting," Jemima murmured, her mind racing. Could this possibly have anything to do with Maria's death? Was Celia trying to tell her this so obliquely that she could deny it later? Why? What did she know? Or was she deliberately leading Jemima astray?

She cleared her throat. "Do you think Mrs. Cardew's opinions were too radical?"

"I?" Celia said with surprise. "No. I admired her for them, as much as I understood what she was doing. I knew that it was dangerous for her." She hesitated so long Jemima thought she was not going to continue. Then suddenly she spoke again. "And I despised myself for not taking the same risks."

"What exactly was she doing?" Jemima was perfectly aware that the question was intrusive, but she had to try.

"Helping black people in trouble to escape the consequences of raising their voices, trying to be like white people, own property, have opinions," Celia said. "After the end of the Civil War, the resistance against change was too strong. The old attitudes were still everywhere."

"She must have been very brave," Jemima said with awe.

"And foolish," Celia added. "I liked her for it."

"But Mr. Albright didn't?"

"I really don't know how much he knew," Celia answered, her voice lifting in surprise as if she had only just realized the fact.

"And Harley?"

Celia smiled. "Certainly not. He would be appalled. All he knew, all he knows, is that she had a certain reputation. Why don't you try the cakes? They are one of Cook's specialties."

Jemima recognized that the discussion was closed. She took one of the cakes, and it was indeed delicious.

*D*inner was long and wretched. Phinnie chattered about her wedding, and never once looked at Jemima. Harley talked about politics, while Brent looked alternately happy and miserable. Mr. Albright spoke to Celia about people Jemima did not know.

Jemima felt awkward remaining downstairs after dinner was finished and they had all retired to the sitting room.

Phinnie sat close to Brent, as if she could not bear to have more distance between them than was necessary.

Mr. Albright sat in the largest armchair. Jemima

imagined the very shape of it had molded itself to his body. Perhaps his father had sat in it before him, and his grandfather also. In time it would be Harley's, who now stood by the mantelpiece, too restless to sit down.

Jemima took one of the smaller chairs, but after only a few minutes she rose to her feet again. Maybe she was running away, but she found she would rather have stood outside in the snow in silence with Patrick Flannery than sit in this warm, lovely room with the Albrights and their stilted conversation.

"It has been a long and interesting day," she said to Mr. Albright. "Will you excuse me if I retire a little early?"

"An excellent idea," Harley replied before his father could. "Good night, Miss Pitt." There was no warmth in his voice.

"Good night, Miss Pitt," Celia echoed. "Sleep well."

Jemima acknowledged the good wishes, then turned and walked out the door, across the huge hall, and up the stairs. She had just reached the landing when she became aware of someone behind her. She turned quickly and saw Phinnie a couple of yards away from her.

"You've been asking about my mother," she accused,

her voice harsh and bitter. "What are you trying to do? The police have been asking me questions, as if they thought I might have asked you to kill her, even paid you to do it!"

Jemima was stung by the injustice of it. "That's their job," she retorted sharply. "They are bound to realize I didn't do it. Why on earth would I?"

"For me, of course," Phinnie responded.

Jemima was stunned. "Don't be ridiculous! Apart from the fact that we have known each other only a short while, why would I do anything so terrible?"

"So that when I marry Brent I can pay you, of course!" Phinnie replied. "Either with money or by making sure you meet all the right people in New York. You are clever enough to have thought of that."

"Oh, yes!" Jemima agreed. "And even blackmail you for the rest of your life?"

Phinnie gasped, her face going pale. "You would, wouldn't you?"

"Well, I suppose if I'd killed poor Maria to stop her from bursting into your wedding and spoiling it, I would probably stoop to pretty much anything," Jemima said cuttingly, with an anger close to despair. "But as I already told you, all I wanted to do was help *Harley* find her so that *he* could pay her to stay away. He was afraid she might make a scene and embarrass everyone, ruin the family's reputation. And you never know, when the president comes to consider him for high office, he might think you an inappropriate relative for a man in the public eye." She knew the last bit would hurt Phinnie, and she meant it to. Phinnie had been willing enough to hurt her.

"So you . . . you didn't . . ." Phinnie said slowly, the angry color draining out of her face leaving her sickly pale.

"No, *of course* I didn't!" Jemima snapped. She was about to turn away and go on to her bedroom when she realized that Phinnie's amazement and relief were real. She had truly feared Jemima had killed her mother. "I saw Maria once, for a moment, in Central Park," she said gently. "When we were following her, and she turned to look back at the snow on the trees. There was such joy on her face at the beauty of them that for a moment she too was beautiful. The next time I saw her she was dead."

Phinnie's eyes filled with tears. "I don't want to like her," she whispered. "She left me! It took me all my life, until I met Brent, to stop wanting her to come back and explain to me what was more important to her than staying with me."

Jemima wanted to put her arms around Phinnie, be—for an instant at least—the sister she did not have. But it was too soon.

"That is what I am trying to find out," she said instead. "I'll start again tomorrow morning. I promise."

Phinnie nodded, too close to losing control to speak.

The next day was bitter. The wind cut like the edge of a knife, and there was ice in the breath of it.

Jemima would rather have stayed inside, but she had very little time left. The memory of the prison always hovered at the edges of her mind like an encroaching darkness. Was it time she sent a telegram to her father and asked him to come? But what could he do here anyway?

Because of course he would come, and he'd find a way to learn the truth and prove it. But part of her didn't want to send for him. Part of her wanted to find out what happened without his help. Was she just being foolish?

She increased her pace, footsteps crunching in the snow. A woman passed her on the pavement, walking briskly, bent forward and huddled into her coat. The man a few steps behind her had his hat jammed on his head and his scarf over half his face.

An automobile passed them all, the driver sitting up rigidly, having difficulty keeping the snow from coating the glass windshield. She smiled to herself, happy to be walking.

At last she reached the coffee shop, her hands so numb she could hardly grasp the door handle. A man opened it for her and she thanked him. Inside she looked around for Patrick. When she saw him, her heart lifted and she found herself smiling as he stood up and came over to her.

"Are you all right?" he said anxiously. "I wish you didn't have to be out today . . ."

"There isn't time," she said simply. "And I have a lot to tell you."

He guided her to the seat where he had been waiting, putting his arm around her shoulders. Even a day ago she would have moved away. Today she let it be. It was comfortable and she was willing to admit it. He held the chair for her, then ordered hot coffee, and more for himself.

Warming her hands on the mug, the chatter of all manner of languages around her, she told him what Celia had said about Harley and his ambitions, about Maria Cardew and her rescue of former slaves in trouble, and then Phinnie's accusation that Jemima had killed Maria—and finally, her belief that Jemima hadn't done it.

"So that makes you sure she wasn't the one who killed Maria?" he said. There was no time to be less than frank.

"Yes, I am. She truly believed I had done it, which means she couldn't have. We need to learn more about that part of her life. But if Maria risked her life helping black people who used to be slaves, she will have made enemies."

He smiled with wry, sad humor. "I know it's 1904, but not everything has changed. Old wounds are slow to heal. We're said to be 'a melting pot,' but there's a lot that hasn't melted yet. Did Celia say anything about Sara Godwin?"

"No. Patrick . . ." A thought occurred to her, and although she hated it, it had to be voiced. "Do you think Sara Godwin could have killed her? Perhaps Maria's death had nothing to do with the Albrights or her past at all but was because of an enmity between the two women?"

There was regret in his face. "It could even be that whoever killed her mistook her for Sara Godwin. I've been asking around more to find anyone who knew them a bit better, and another woman in the same building said they were always very careful, as if they were constantly afraid of something. According to Ellie, Maria said Sara thought someone had been following her, and she was afraid that he knew where she lived. But we have no description of him."

"He could be anyone," she said, a wave of hopelessness overwhelming her. "How can we even look for him?"

Patrick reached across the table and put his hand over hers, holding her when she tried to pull away. She stopped pulling. His touch was warm and strong.

"I don't need to find him to prove he existed," he told her. "Two witnesses, independent of each other, and a little more about her past, will be enough to prove he

341

could have killed her. We just have to know what kind of woman she was, and make a case for why it is believable that he mistook Maria for her. They did look alike. That much I know already, from questioning their neighbors."

"Will it be enough?" she said anxiously. "Won't they still think it's me, because I was there and we don't know anything about this man?"

"I won't let them think that," he promised.

She looked away. Suddenly it mattered more that he believed her, that he did not for a moment think she was guilty, than that she still might face trial for murder and not be able to prove her innocence.

He interrupted her thoughts. "Finish your coffee. We have a lot to do." He said it gently, but it was an instruction, almost an order.

Toward the end of the day they met with an old man, nearly blind, who said he had known Sara well. He had been a cobbler. He knew everyone's feet.

Jemima and Patrick sat with him in his small tenement room sharing hot food that Patrick had bought from a shop in the narrow street opposite. It was very savory meat cooked and then wrapped in leaves. Patrick told her the shop owners were Russian immigrants and they had told him the name of the dish, but he couldn't now pronounce it. It was delicious, though, and Jemima told him so.

The cobbler also ate his with relish.

"Sara," he said with a smile of memory. "Good feet, she had. But sickly, even then."

"Even then?" Patrick said quickly. "How long ago was that?"

"Oh, thirty years or so. Had a hard time, Sara did. Wonder she lived so long." He blinked several times, as if to hide tears. "Wouldn't have made it without Maria."

Jemima leaned forward quickly. "I thought that thirty years ago Maria was busy helping people fight against injustice? Is that not true?"

The cobbler stared at her, a touch of anger in his eyes. "Course she did! Both of them. That's when it all happened. In the seventies, before they came to this part of the city."

Patrick started to speak, then stopped. He nodded to Jemima.

"If you knew them, then I'd really like to hear the truth," Jemima said. "Her daughter is my friend and I think she deserves to hear something more than gossip, a lot of which is unkind."

"Unkind!" the cobbler snorted. It was dim inside the small room. He burned a stove to keep the air from freezing but he clearly could not afford to burn a light as well, and the window was blurring over with snow. "That what you call it? Bastards deserve to be hanged themselves."

Jemima waited. She did not even dare glance at Patrick, but she was acutely aware of his presence in the room, sitting opposite her, their knees almost touching.

"Them as used to be slaves got into a bit of trouble back then," the cobbler began. "Blacks, you know? Some folks were fine, but in some ways it seemed we weren't so very far from the South. The ones who'd run away were here and there. Some folks didn't think they should own things, like horses and land and such. You know?" He looked at Patrick, his eyebrows raised in question. He had caught Jemima's English accent and clearly did not expect her to understand.

"I've heard," Patrick said, nodding. He was Irish; he knew about discrimination.

"Sara used to help people," the cobbler went on. "Got

into it with Maria. There was one real bad time. Black man been a slave, owned a real nice place. Some folks got very upset about it. Spread around stories that he'd stole it, that they should turn him out of it. It turned into a big fight on the street. Women and children in it too. Sara and Maria were both there. Feller who used to be a slave fought to get the women out. In the end, one man was killed. Son of a bitch had it coming. He had no regard for the safety of the women or the children, injured a few in that fight. But he was white. Maria fell in love with the man what did it. Married him, she did. Some folks never forgave her for that."

"That was the scandal?" Jemima asked. She didn't know what to make of this information. How could Maria have been married once before? Did the Albrights know about it? Her heart was racing.

"It's enough," the cobbler replied, pursing his lips. "Black don't marry white. Some folks consider it unnatural, a sin against God, like."

"Where is that man now?" Jemima forced herself to ask, and yet she dreaded the answer. Maria had lived in an apartment with Sara Godwin. Had she had a falling out with this other man? Could he have done it?

"Don't know," the cobbler replied with a sniff. "He was taken down here in New York, to be tried for killing that white son of a bitch. Pardon my language, miss."

Jemima shivered at the word "tried." She felt Patrick's knees touch hers, just for a moment. Had he meant to, or was he just moving because he was stiff?

"What happened?" she whispered.

"They told her he died in prison," the cobbler replied, his voice hoarse. "But I heard after that he hadn't. Don't know what was true."

"What happened to Maria?" Patrick asked.

"Some rich white feller kind of looked after her. She were a real handsome woman. His name was All-something . . ."

"Albright?" Jemima filled in.

"Yes, something like that. He was married, of course. Men like that always are. Got to keep the family going. Anyway, she married his business partner, or something. English . . . like you," he said to Jemima. "Is that why you're asking all this?"

"Yes. Maria's daughter is my friend."

"Well, ain't it a small world. And this daughter come here just as poor Maria's killed? That's a terrible shame.

You tell her that her mother was one of the best ladies that ever drew breath, you hear me?"

"Yes," Jemima answered. "Yes, I will. I promise."

*O*utside again in the more heavily falling snow, Jemima turned to Patrick. He was standing to the windward of her, sheltering her from the worst of it. It blew against him and piled on his shoulders.

"Do you think someone killed her because years ago she married a black man who used to be a slave?" she asked.

"I think that's very possible, though it's a shame that it is," he replied. "Are you prepared for Delphinia to learn this?"

"No!" She looked away from him, down at the snow around her boots. "No. She might not mind, but imagine what the Albrights would make of it if they don't already know!"

"Delphinia's a Cardew," he pointed out. "Come out of the snow. We can find somewhere better than this to talk." He took her arm as he said it, gently but too firmly for her to resist.

Jemima said nothing. It was difficult to talk out here in the street because the wind snatched her words and the freezing air almost choked her.

They walked side by side until they came to an alley and found room to stand in a recessed doorway, sheltered from the worst of the weather.

She remembered Harley Albright's words to her, before they had even found Maria's body, when it was still a matter of stopping her from creating a scene at the wedding.

"Marguerite Albright, Harley's mother," she began. "He said to me that she had told him about Maria and what a terrible woman she was."

"Well, if the cobbler is right, then Mr. Albright was very fond of Maria, and Mrs. Albright was probably jealous," he pointed out.

"Do you suppose she knew about Maria's first husband?"

"It's definitely possible. What are you thinking, Jemima? That it was one of the Albrights after all?"

He was worried, she could see. It would be difficult to prove; might his superiors try to prevent him from even suggesting it? Jemima would be a much easier target, much more comfortable. Nobody in New York would care if she was convicted. Would it matter to them that her father was important in England? The fear came back over her like an icy wave.

Patrick saw it in her eyes. "Jemima, don't! I won't let that happen," he promised.

"You might not be able to stop it," she replied. "If Mrs. Albright knew the truth about Maria, then she would've cared very much indeed that Phinnie didn't marry into the Albright family."

"Then why wouldn't she just tell Brent the truth?" he asked."

"Maybe she died before she had the chance? Or Brent doesn't care as much?" Another thought occurred to her. "What if . . . what if Marguerite Albright had written to Maria back when she was in England and told her that her first husband was alive after all? Then she was not a widow! She was a bigamist! Her marriage to Edward Cardew was not legal."

He was watching her closely, trying to read what she was thinking now.

"Phinnie would be illegitimate," she told him. "Would she still be Cardew's heir?"

"She's still his daughter!" He was angry at the injustice and it was naked in his face. "Maria thought she was a widow. In fact, we don't know for certain that she wasn't. Mrs. Albright could have said her husband was alive simply out of . . ." He stopped.

"Out of spite?" Jemima finished. "Revenge, for Mr. Albright having liked Maria so much?"

He shook his head, his eyes very grave. "Not just that. More importantly, so the company's power and money will stay with the Albright family."

"But she died well before Brent proposed marriage to Phinnie . . . oh." Now it was there, real and cold as ice. "She told Harley. Of course. And if Brent married Phinnie, then between the two of them they would own three-quarters of the company: Phinnie's entire Cardew share from her father, and Brent's half of the Albright share. She leaned forward and put her hands over her face, pushing her fingers through her hair, heedless of the mess she made of it. "Poor Phinnie."

Patrick said nothing. He understood too well to say something meaningless.

"She's so much in love with him," Jemima went on. "Do you think he is even half as much in love with her?"

She did not look up at him. She was afraid he was going to struggle to find some comfortable half-truth.

"No," he said softly. "If you really love someone you stick by them, no matter what. You don't doubt them, or make a way to get out of it."

Now she did look up. "What makes you say that? Did he make a way to get out of it?"

"Yes. When I questioned him, he didn't defend her— not completely. If anyone said that about you, I would have defended you, whether I had the right to or not."

She tried to smile through the emotion that was beating so hard inside her it almost robbed her of breath.

"Thanks to Harley they *are* saying it about me," she pointed out. "He tricked me well. He spent enough time with me to guess I would get impatient and leave the coffee shop. He must've also sent the young boy to tell me the room number. I'm sure he had a backup plan, but he didn't need one. I played right into his hands." Jemima's voice was bitter.

"I know what people are saying thanks to Harley." Now his eyes hid nothing. "And I am defending you. I'll prove you didn't do it. We're nearly there now. But you can't help Delphinia, except maybe to make her see the truth about the Albrights, and to give her the knowledge that her mother was a good woman who got caught up in a tragedy that wasn't of her making."

"Why did she leave Phinnie? She was only two years old!" Jemima protested.

"What if Mrs. Albright didn't write to Maria, as we supposed, but to Cardew, telling him all about Maria's first marriage? Cardew may have given Maria no choice. And she certainly wouldn't be allowed to take Phinnie with her, even if she had the means to look after her. But he must've loved Phinnie enough to leave it at that, at least."

"I suppose I should have known that," she said. "It explains everything, doesn't it?"

"Except what happened to Sara Godwin," Patrick agreed.

"Why did she run off, and where is she now? Hadn't she enough loyalty to see that Maria at least had a decent burial?" Jemima asked, somewhat angry.

"Perhaps she is afraid they'll come after her too?" Patrick said.

Jemima tried to imagine the conflict in Sara Godwin. She owed Maria her life, but she was ill, alone now, and knew that Maria had been murdered. Perhaps she even knew who had done it. And the woman in the same building had said Sara had been followed . . .

Patrick must have been thinking the same thing.

"We must find her," he said with sudden urgency. "If she saw the man following her, she might know who it was, or at least be able to describe him. I suspect that it was Harley, though. I think he killed Maria and then very neatly organized it so you would be the one to find her. But we need to prove that."

Jemima nodded hesitantly. "Yes."

"What is it?" he asked. "Why don't you want to? Are you afraid we're wrong?" He put his hand over hers. "Jemima, we aren't wrong. It all fits together and makes sense of all the bits we couldn't understand before."

She met his eyes. "I know. I just hate that Sara owed so much to Maria but just ran away when she was dead, instead of staying to help. I understand! Maybe I wouldn't have done better. But I still hate it."

"I'll find her alone, then," he answered.

She glared at him. "No, you won't! I'm coming with you."

This time he laughed, his face eased in relief. She realized that it very much mattered to him that she came, and the feeling was wonderful, as if the cold outside barely existed. She withdrew her hand from his. "Let's begin."

*I*t took them all that day, and the next. It was almost Christmas when, after much questioning, pleading, and even promises, they finally climbed the rickety stairs in the tenement building where Sara Godwin had supposedly taken refuge. They had found her largely by trailing her attempts to earn money by taking small jobs, never staying in one dwelling more than two days at most, as if she was afraid that someone was pursuing her.

The snow had eased and the east wind had dropped when finally, feet aching and bones cold, they knocked on the door of the smallest apartment on the top floor.

The door opened tentatively and a woman looked out, keeping her weight behind the door so she could close it if needed. Her face was filled with alarm.

Jemima recognized her immediately. It was the same woman who had been walking in Central Park and had turned back to gaze up at the snow-laden branches with such joy. Suddenly she understood. "Maria?" Jemima said gently.

The woman's face filled with terror and she tried to push the door closed.

Patrick leaned his weight against it, forcing it to stay open.

"I'm Jemima Pitt," Jemima said gently. "I'm Phinnie's friend. I've come over from England to be with her for her wedding. I understand that you can't be . . . and why."

Tenderness and grief filled the woman's eyes. She must have been over fifty, and had certainly not had an easy life, but she was still beautiful.

"You don't know why," she said quietly. "I . . . I wish I could . . ."

"I do know," Jemima said, contradicting her. "Mrs. Albright wrote to Mr. Cardew and told him about your first husband. You had no choice."

Maria's grief was impossible to hide. She pulled the door open and Jemima and Patrick went inside. The room was tiny and the air was chill, but it was clean and there was a feeling of hominess to it because of the few personal belongings scattered about: There were embroidered pillow covers on the narrow bed, half a dozen books on a shelf, and a photograph of a handsome black man, smiling, on the bedside table.

"I never stopped thinking about her," Maria said as Patrick closed the door. "But I couldn't even see her. It would have spoiled things for her. Why have you come here?"

Jemima hesitated, and it was Patrick who answered.

"Because they are blaming Jemima for killing you, either with Phinnie's help, or at the least for her sake."

Maria paled. "Why? That's . . ." Then she understood. "It was Harley, wasn't it?" She closed her eyes, and for a moment she swayed a little, as if she might fall.

Patrick took hold of her, supporting part of her weight, and eased her to the one moderately comfortable chair in the room.

She waited a moment, then opened her eyes. "Sara was dying," she said with difficulty, her voice thick with tears. "She tricked me. She sent me on an errand to help someone, and she took my place. She wore my clothes—we were always the same size—and I suppose we look a bit alike. Harley hadn't seen me for years."

"It wouldn't matter if he had, and knew he was wrong," Patrick pointed out. "He identified the body as yours, so it served his purpose well enough. You weren't going to come forward and say he was wrong."

"I couldn't! Not without Phinnie learning all about me, and that she was illegitimate." She said the word as if it hurt her. "Even though I thought Joe was dead at the time. Of course I would never have married Albert and left America if I'd known he was still alive!"

"And Phinnie's wedding?" Jemima asked.

"I just wanted to see her. I wouldn't have spoken to her, just watched. There'll be a crowd. No one would have seen me."

"And Sara Godwin?" This time it was Patrick who asked the question.

"There was no one else to look after her properly. No matter what, I couldn't leave her to die alone—and yet that's just what I did!"

"She chose to." Jemima shook her head. "She did that for you, perhaps to thank you for all you'd done for her."

"I've got to bury her properly. They're not putting her in a pauper's grave. I've got nearly enough money." She looked from Jemima to Patrick. "Whatever you think of me, please see that that happens?"

"We will," Patrick promised instantly. "But before

that, we have to make sure we have the evidence to prove it was Harley Albright who killed Sara, whether he thought she was you or not."

"How are you going to do that?" Maria asked doubtfully.

Patrick smiled at her. "You're coming to the police station and you'll tell my bosses the whole story, including that Harley was following you a day or so before Sara was killed. We all know he identified her as you. We know that Phinnie is Mr. Cardew's heir, and that when she marries Brent he will become heir to three-quarters of the Albright and Cardew business. The only way for Harley to keep his power and fortune is to discredit Phinnie, either so Brent doesn't marry her and the shares stay equal among the three of them—or, better still, so that she is written off as illegitimate, Mr. Cardew has no heirs, and the power reverts to the Albrights."

"Poor Harley," Maria said with regret. "He was a nice child. So handsome, with all that fair hair. Marguerite adored him. One loves one's children . . . so much."

"When this is settled, will you meet Phinnie?" Jemima asked urgently.

"Oh, no. I won't spoil her happiness. It will be terribly hard for Brent to come to terms with his brother's crime. He will need her support. And Celia will help. She was always strong . . . and loyal, as much as they would allow."

Jemima glanced at Patrick and saw him nod very slightly. Did he really know her so well he understood what she was asking? She realized that the joy that Maria was alive, and the relief that she herself would be cleared of any suspicion, was suddenly horribly overshadowed by the thought of leaving New York after the wedding . . . if it proceeded! She might never see Patrick again, and that hurt more than she had thought possible.

Her own mother had come from a very good family, and scandalized them all by marrying a policeman at a time when policemen were socially regarded as little better than bailiffs or dustmen. Early in their marriage times had been hard and money scarce, but she had been, and still was, extraordinarily happy. And unlike so many women, she had never been bored . . . or lonely.

This was ridiculous! Yes, she admitted to herself, she was in love with Patrick Flannery, very much in love. But he had not mentioned marriage, and had probably not given it a thought!

Jemima looked at Maria, and read in the older woman's eyes an understanding so complete that it made the color burn up Jemima's cheeks. But then, Maria had married the man she loved, in spite of the fact that he was black, and had once been owned, like an animal. It had not stopped her.

"Brent might not marry Phinnie," Jemima said aloud. "She deserves someone who loves her wholeheartedly, whoever her mother is and whatever the circumstances. You don't become a different person just because you discover something about your birth. And money is nice, but it has nothing to do with real happiness. You and I both know that." It was a challenge, and she wanted an answer.

Maria smiled and touched Jemima's hand lightly. "Of course we do. Although hunger is hard, perhaps harder than you know."

"Isn't hunger of the heart because you denied yourself even harder?" Jemima asked.

"I don't know, because I was always rash enough not to try it," Maria answered. "And it cost me dear . . . but I never doubted it was worth it."

*T*wo days later, Harley was arrested. Brent postponed indefinitely his marriage to Phinnie. It was a polite fiction. Everyone knew that it would never take place. Celia stepped forward to comfort her family and support them, especially Rothwell, as she had done discreetly all their lives.

Phinnie and Jemima left the Albright house and took lodgings in the city, until they should find passage home, early in the New Year. Phinnie's means were more than sufficient to look after all their needs.

Early on Christmas morning, Jemima persuaded Phinnie to meet Maria.

It was awkward at first.

"I don't wish to," Phinnie said miserably. "I don't know what to say!"

"Start with 'Hello,'" Jemima replied. "I know everything fell apart and nothing was the way you hoped it would be, but don't let go of what is good. You have plenty of time to meet someone who loves you, no matter who your family is or what's happened."

"I thought Brent loved me . . ."

"I know. And maybe he thought so too," Jemima said. "But none of that has anything to do with meeting Maria. Come on."

Reluctantly, Phinnie agreed. They put on their best winter coats and hats and walked down to Central Park, to the place where Harley and Jemima had seen Maria turn back to gaze at the snow-laden trees. They were edged with snow again today, glittering white for Christmas.

"There," Jemima pointed. Fifty yards ahead of them she saw Patrick. It took her a moment to be certain it was him: He was wearing not his police uniform but a plain dark overcoat, and he was bareheaded. Beside him was Maria, looking at them as if she had known them even in the farthest distance. She took a tentative step forward, then another.

"I'm frightened," Phinnie whispered to Jemima. "What if she doesn't like me?"

"She loves you!" Jemima replied. "She always did. Come on!" She stepped out, taking Phinnie by the arm and pulling her forward.

There were other people on the path as well, but none of them took any notice. It was only as they came much closer that Jemima realized that the black man a little behind Maria was the same man she had seen in the photograph beside Maria's bed. He was older, grayer at the temples, but the smile had not changed, nor the curious mixture of shyness and inner confidence on display in the picture.

Phinnie stopped in front of Maria. They were the same height, and had the same soft features and dark eyes, the same grace of movement.

Maria held out her hands. Slowly Phinnie took them and held on.

When Jemima looked at Patrick she knew that it was going to be all right. She forgot about Phinnie and Maria, even about the man, Joe, whom Maria introduced quietly and with pride.

"I think you took care of Phinnies happiness," Patrick said, taking Jemima's arm and beginning to walk toward the edge of the path.

"But what about us?" he asked, stopping and turning to face her. "Are we going to be all right too?"

She looked up at him. She was almost certain of what he meant. It was there in his eyes, his whole face, but she needed to hear him say it.

"I don't know," she answered. "Are we?"

"I will be, if you marry me. Will you?"

"I think I probably will."

He looked startled. "What?"

Jemima laughed and reached up to touch his cheek with her gloved fingers. "I will marry you, and I think I will probably be all right, for always."

He leaned forward and kissed her.

The passersby smiled, and in the distance Christmas bells began to ring.

ANNE PERRY is the bestselling author of thirteen holiday novels: *A Christmas Escape, A New York Christmas, A Christmas Hope, A Christmas Garland, A Christmas Homecoming, A Christmas Odyssey, A Christmas Promise, A Christmas Grace, A Christmas Beginning, A Christmas Secret, A Christmas Guest, A Christmas Visitor,* and *A Christmas Journey.* She is also the author of two acclaimed series set in Victorian England—the William Monk novels and the Charlotte and Thomas Pitt novels—five World War I novels, and a work of historical fiction, *The Sheen on the Silk.*

anneperry.co.uk
@AnnePerryWriter

Anne Perry is available for select readings and lectures. To inquire about a possible appearance, please contact the Penguin Random House Speakers Bureau at 212-572-2013 or speakers@penguinrandomhouse.com.

ABOUT THE TYPE

This book was set in Century Schoolbook, a member of the Century family of typefaces. It was designed in the 1890s by Theodore Low De Vinne (1828–1914) of the American Type Founders Company, in collaboration with Linn Boyd Benton (1844–1932). It was one of the earliest types designed for a specific purpose, the *Century* magazine, because it was able to maintain the economies of a narrower typeface while using stronger serifs and thickened verticals.